Winx Club 6

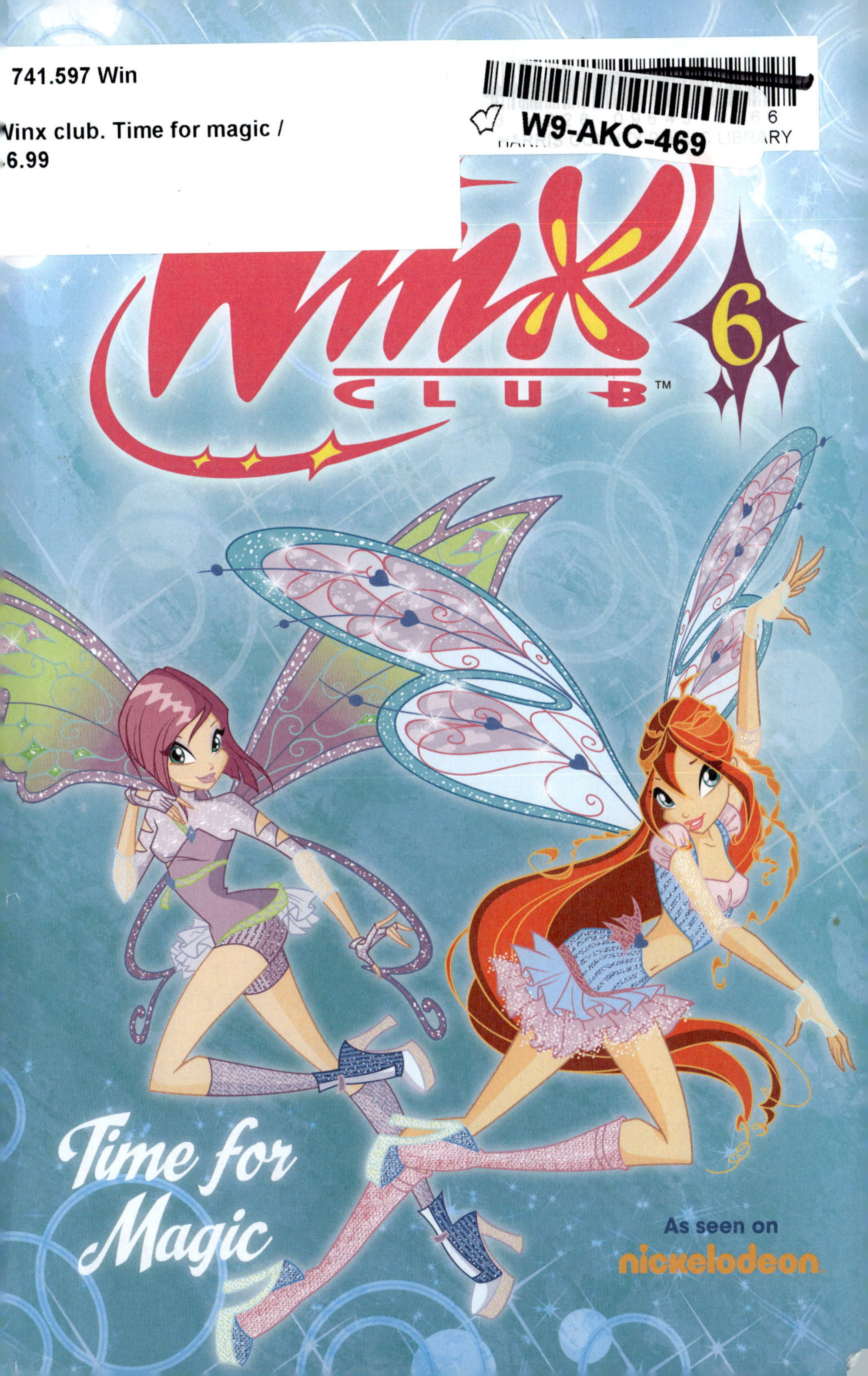

Time for Magic

As seen on nickelodeon

Winx Club
Volume 6

Designer • Fawn Lau
Letterer • John Hunt
Editor • Amy Yu

Printed in China

Published by VIZ Media, LLC
P.O. Box 77010
San Francisco, CA 94107

10 9 8 7 6 5 4 3 2 1
First printing, March 2013

www.vizkids.com
www.viz.com

PARENTAL ADVISORY
WINX CLUB is rated A and is suitable for readers of all ages.
RATED A FOR ALL AGES
ratings.viz.com

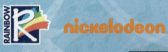

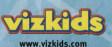

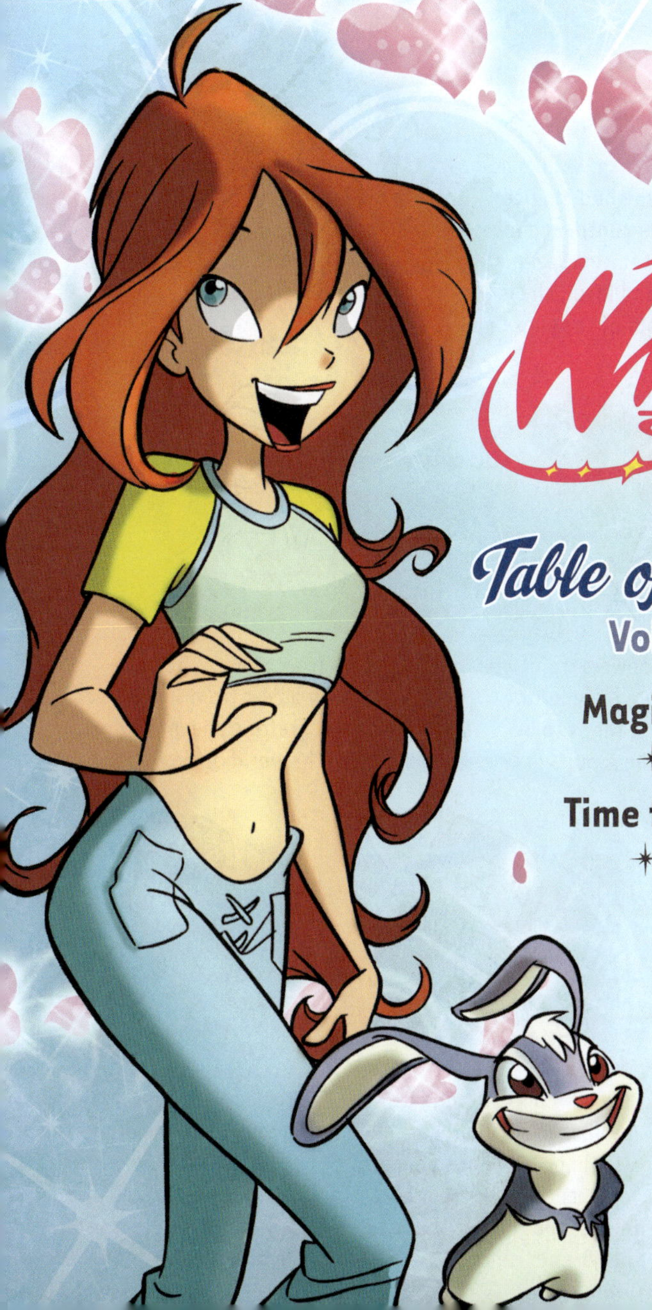

Winx Club™

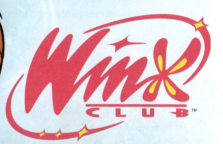

Table of Contents
Volume 6

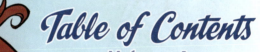

Meet the Winx Club

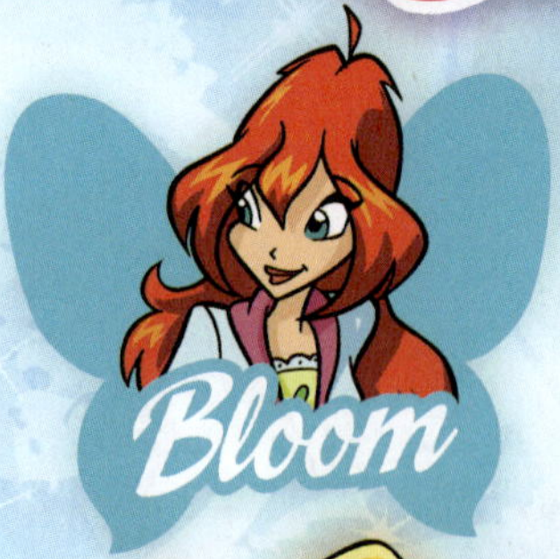
Bloom

Raised on Earth, **BLOOM** had no idea she had magical fairy powers until a chance encounter with Stella. Intelligent and loyal, she is the heart and soul of the Winx Club.

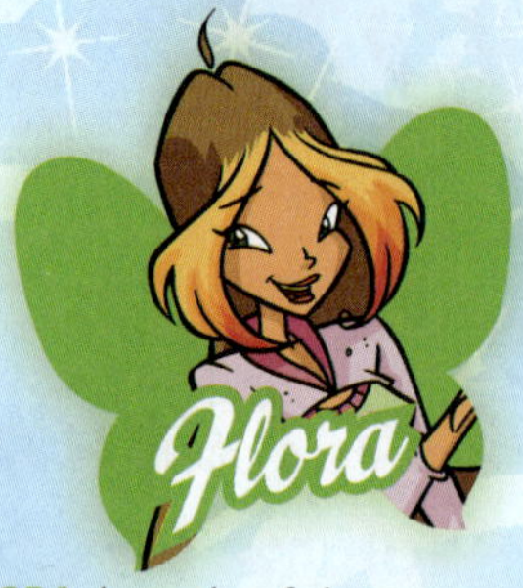
Flora

FLORA draws her fairy powers from flowers, plants and nature in general. Sweet and thoughtful, she tends to be the peacemaker in the group.

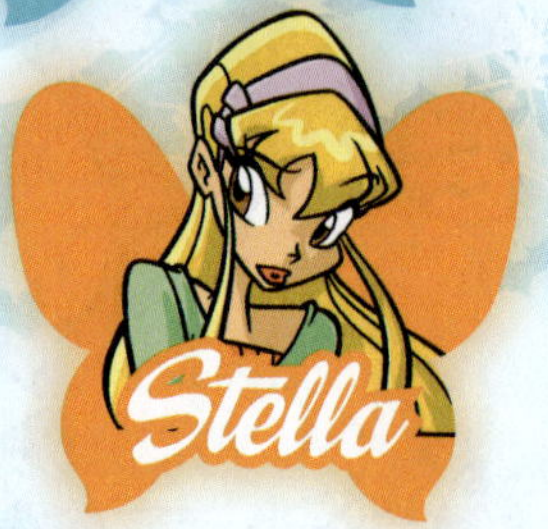
Stella

A princess from Solaria, **STELLA** draws her fairy power from sunlight. Optimistic and carefree, she introduces Bloom to the world of Magix.

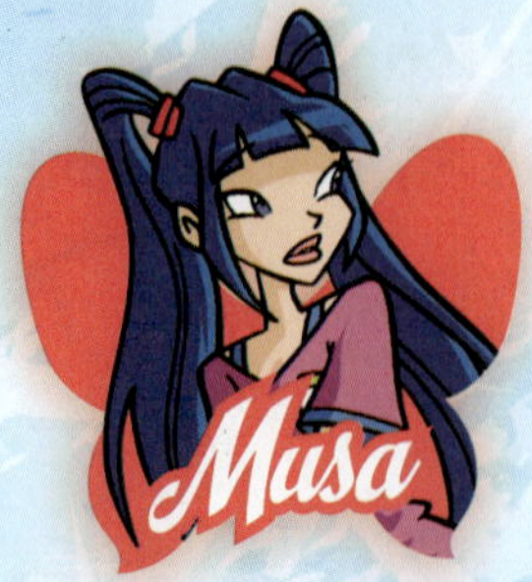
Musa

MUSA draws power from the music she plays. She has a natural talent for investigating, and she's got a keen eye for details.

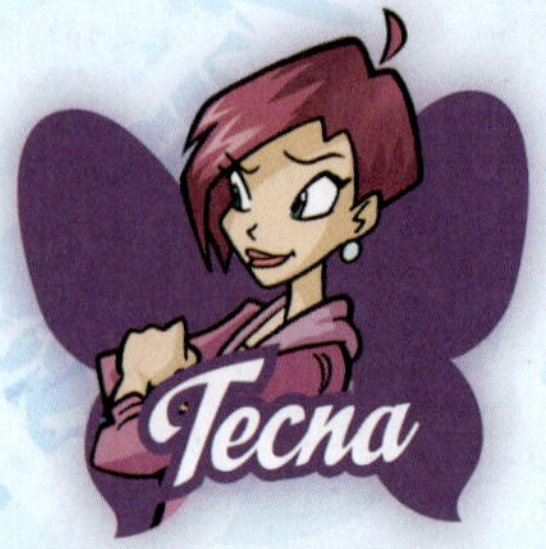
Tecna

Self-confident and a perfectionist, **TECNA** has a vast knowledge of science, which enables her to create devices that can get her and her friends out of trouble.

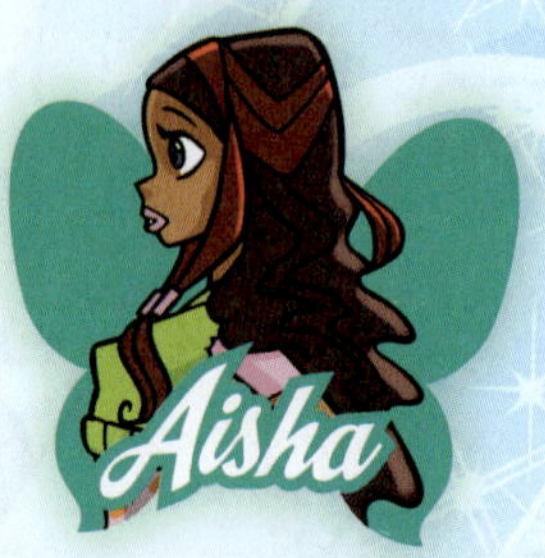
Aisha

Strong and fearless, **AISHA** is able to control the properties of liquids like water. She joined the Winx Club after they saved her from some powerful nightmares.

Their Friends

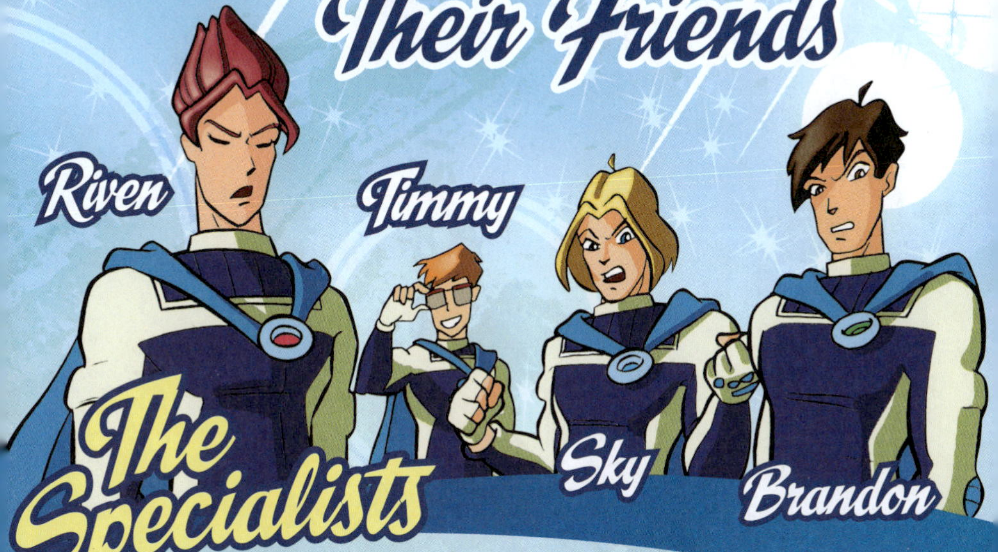
Riven
Timmy
Sky
Brandon

The Specialists

These boys from Red Fountain School are friends with the Winx Club girls and sometimes team up with them to fight trolls and other magical monsters.

Their Foes

THE TRIX are an evil trio of witches from Cloudtower Academy who battle the Winx Club regularly. With leader Icy's freezing powers, Stormy's weather-controlling powers, and Darcy's powers of darkness, these girls love to wreak havoc!

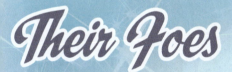

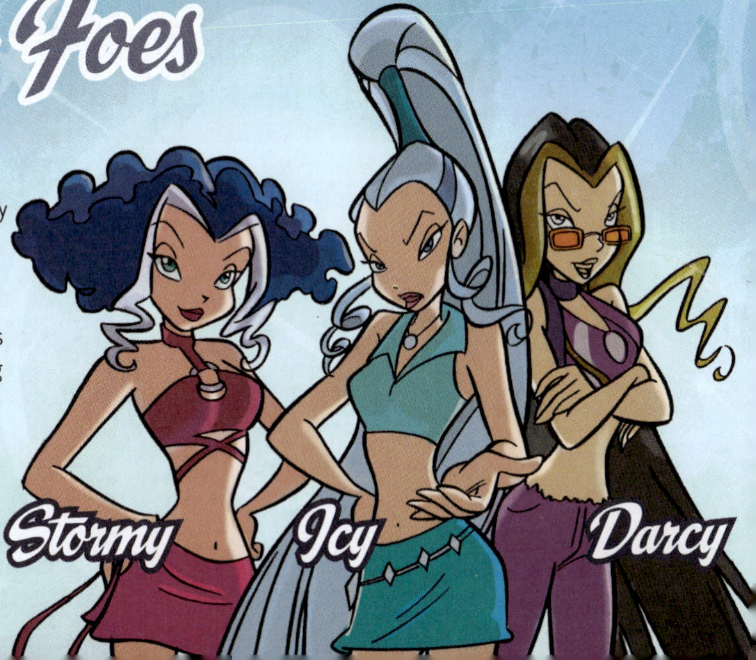
Stormy
Icy
Darcy

Magix on Ice

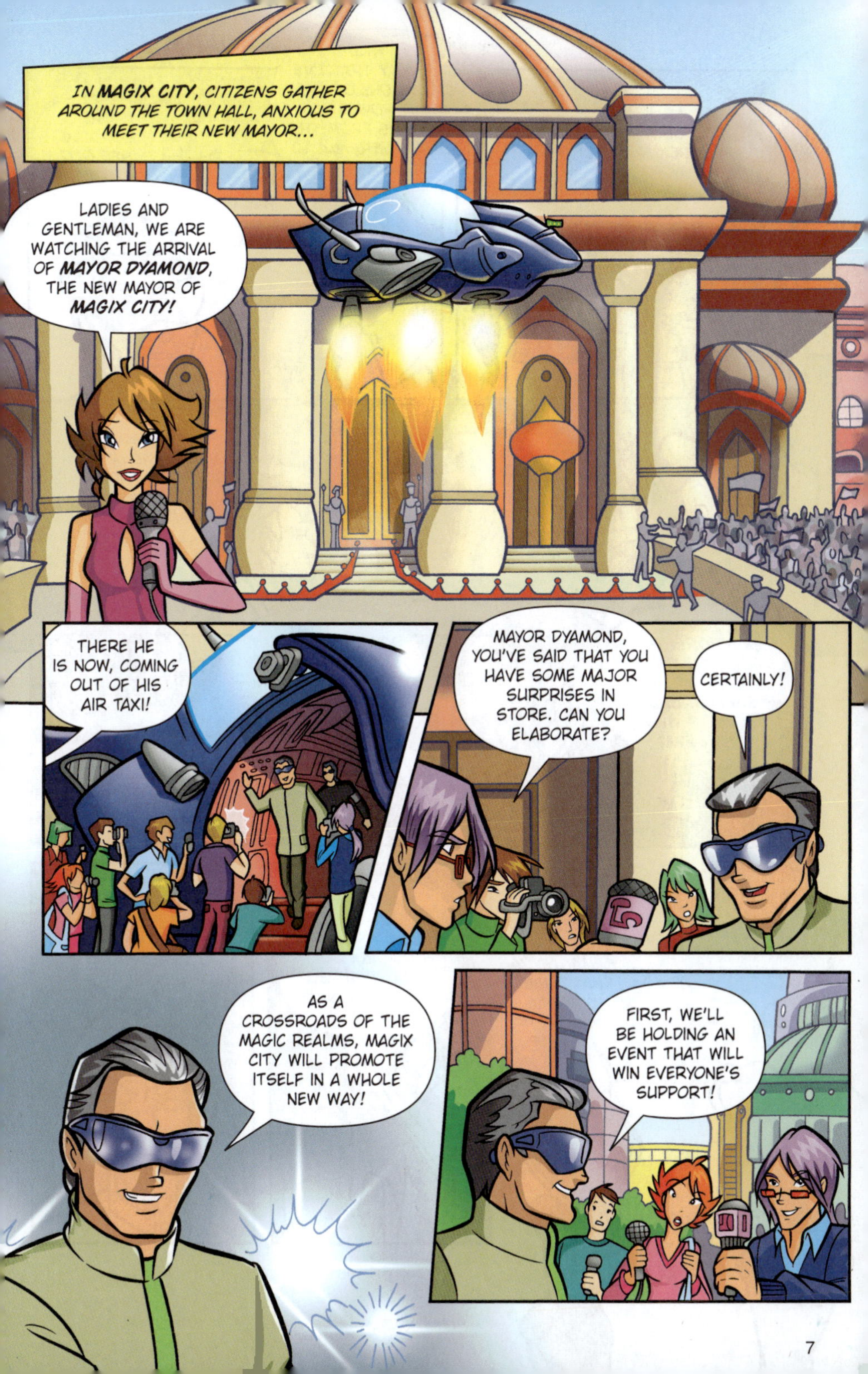
IN MAGIX CITY, CITIZENS GATHER AROUND THE TOWN HALL, ANXIOUS TO MEET THEIR NEW MAYOR...
LADIES AND GENTLEMAN, WE ARE WATCHING THE ARRIVAL OF MAYOR DYAMOND, THE NEW MAYOR OF MAGIX CITY!
THERE HE IS NOW, COMING OUT OF HIS AIR TAXI!
MAYOR DYAMOND, YOU'VE SAID THAT YOU HAVE SOME MAJOR SURPRISES IN STORE. CAN YOU ELABORATE?
CERTAINLY!
AS A CROSSROADS OF THE MAGIC REALMS, MAGIX CITY WILL PROMOTE ITSELF IN A WHOLE NEW WAY!
FIRST, WE'LL BE HOLDING AN EVENT THAT WILL WIN EVERYONE'S SUPPORT!

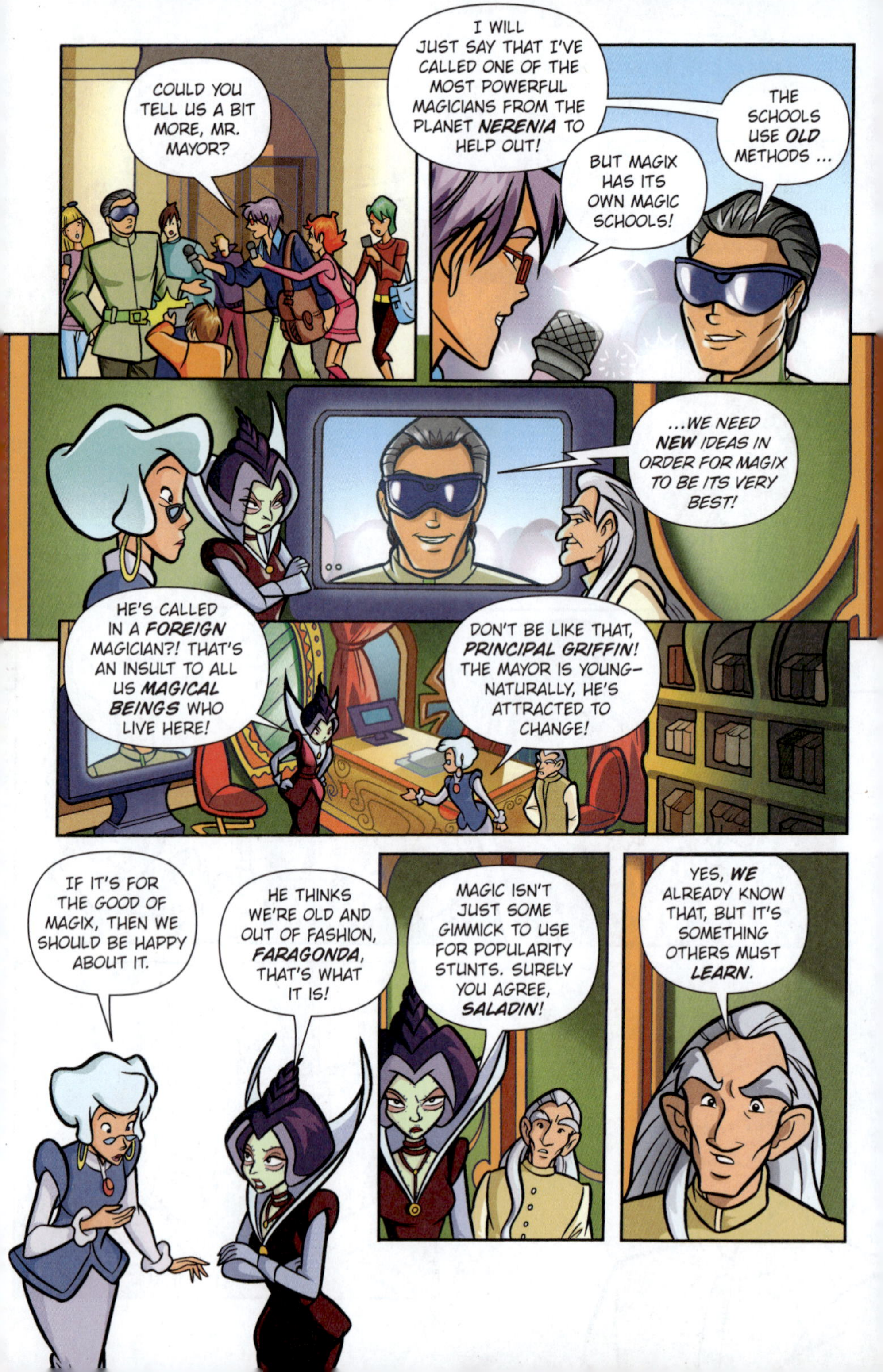
COULD YOU TELL US A BIT MORE, MR. MAYOR?
I WILL JUST SAY THAT I'VE CALLED ONE OF THE MOST POWERFUL MAGICIANS FROM THE PLANET NERENIA TO HELP OUT!
BUT MAGIX HAS ITS OWN MAGIC SCHOOLS!
THE SCHOOLS USE OLD METHODS ...
...WE NEED NEW IDEAS IN ORDER FOR MAGIX TO BE ITS VERY BEST!
HE'S CALLED IN A FOREIGN MAGICIAN?! THAT'S AN INSULT TO ALL US MAGICAL BEINGS WHO LIVE HERE!
DON'T BE LIKE THAT, PRINCIPAL GRIFFIN! THE MAYOR IS YOUNG-NATURALLY, HE'S ATTRACTED TO CHANGE!
IF IT'S FOR THE GOOD OF MAGIX, THEN WE SHOULD BE HAPPY ABOUT IT.
HE THINKS WE'RE OLD AND OUT OF FASHION, FARAGONDA, THAT'S WHAT IT IS!
MAGIC ISN'T JUST SOME GIMMICK TO USE FOR POPULARITY STUNTS. SURELY YOU AGREE, SALADIN!
YES, WE ALREADY KNOW THAT, BUT IT'S SOMETHING OTHERS MUST LEARN.

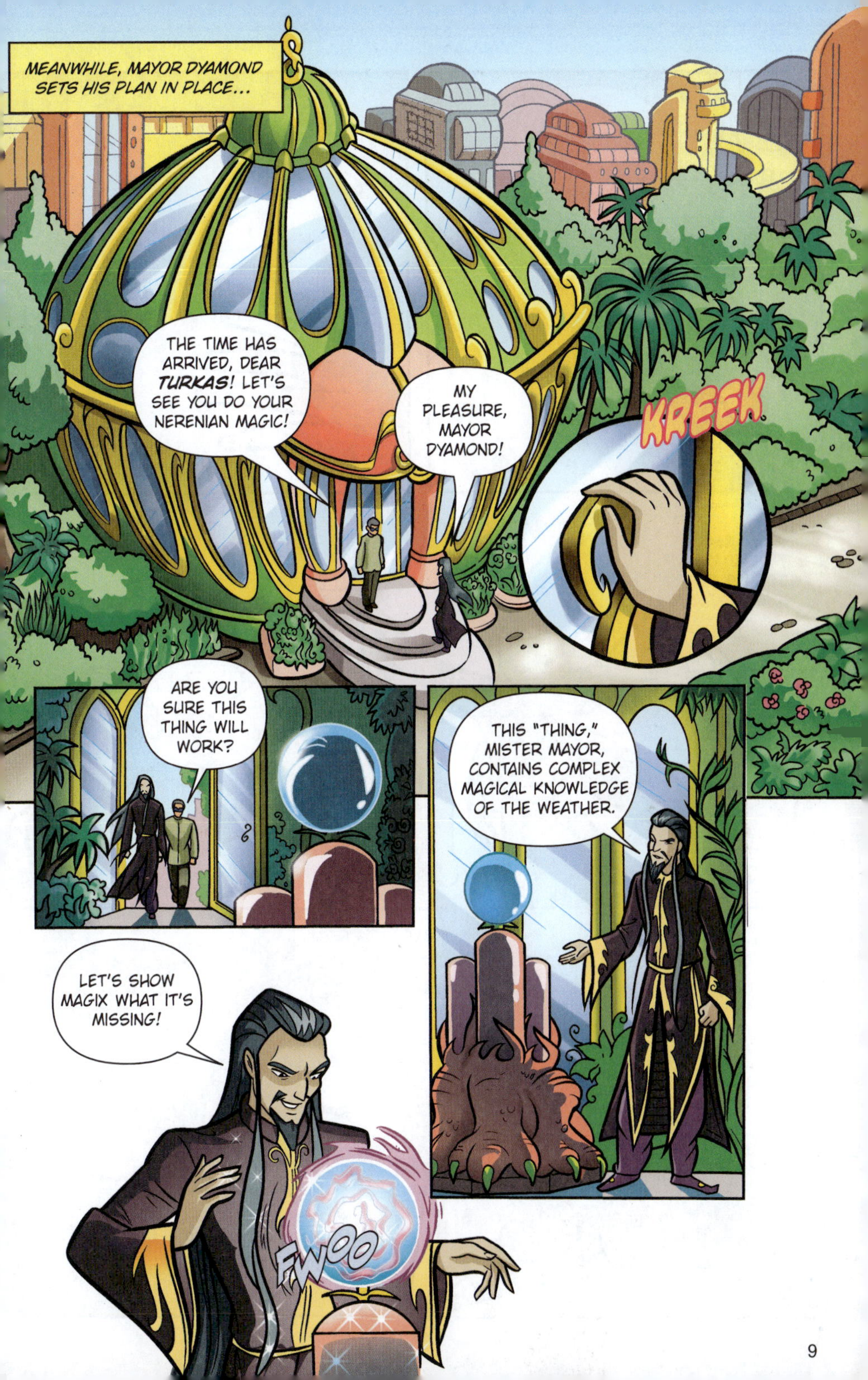
MEANWHILE, MAYOR DYAMOND SETS HIS PLAN IN PLACE...
THE TIME HAS ARRIVED, DEAR TURKAS! LET'S SEE YOU DO YOUR NERENIAN MAGIC!
MY PLEASURE, MAYOR DYAMOND!
KREEK
ARE YOU SURE THIS THING WILL WORK?
THIS "THING," MISTER MAYOR, CONTAINS COMPLEX MAGICAL KNOWLEDGE OF THE WEATHER.
LET'S SHOW MAGIX WHAT IT'S MISSING!
FWOO

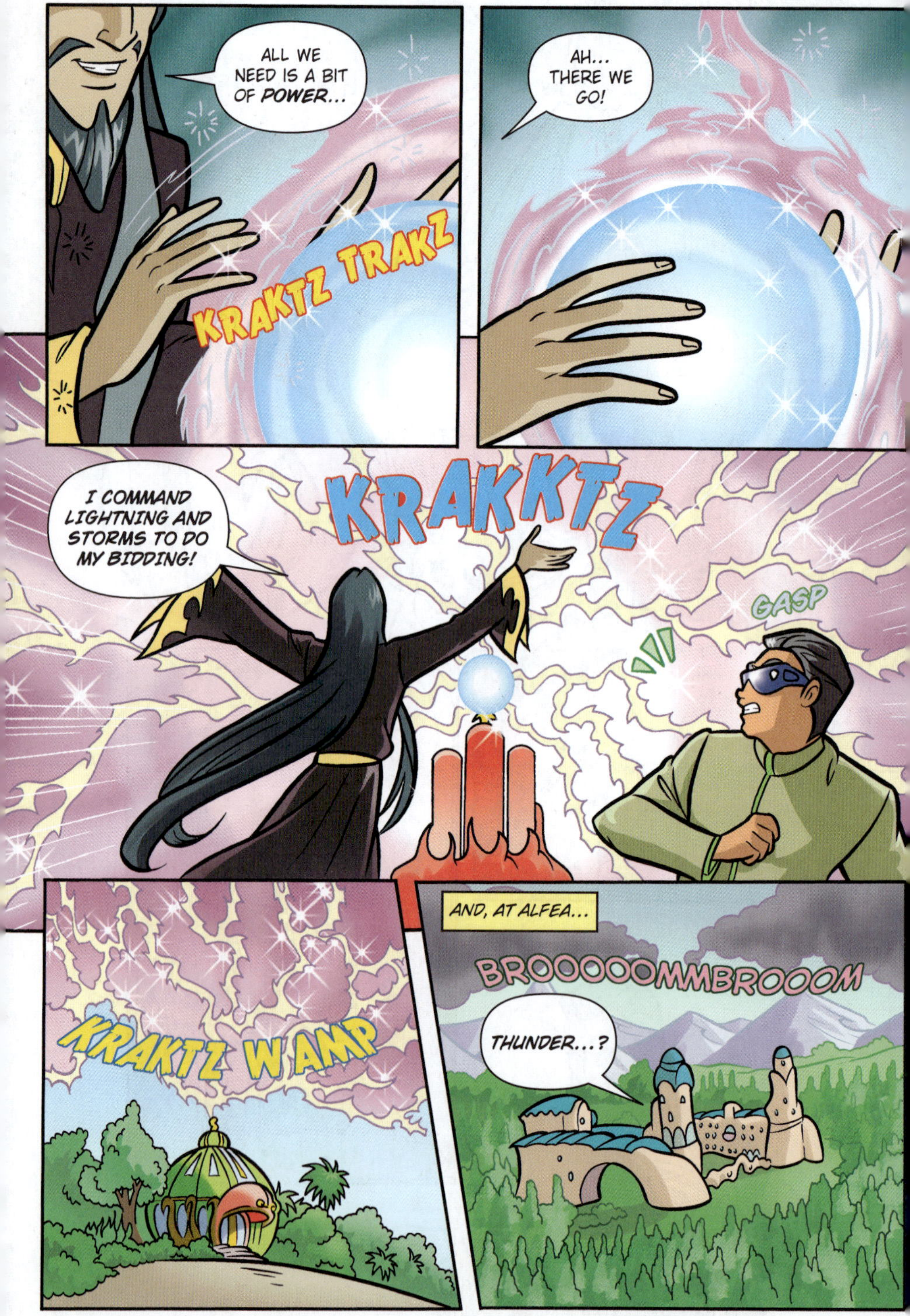
ALL WE NEED IS A BIT OF POWER...
KRAKTZ TRAKZ
AH... THERE WE GO!
I COMMAND LIGHTNING AND STORMS TO DO MY BIDDING!
KRAKKTZ
GASP
KRAKTZ WAMP
AND, AT ALFEA...
BROOOOOMMBROOOM
THUNDER...?

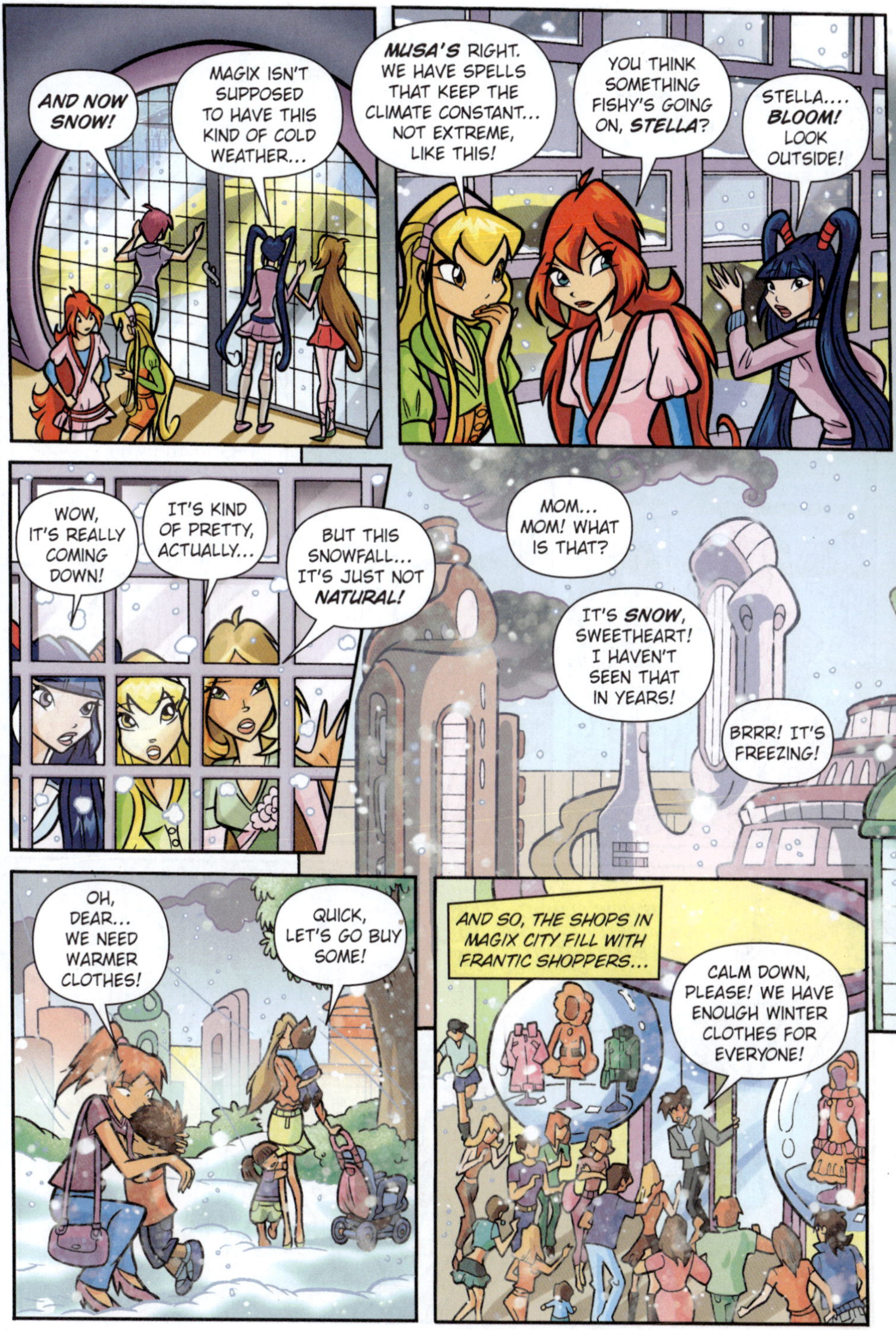
AND NOW SNOW!
MAGIX ISN'T SUPPOSED TO HAVE THIS KIND OF COLD WEATHER...
MUSA'S RIGHT. WE HAVE SPELLS THAT KEEP THE CLIMATE CONSTANT... NOT EXTREME, LIKE THIS!
YOU THINK SOMETHING FISHY'S GOING ON, STELLA?
STELLA.... BLOOM! LOOK OUTSIDE!
WOW, IT'S REALLY COMING DOWN!
IT'S KIND OF PRETTY, ACTUALLY...
BUT THIS SNOWFALL... IT'S JUST NOT NATURAL!
MOM... MOM! WHAT IS THAT?
IT'S SNOW, SWEETHEART! I HAVEN'T SEEN THAT IN YEARS!
BRRR! IT'S FREEZING!
OH, DEAR... WE NEED WARMER CLOTHES!
QUICK, LET'S GO BUY SOME!
AND SO, THE SHOPS IN MAGIX CITY FILL WITH FRANTIC SHOPPERS...
CALM DOWN, PLEASE! WE HAVE ENOUGH WINTER CLOTHES FOR EVERYONE!

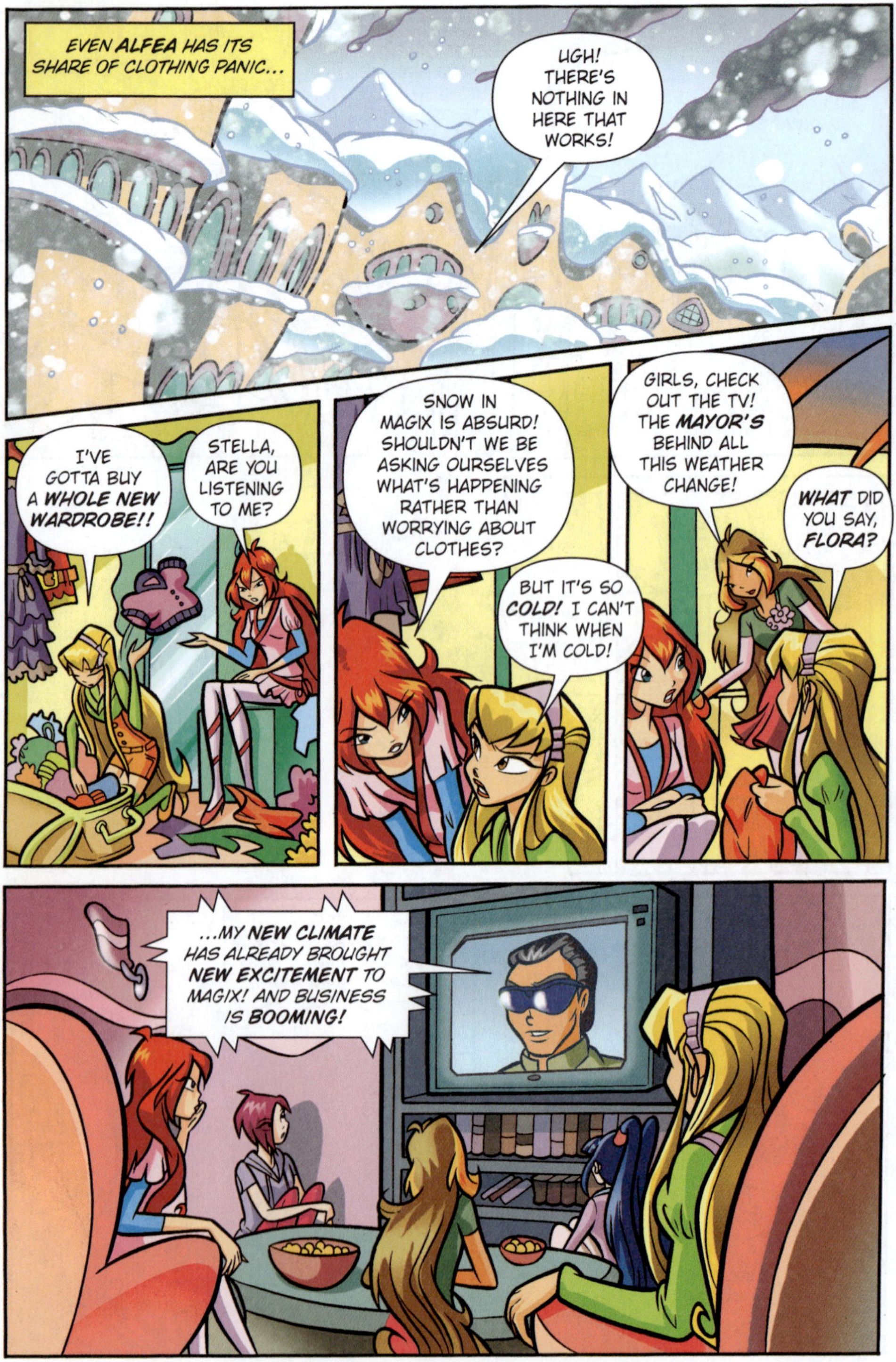
EVEN ALFEA HAS ITS SHARE OF CLOTHING PANIC...
UGH! THERE'S NOTHING IN HERE THAT WORKS!
I'VE GOTTA BUY A WHOLE NEW WARDROBE!!
STELLA, ARE YOU LISTENING TO ME?
SNOW IN MAGIX IS ABSURD! SHOULDN'T WE BE ASKING OURSELVES WHAT'S HAPPENING RATHER THAN WORRYING ABOUT CLOTHES?
BUT IT'S SO COLD! I CAN'T THINK WHEN I'M COLD!
GIRLS, CHECK OUT THE TV! THE MAYOR'S BEHIND ALL THIS WEATHER CHANGE!
WHAT DID YOU SAY, FLORA?
...MY NEW CLIMATE HAS ALREADY BROUGHT NEW EXCITEMENT TO MAGIX! AND BUSINESS IS BOOMING!

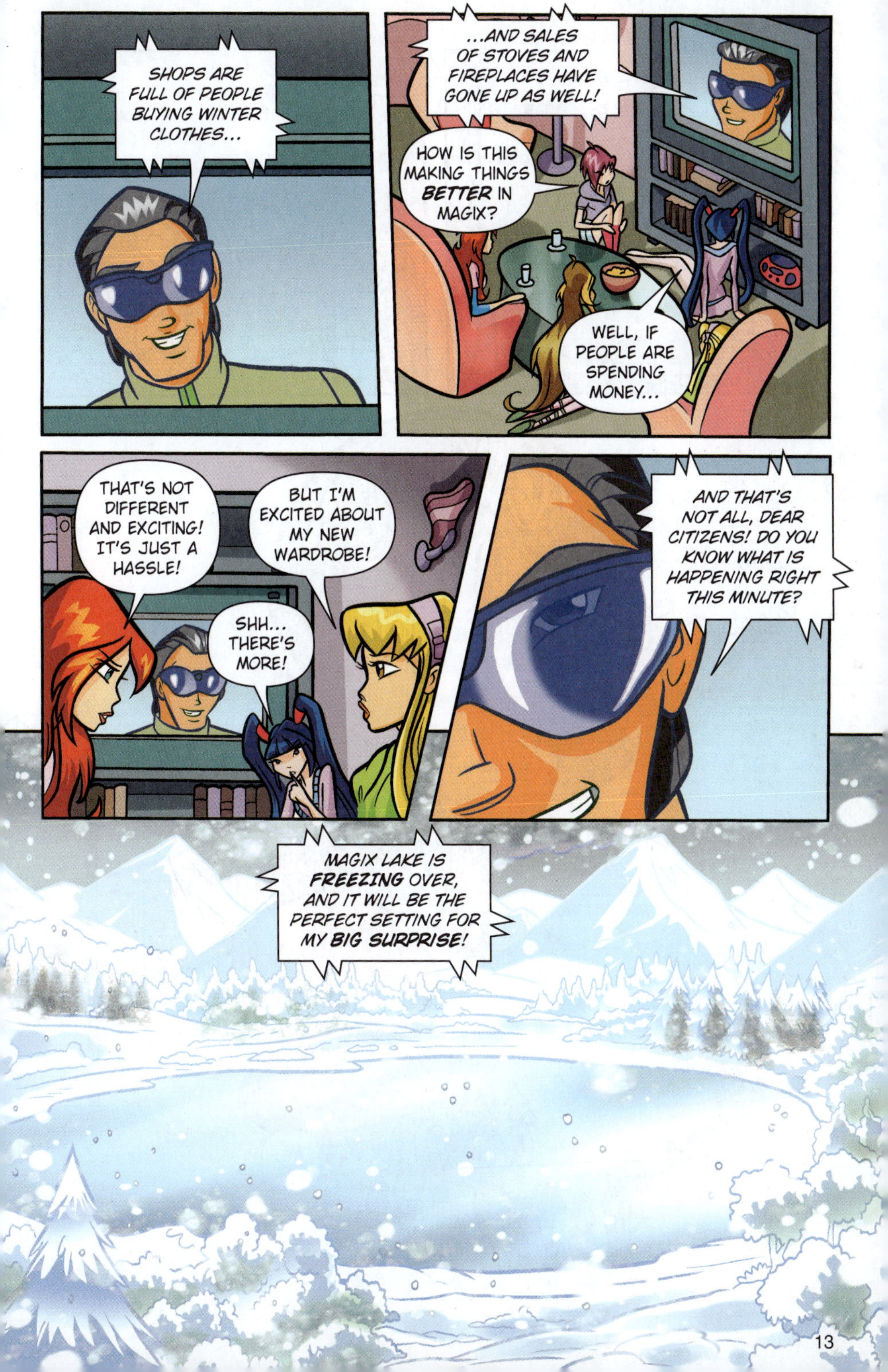
SHOPS ARE FULL OF PEOPLE BUYING WINTER CLOTHES...
...AND SALES OF STOVES AND FIREPLACES HAVE GONE UP AS WELL!
HOW IS THIS MAKING THINGS **BETTER** IN MAGIX?
WELL, IF PEOPLE ARE SPENDING MONEY...
THAT'S NOT DIFFERENT AND EXCITING! IT'S JUST A HASSLE!
BUT I'M EXCITED ABOUT MY NEW WARDROBE!
SHH... THERE'S MORE!
AND THAT'S NOT ALL, DEAR CITIZENS! DO YOU KNOW WHAT IS HAPPENING RIGHT THIS MINUTE?
MAGIX LAKE IS **FREEZING** OVER, AND IT WILL BE THE PERFECT SETTING FOR MY **BIG SURPRISE**!

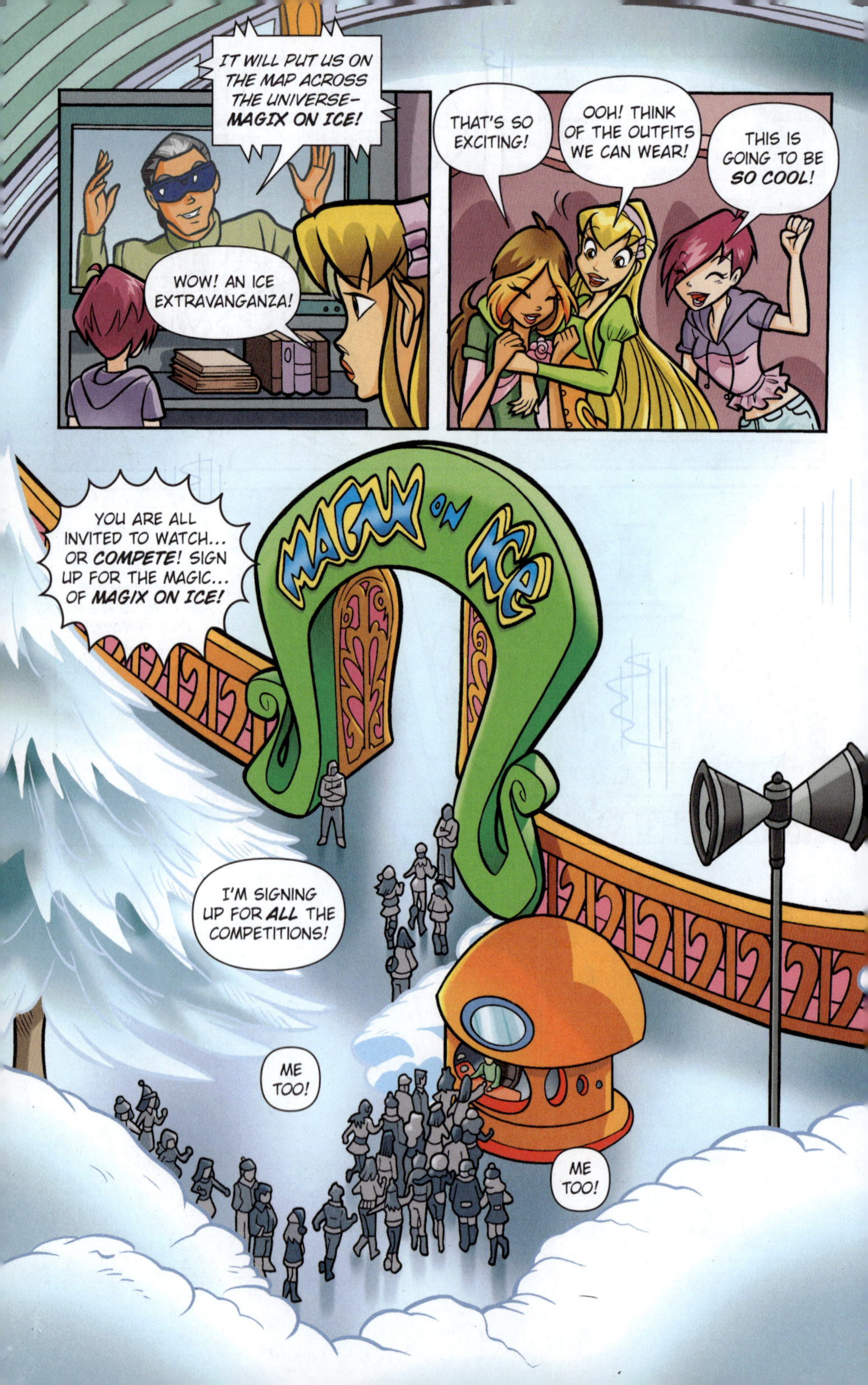

IT WILL PUT US ON THE MAP ACROSS THE UNIVERSE- MAGIX ON ICE!
WOW! AN ICE EXTRAVANGANZA!
THAT'S SO EXCITING!
OOH! THINK OF THE OUTFITS WE CAN WEAR!
THIS IS GOING TO BE SO COOL!
MAGIX ON ICE
YOU ARE ALL INVITED TO WATCH... OR COMPETE! SIGN UP FOR THE MAGIC... OF MAGIX ON ICE!
I'M SIGNING UP FOR ALL THE COMPETITIONS!
ME TOO!
ME TOO!

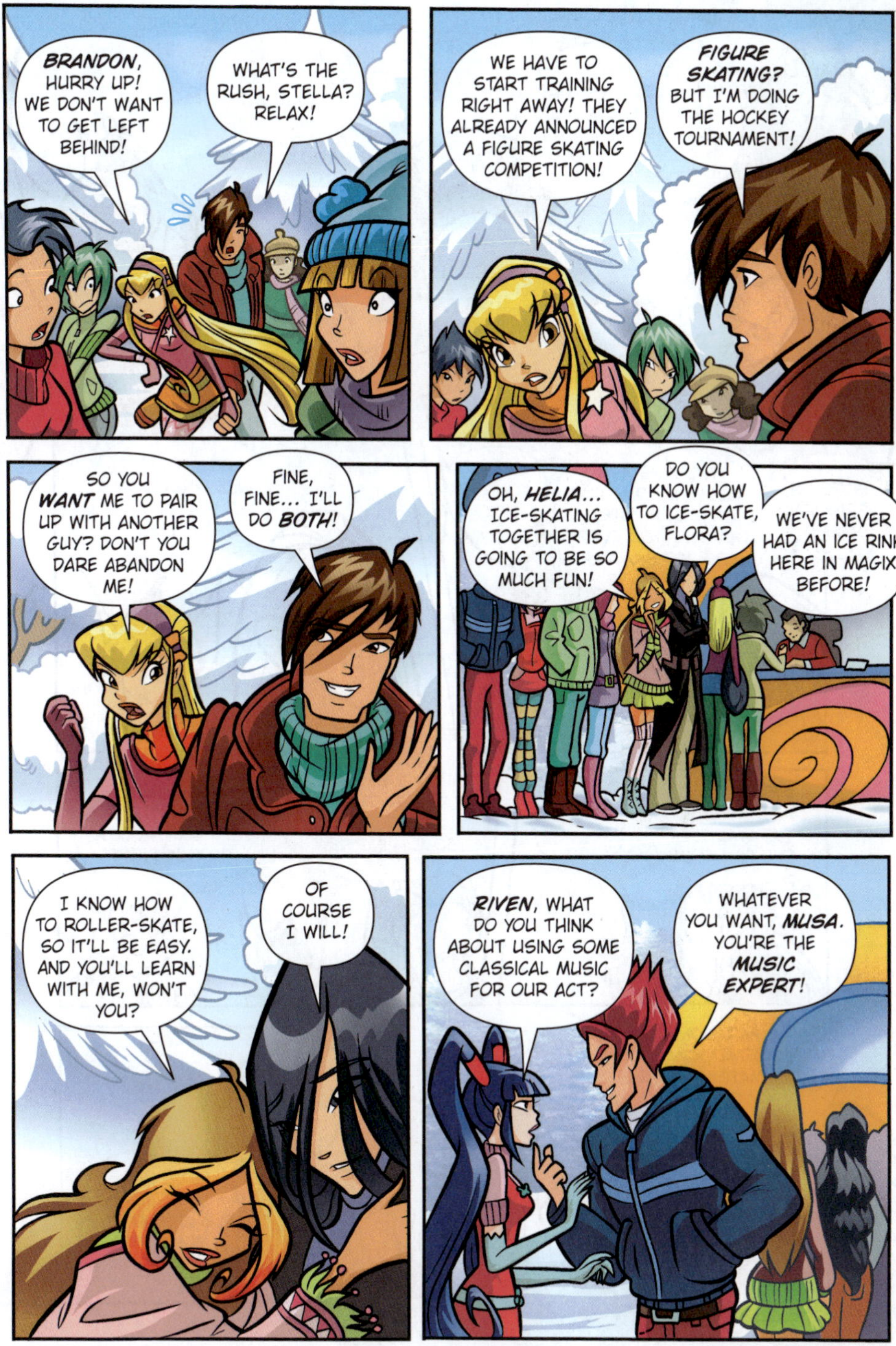
BRANDON, HURRY UP! WE DON'T WANT TO GET LEFT BEHIND!
WHAT'S THE RUSH, STELLA? RELAX!
WE HAVE TO START TRAINING RIGHT AWAY! THEY ALREADY ANNOUNCED A FIGURE SKATING COMPETITION!
FIGURE SKATING? BUT I'M DOING THE HOCKEY TOURNAMENT!
SO YOU WANT ME TO PAIR UP WITH ANOTHER GUY? DON'T YOU DARE ABANDON ME!
FINE, FINE... I'LL DO BOTH!
OH, HELIA... ICE-SKATING TOGETHER IS GOING TO BE SO MUCH FUN!
DO YOU KNOW HOW TO ICE-SKATE, FLORA?
WE'VE NEVER HAD AN ICE RINK HERE IN MAGIX BEFORE!
I KNOW HOW TO ROLLER-SKATE, SO IT'LL BE EASY. AND YOU'LL LEARN WITH ME, WON'T YOU?
OF COURSE I WILL!
RIVEN, WHAT DO YOU THINK ABOUT USING SOME CLASSICAL MUSIC FOR OUR ACT?
WHATEVER YOU WANT, MUSA. YOU'RE THE MUSIC EXPERT!

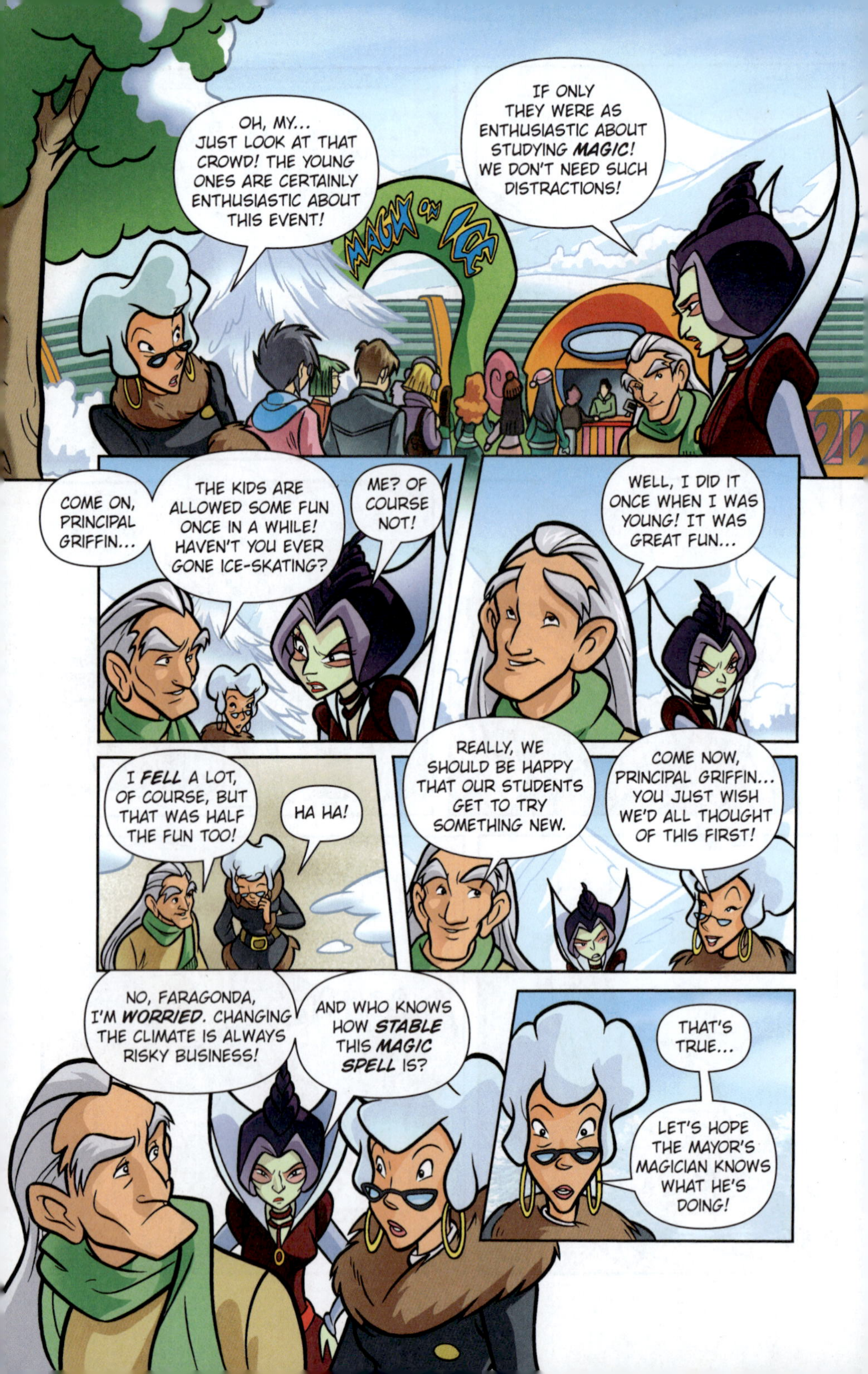
OH, MY... JUST LOOK AT THAT CROWD! THE YOUNG ONES ARE CERTAINLY ENTHUSIASTIC ABOUT THIS EVENT!
IF ONLY THEY WERE AS ENTHUSIASTIC ABOUT STUDYING *MAGIC*! WE DON'T NEED SUCH DISTRACTIONS!
MAGIX ON ICE
COME ON, PRINCIPAL GRIFFIN...
THE KIDS ARE ALLOWED SOME FUN ONCE IN A WHILE! HAVEN'T YOU EVER GONE ICE-SKATING?
ME? OF COURSE NOT!
WELL, I DID IT ONCE WHEN I WAS YOUNG! IT WAS GREAT FUN...
I *FELL* A LOT, OF COURSE, BUT THAT WAS HALF THE FUN TOO!
HA HA!
REALLY, WE SHOULD BE HAPPY THAT OUR STUDENTS GET TO TRY SOMETHING NEW.
COME NOW, PRINCIPAL GRIFFIN... YOU JUST WISH WE'D ALL THOUGHT OF THIS FIRST!
NO, FARAGONDA, I'M *WORRIED*. CHANGING THE CLIMATE IS ALWAYS RISKY BUSINESS!
AND WHO KNOWS HOW *STABLE* THIS *MAGIC SPELL* IS?
THAT'S TRUE...
LET'S HOPE THE MAYOR'S MAGICIAN KNOWS WHAT HE'S DOING!

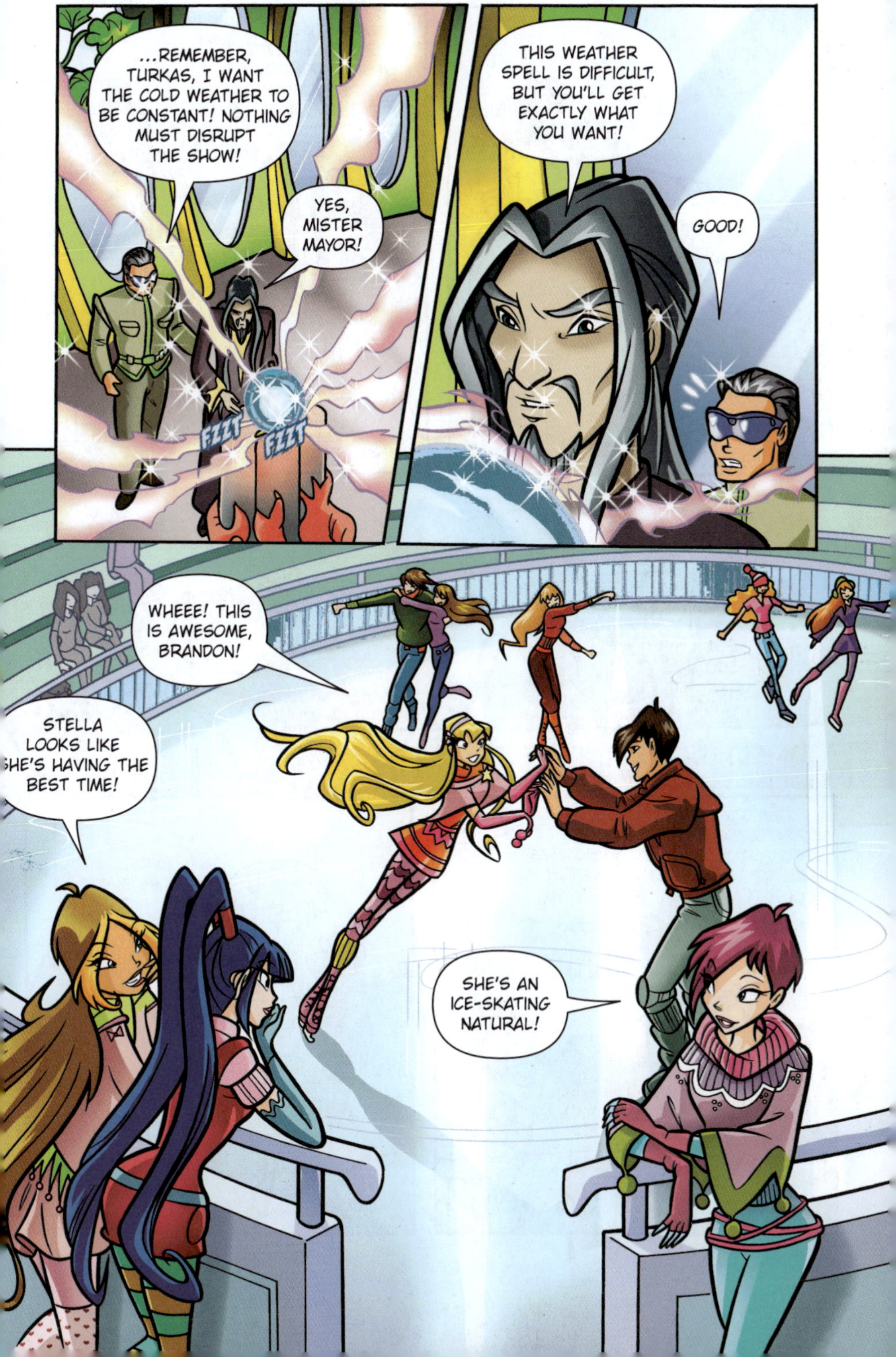
...REMEMBER, TURKAS, I WANT THE COLD WEATHER TO BE CONSTANT! NOTHING MUST DISRUPT THE SHOW!
YES, MISTER MAYOR!
FZZT
FZZT
THIS WEATHER SPELL IS DIFFICULT, BUT YOU'LL GET EXACTLY WHAT YOU WANT!
GOOD!
WHEEE! THIS IS AWESOME, BRANDON!
STELLA LOOKS LIKE SHE'S HAVING THE BEST TIME!
SHE'S AN ICE-SKATING NATURAL!

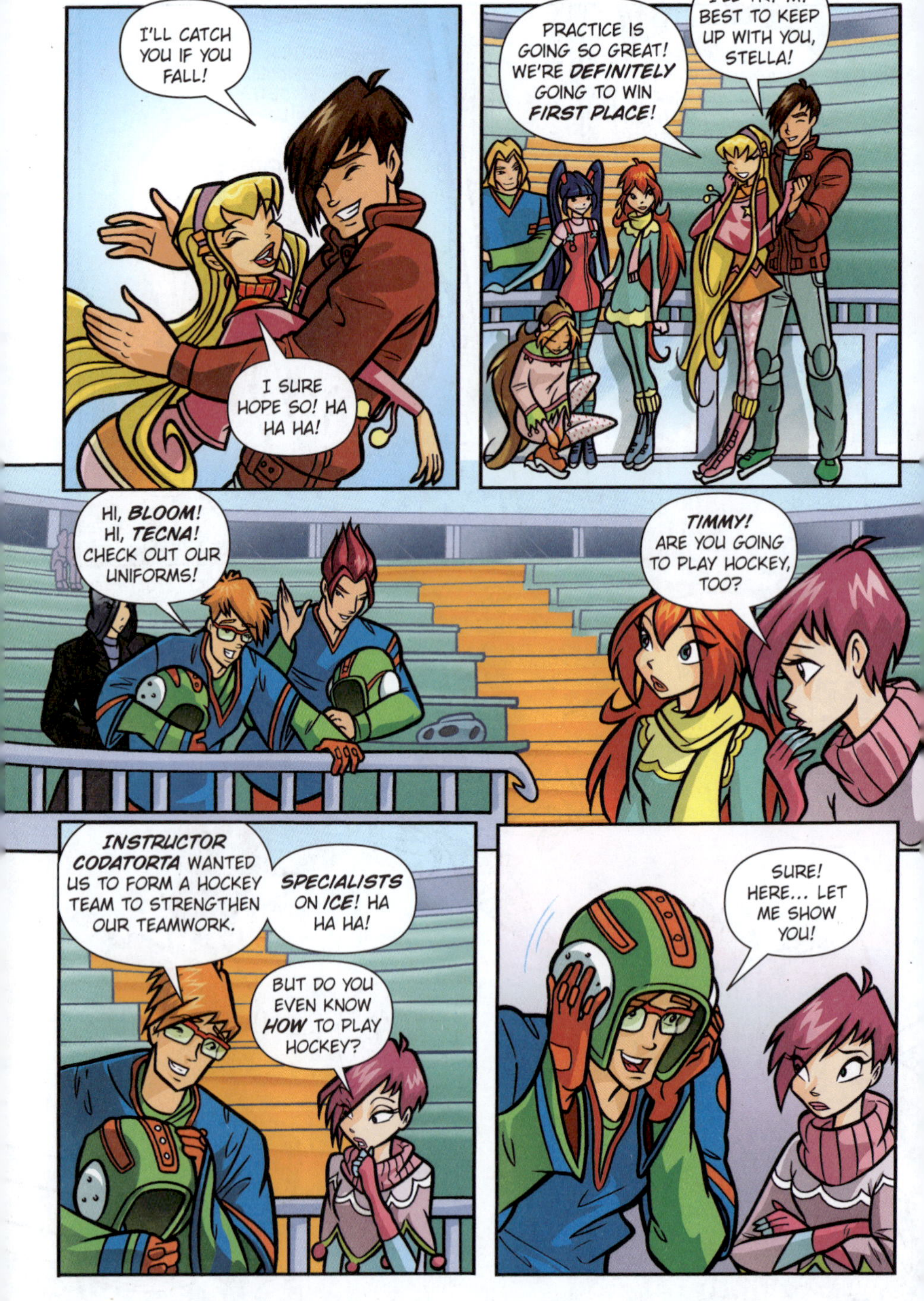
I'LL CATCH YOU IF YOU FALL!
I SURE HOPE SO! HA HA HA!
PRACTICE IS GOING SO GREAT! WE'RE DEFINITELY GOING TO WIN FIRST PLACE!
I'LL TRY MY BEST TO KEEP UP WITH YOU, STELLA!
HI, BLOOM! HI, TECNA! CHECK OUT OUR UNIFORMS!
TIMMY! ARE YOU GOING TO PLAY HOCKEY, TOO?
INSTRUCTOR CODATORTA WANTED US TO FORM A HOCKEY TEAM TO STRENGTHEN OUR TEAMWORK.
SPECIALISTS ON ICE! HA HA HA!
BUT DO YOU EVEN KNOW HOW TO PLAY HOCKEY?
SURE! HERE... LET ME SHOW YOU!

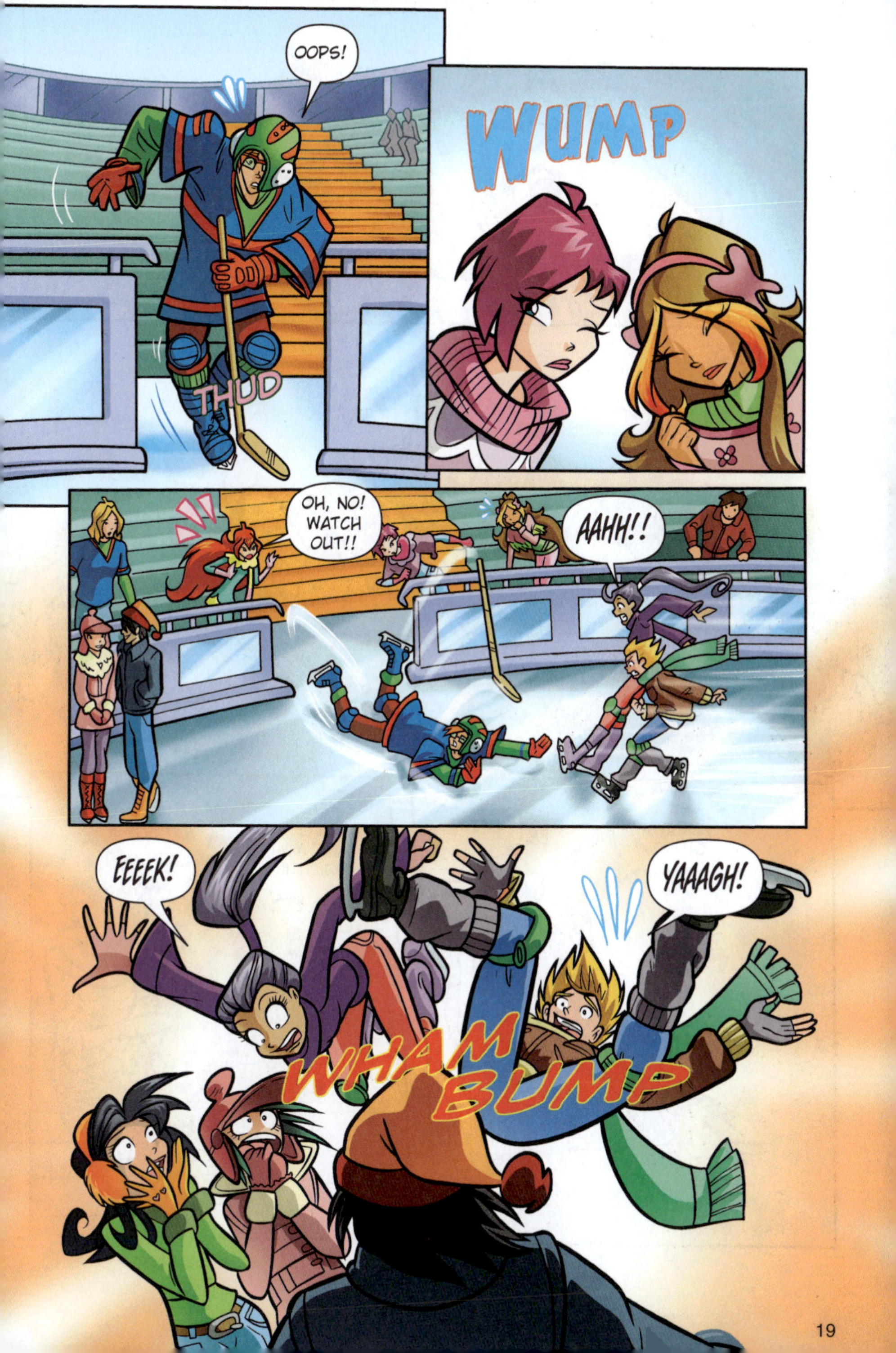
OOPS!
THUD
WUMP
OH, NO! WATCH OUT!!
AAHH!!
EEEEK!
YAAAGH!
WHAM
BUMP

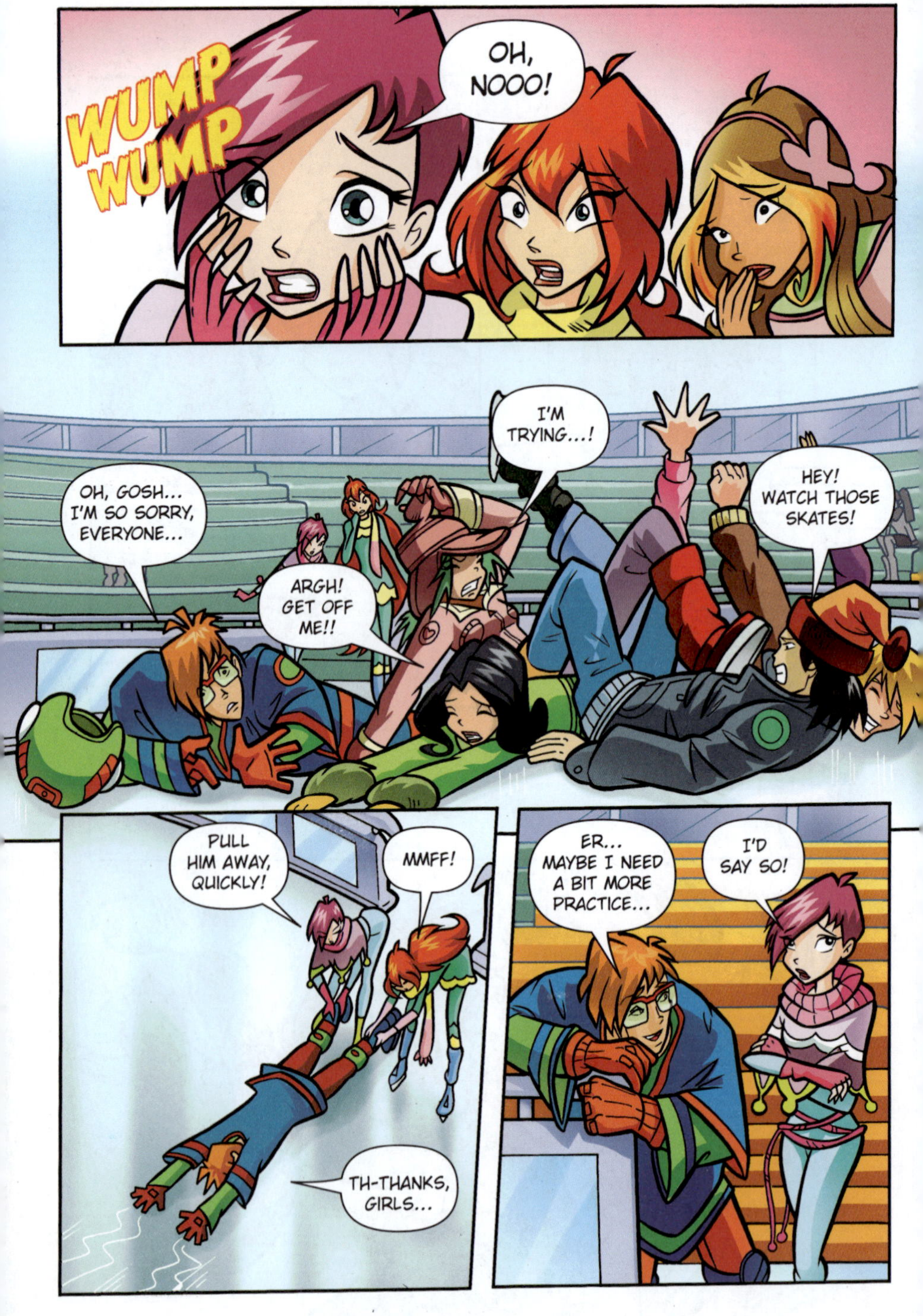
WUMP WUMP
OH, NOOO!
I'M TRYING...!
OH, GOSH... I'M SO SORRY, EVERYONE...
ARGH! GET OFF ME!!
HEY! WATCH THOSE SKATES!
PULL HIM AWAY, QUICKLY!
MMFF!
TH-THANKS, GIRLS...
ER... MAYBE I NEED A BIT MORE PRACTICE...
I'D SAY SO!

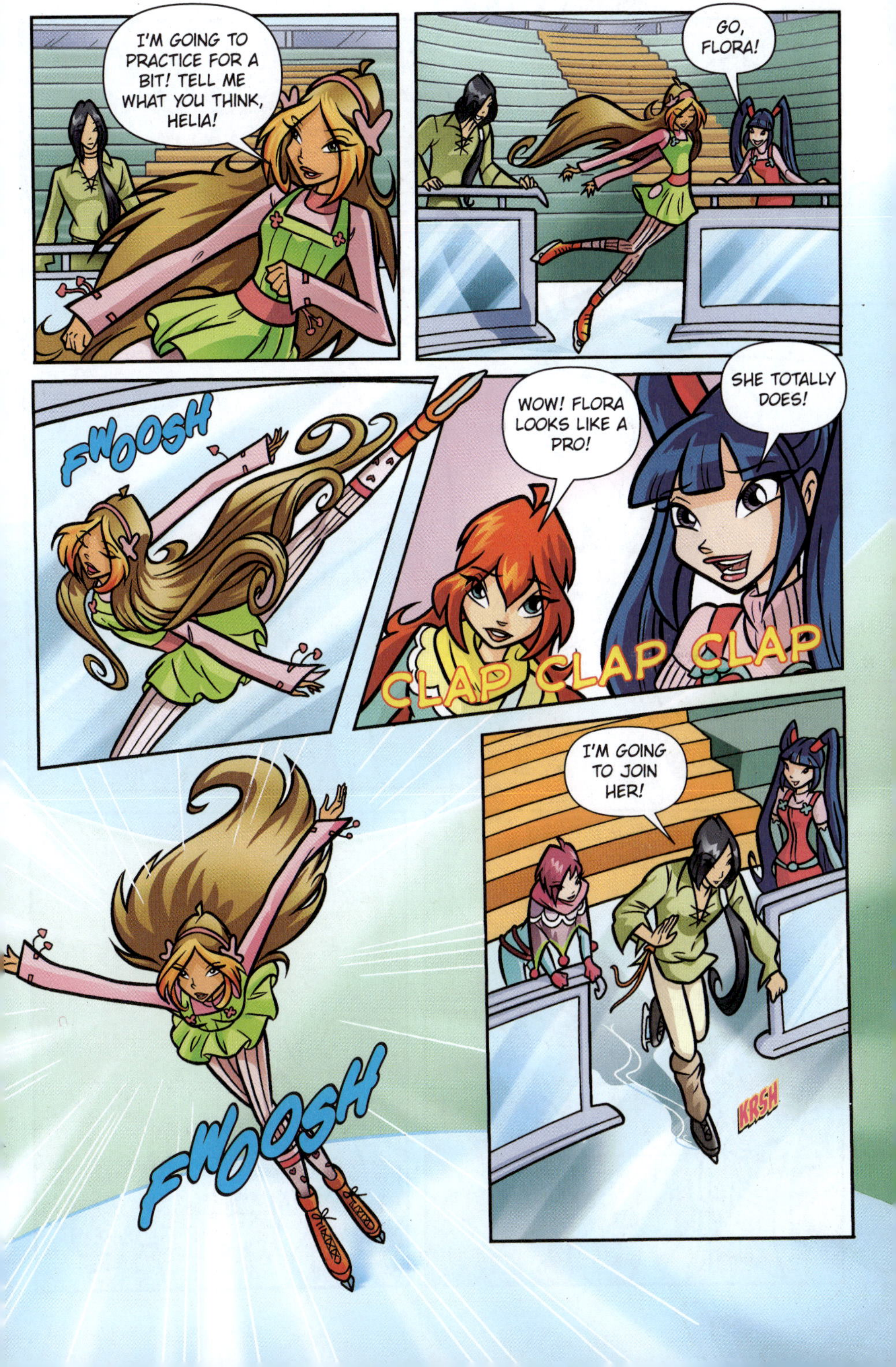
I'M GOING TO PRACTICE FOR A BIT! TELL ME WHAT YOU THINK, HELIA!
GO, FLORA!
FWOOSH
WOW! FLORA LOOKS LIKE A PRO!
SHE TOTALLY DOES!
CLAP CLAP CLAP
FWOOSH
I'M GOING TO JOIN HER!
KRSH

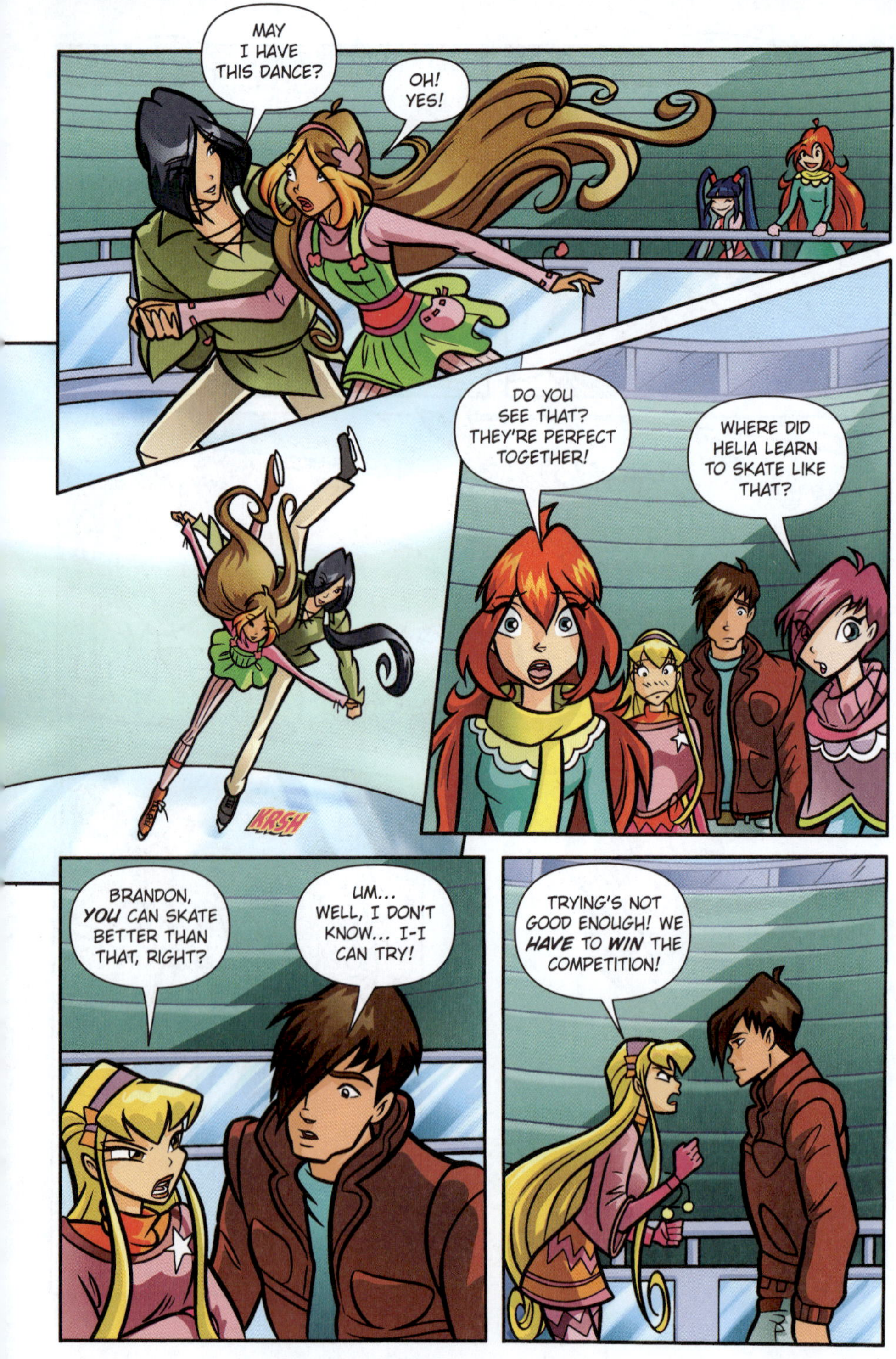
MAY I HAVE THIS DANCE?
OH! YES!
KRSH
DO YOU SEE THAT? THEY'RE PERFECT TOGETHER!
WHERE DID HELIA LEARN TO SKATE LIKE THAT?
BRANDON, *YOU* CAN SKATE BETTER THAN THAT, RIGHT?
UM... WELL, I DON'T KNOW... I-I CAN TRY!
TRYING'S NOT GOOD ENOUGH! WE *HAVE* TO *WIN* THE COMPETITION!

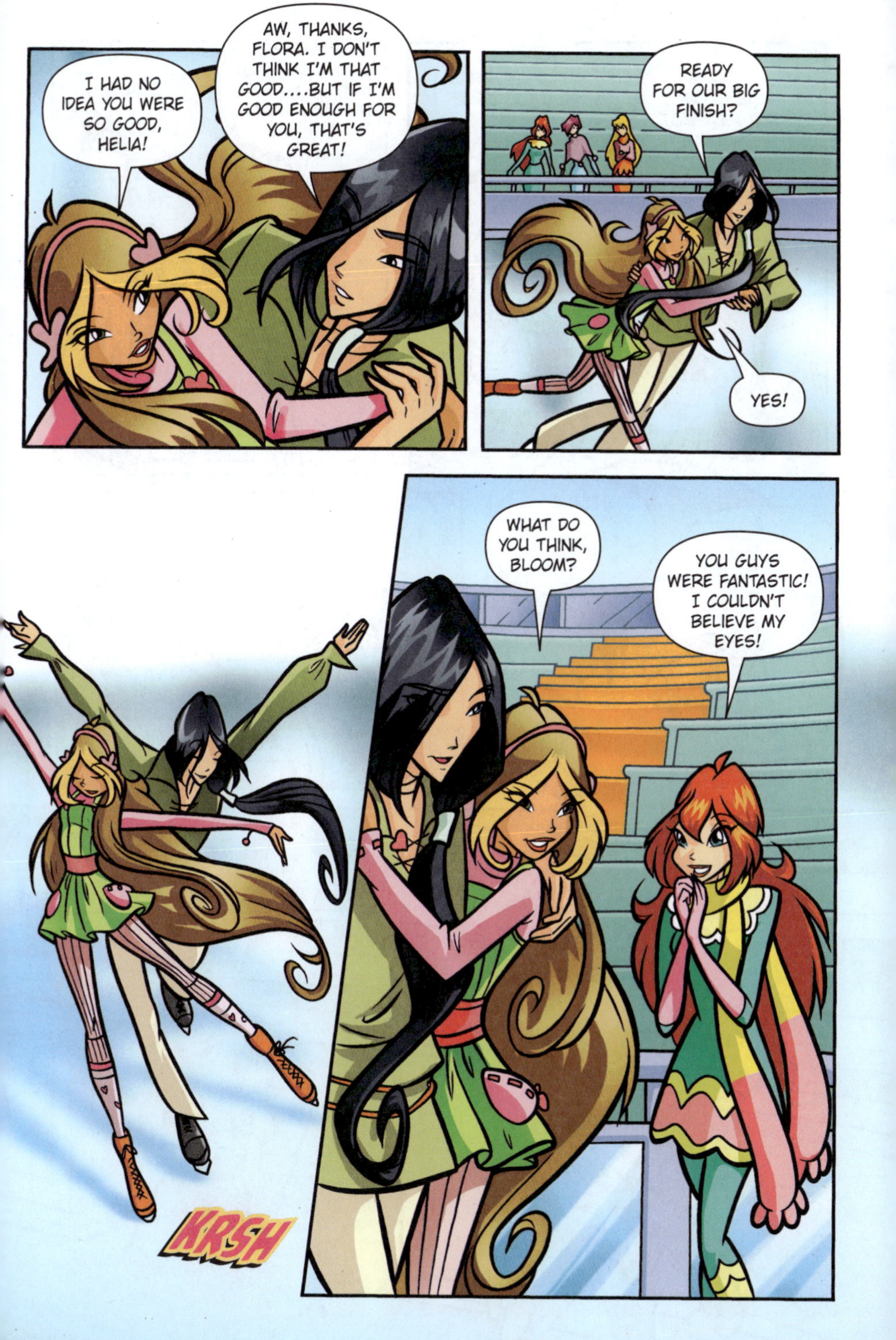

I HAD NO IDEA YOU WERE SO GOOD, HELIA!
AW, THANKS, FLORA. I DON'T THINK I'M THAT GOOD....BUT IF I'M GOOD ENOUGH FOR YOU, THAT'S GREAT!
READY FOR OUR BIG FINISH?
YES!
KRSH
WHAT DO YOU THINK, BLOOM?
YOU GUYS WERE FANTASTIC! I COULDN'T BELIEVE MY EYES!

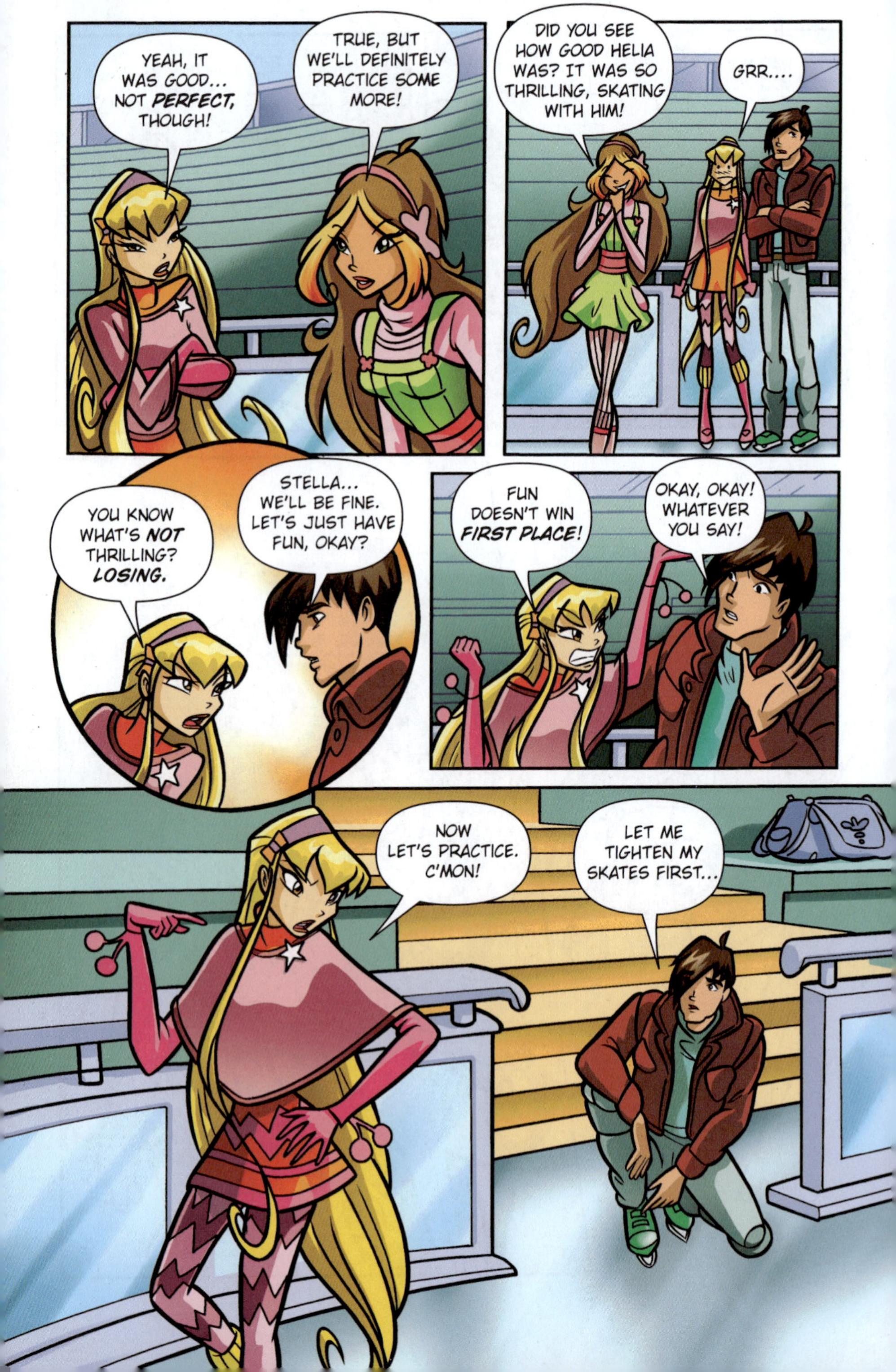
YEAH, IT WAS GOOD... NOT *PERFECT,* THOUGH!
TRUE, BUT WE'LL DEFINITELY PRACTICE SOME MORE!
DID YOU SEE HOW GOOD HELIA WAS? IT WAS SO THRILLING, SKATING WITH HIM!
GRR....
YOU KNOW WHAT'S **NOT** THRILLING? ***LOSING.***
STELLA... WE'LL BE FINE. LET'S JUST HAVE FUN, OKAY?
FUN DOESN'T WIN ***FIRST PLACE!***
OKAY, OKAY! WHATEVER YOU SAY!
NOW LET'S PRACTICE. C'MON!
LET ME TIGHTEN MY SKATES FIRST...

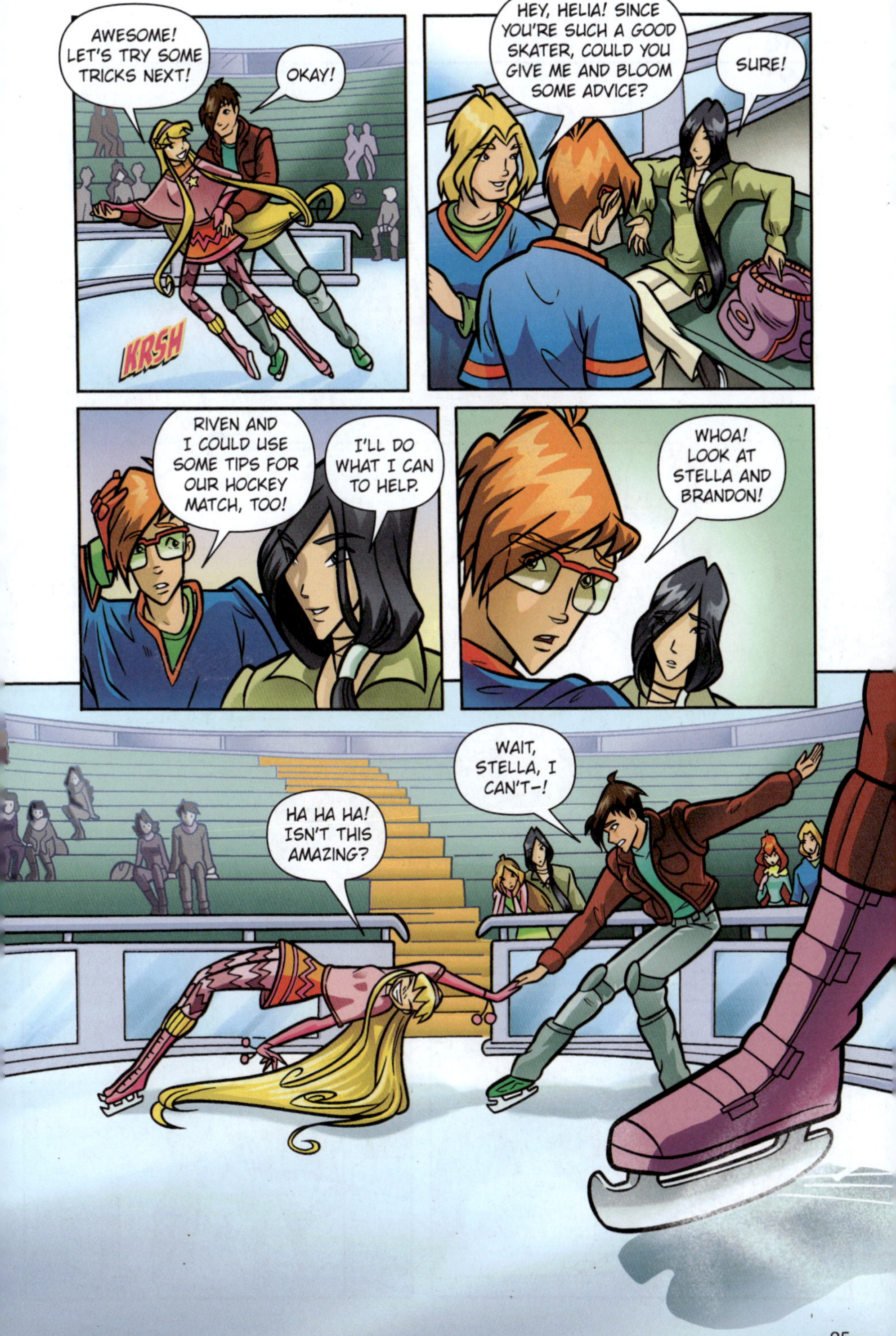
AWESOME! LET'S TRY SOME TRICKS NEXT!
OKAY!
KRSH
HEY, HELIA! SINCE YOU'RE SUCH A GOOD SKATER, COULD YOU GIVE ME AND BLOOM SOME ADVICE?
SURE!
RIVEN AND I COULD USE SOME TIPS FOR OUR HOCKEY MATCH, TOO!
I'LL DO WHAT I CAN TO HELP.
WHOA! LOOK AT STELLA AND BRANDON!
WAIT, STELLA, I CAN'T-!
HA HA HA! ISN'T THIS AMAZING?

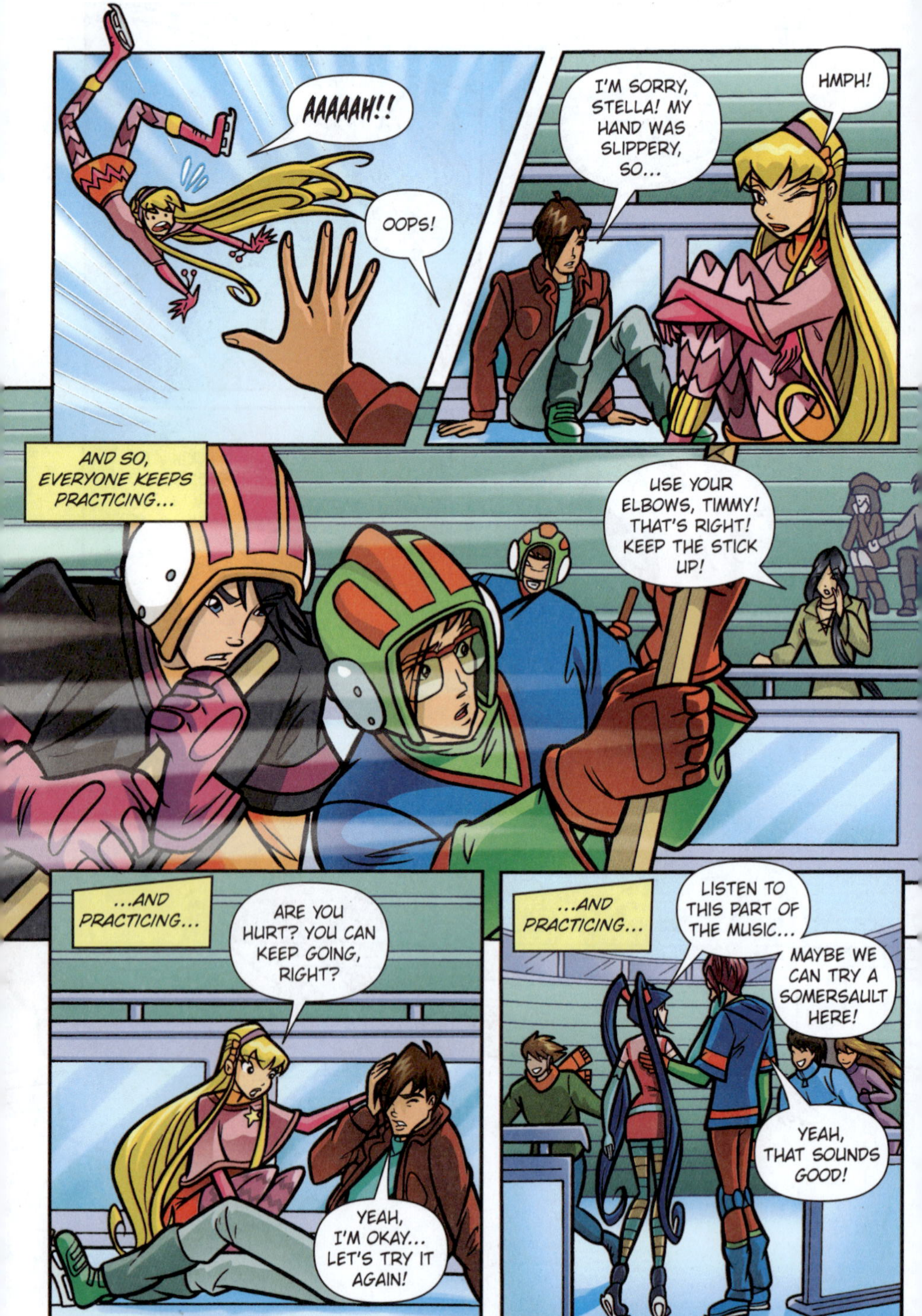
AAAAAH!!
OOPS!
I'M SORRY, STELLA! MY HAND WAS SLIPPERY, SO...
HMPH!
AND SO, EVERYONE KEEPS PRACTICING...
USE YOUR ELBOWS, TIMMY! THAT'S RIGHT! KEEP THE STICK UP!
...AND PRACTICING...
ARE YOU HURT? YOU CAN KEEP GOING, RIGHT?
YEAH, I'M OKAY... LET'S TRY IT AGAIN!
...AND PRACTICING...
LISTEN TO THIS PART OF THE MUSIC...
MAYBE WE CAN TRY A SOMERSAULT HERE!
YEAH, THAT SOUNDS GOOD!

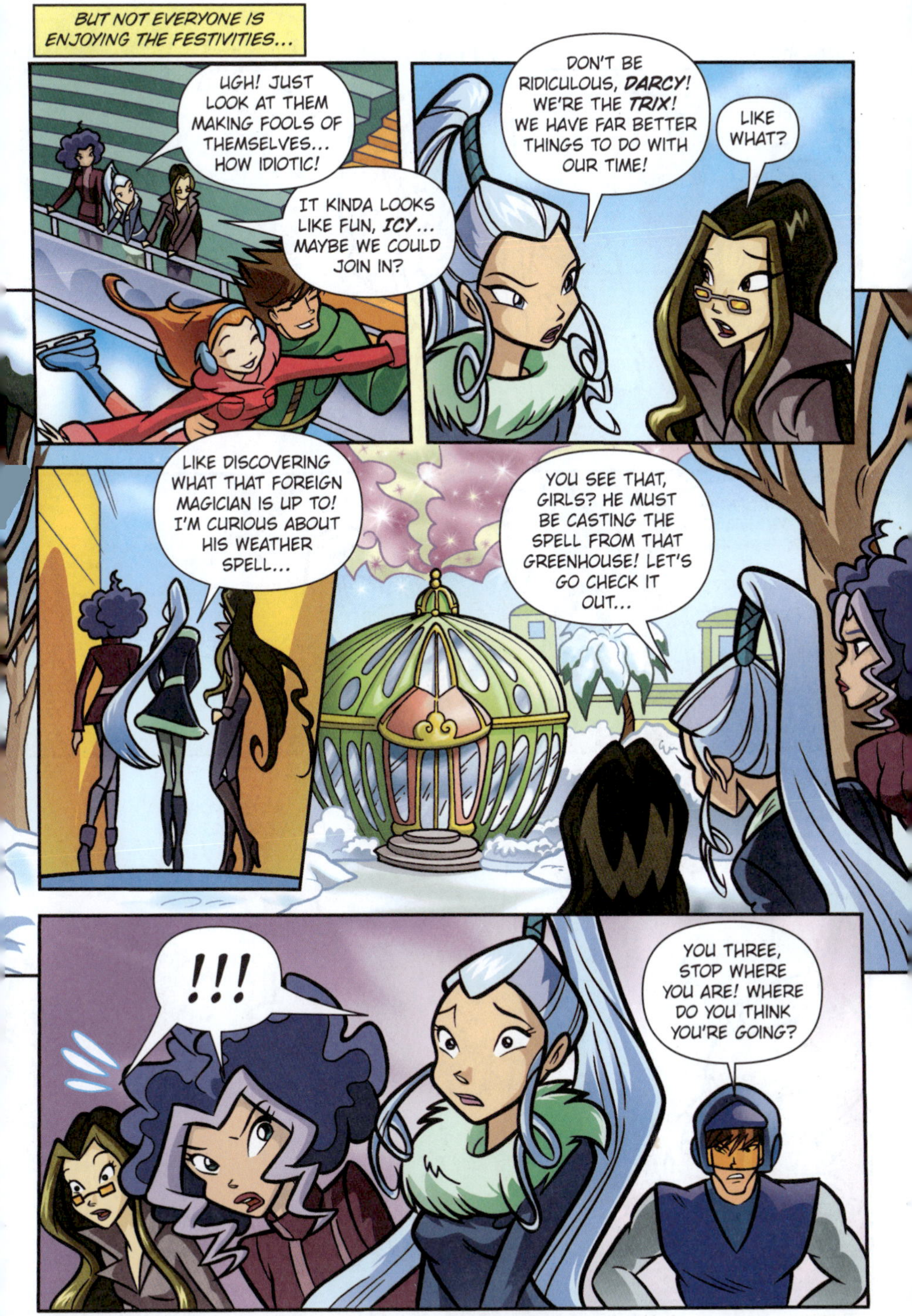

BUT NOT EVERYONE IS ENJOYING THE FESTIVITIES...
UGH! JUST LOOK AT THEM MAKING FOOLS OF THEMSELVES... HOW IDIOTIC!
IT KINDA LOOKS LIKE FUN, ICY... MAYBE WE COULD JOIN IN?
DON'T BE RIDICULOUS, DARCY! WE'RE THE TRIX! WE HAVE FAR BETTER THINGS TO DO WITH OUR TIME!
LIKE WHAT?
LIKE DISCOVERING WHAT THAT FOREIGN MAGICIAN IS UP TO! I'M CURIOUS ABOUT HIS WEATHER SPELL...
YOU SEE THAT, GIRLS? HE MUST BE CASTING THE SPELL FROM THAT GREENHOUSE! LET'S GO CHECK IT OUT...
!!!
YOU THREE, STOP WHERE YOU ARE! WHERE DO YOU THINK YOU'RE GOING?

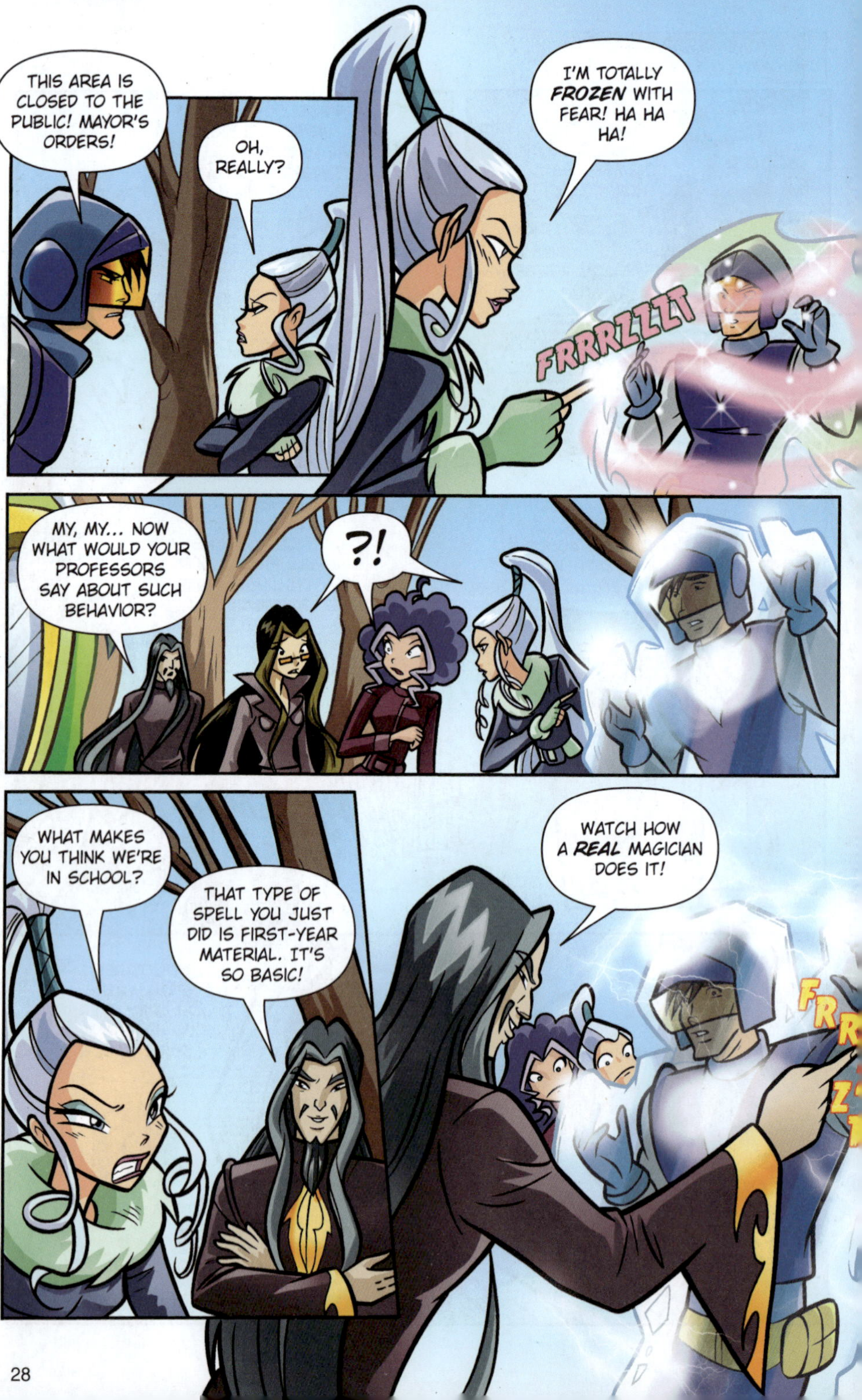
THIS AREA IS CLOSED TO THE PUBLIC! MAYOR'S ORDERS!
OH, REALLY?
I'M TOTALLY FROZEN WITH FEAR! HA HA HA!
FRRRZZZT
MY, MY... NOW WHAT WOULD YOUR PROFESSORS SAY ABOUT SUCH BEHAVIOR?
?!
WHAT MAKES YOU THINK WE'RE IN SCHOOL?
THAT TYPE OF SPELL YOU JUST DID IS FIRST-YEAR MATERIAL. IT'S SO BASIC!
WATCH HOW A REAL MAGICIAN DOES IT!

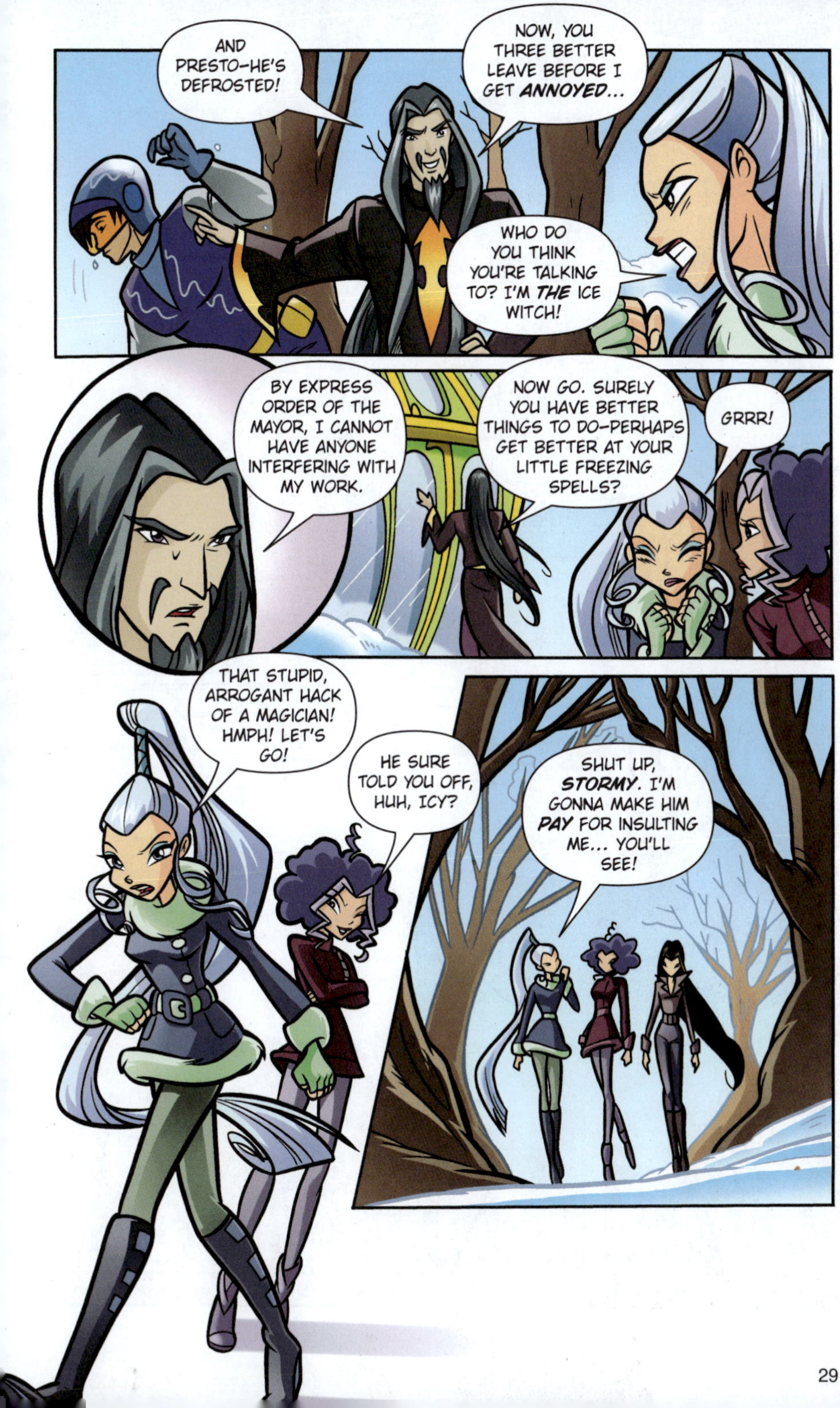

AND PRESTO–HE'S DEFROSTED!
NOW, YOU THREE BETTER LEAVE BEFORE I GET ANNOYED...
WHO DO YOU THINK YOU'RE TALKING TO? I'M THE ICE WITCH!
BY EXPRESS ORDER OF THE MAYOR, I CANNOT HAVE ANYONE INTERFERING WITH MY WORK.
NOW GO. SURELY YOU HAVE BETTER THINGS TO DO–PERHAPS GET BETTER AT YOUR LITTLE FREEZING SPELLS?
GRRR!
THAT STUPID, ARROGANT HACK OF A MAGICIAN! HMPH! LET'S GO!
HE SURE TOLD YOU OFF, HUH, ICY?
SHUT UP, STORMY. I'M GONNA MAKE HIM PAY FOR INSULTING ME... YOU'LL SEE!

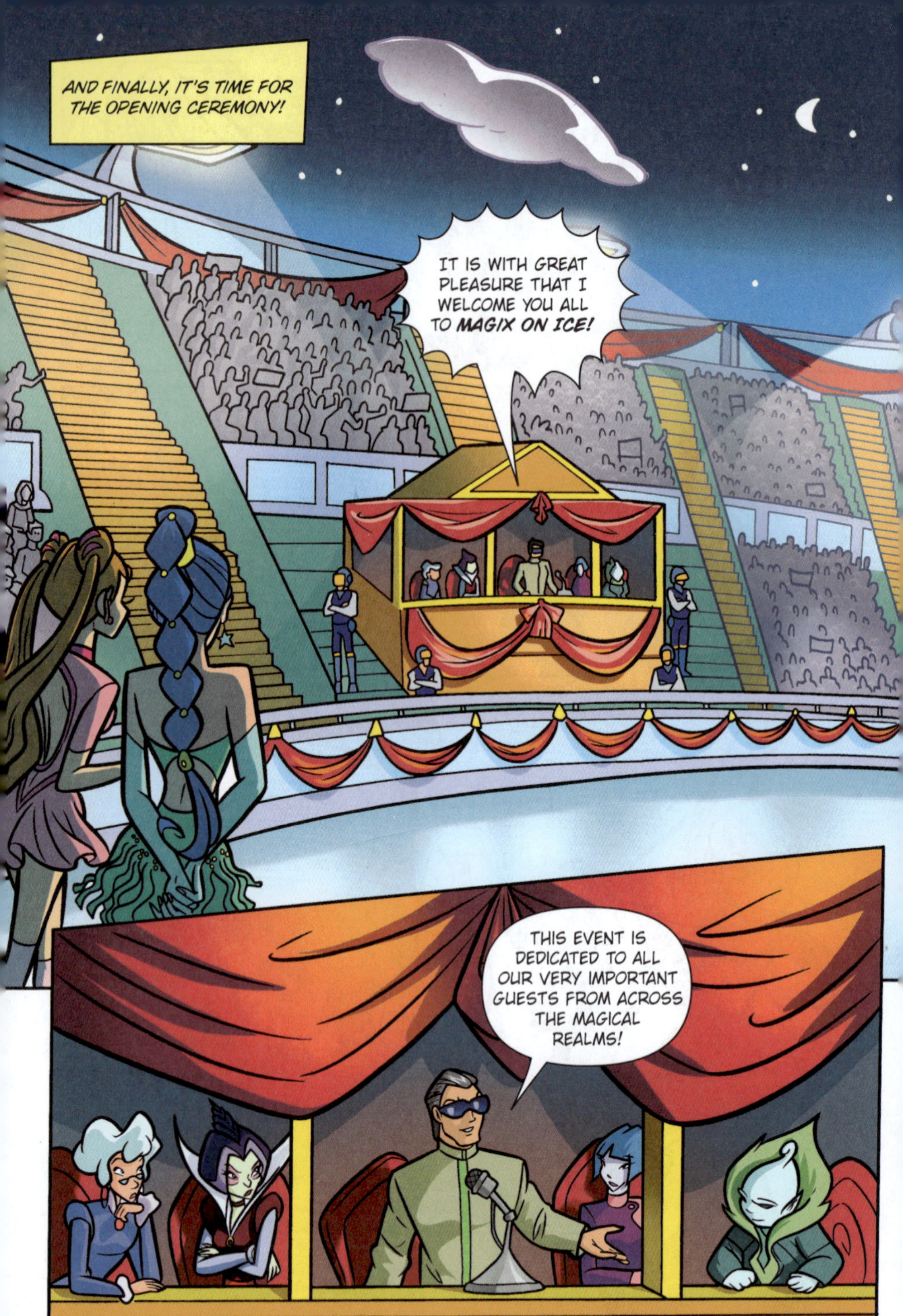
AND FINALLY, IT'S TIME FOR THE OPENING CEREMONY!
IT IS WITH GREAT PLEASURE THAT I WELCOME YOU ALL TO MAGIX ON ICE!
THIS EVENT IS DEDICATED TO ALL OUR VERY IMPORTANT GUESTS FROM ACROSS THE MAGICAL REALMS!

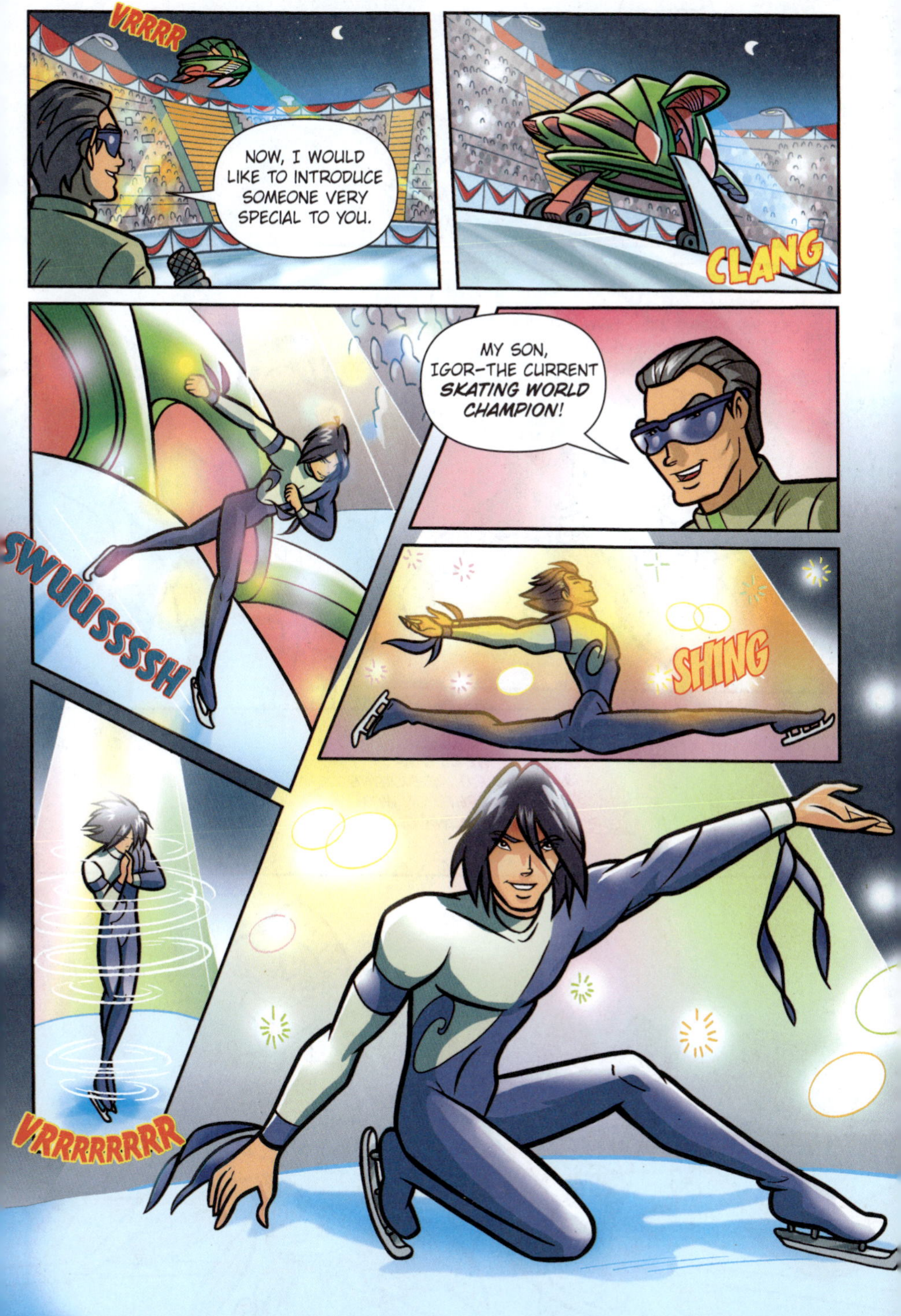
VRRRR
NOW, I WOULD LIKE TO INTRODUCE SOMEONE VERY SPECIAL TO YOU.
CLANG
SWUUSSSSH
MY SON, IGOR—THE CURRENT ***SKATING WORLD CHAMPION!***
SHING
VRRRRRRRRR

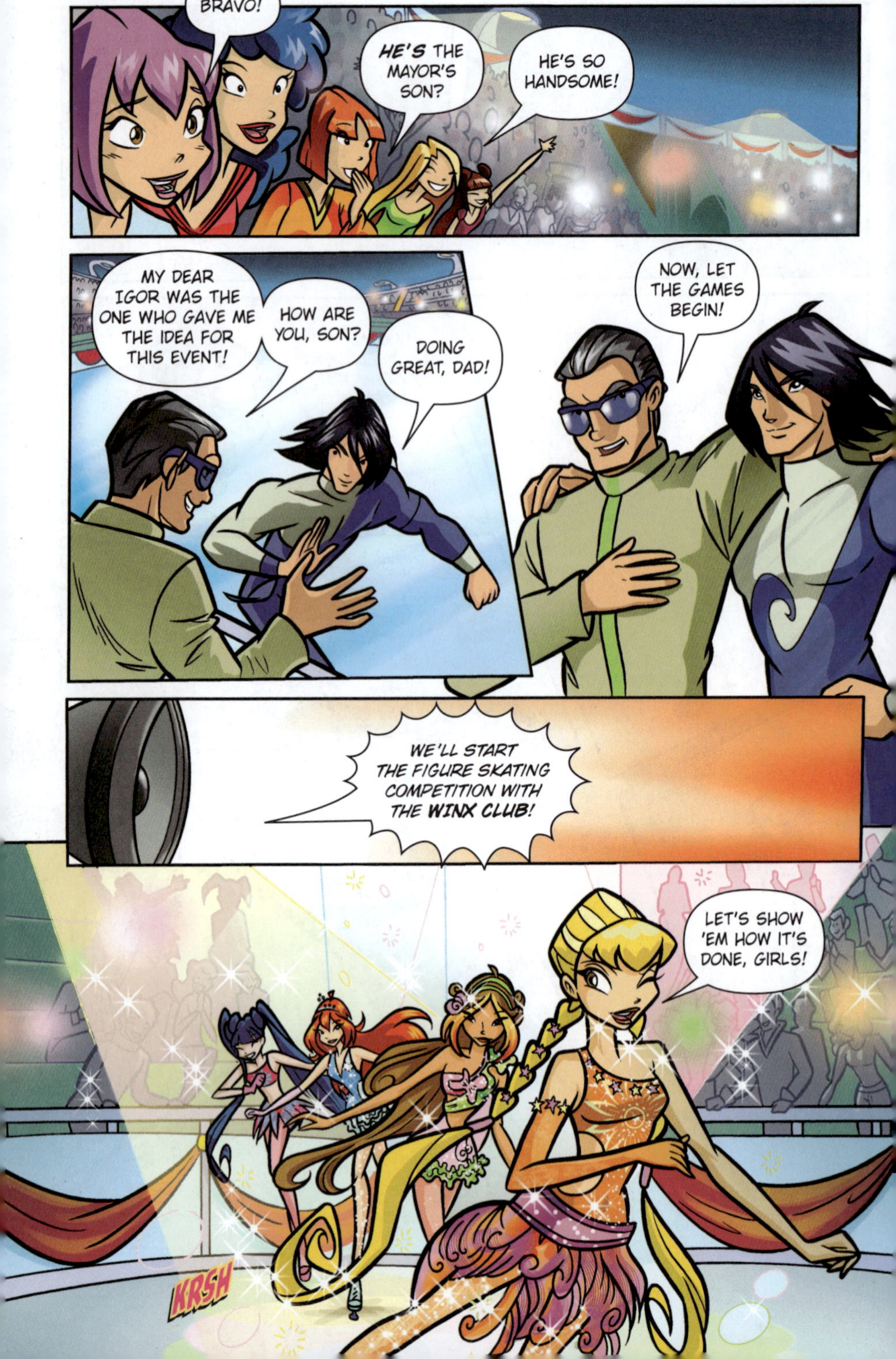
BRAVO!
HE'S THE MAYOR'S SON?
HE'S SO HANDSOME!
MY DEAR IGOR WAS THE ONE WHO GAVE ME THE IDEA FOR THIS EVENT!
HOW ARE YOU, SON?
DOING GREAT, DAD!
NOW, LET THE GAMES BEGIN!
WE'LL START THE FIGURE SKATING COMPETITION WITH THE WINX CLUB!
LET'S SHOW 'EM HOW IT'S DONE, GIRLS!
KRSH

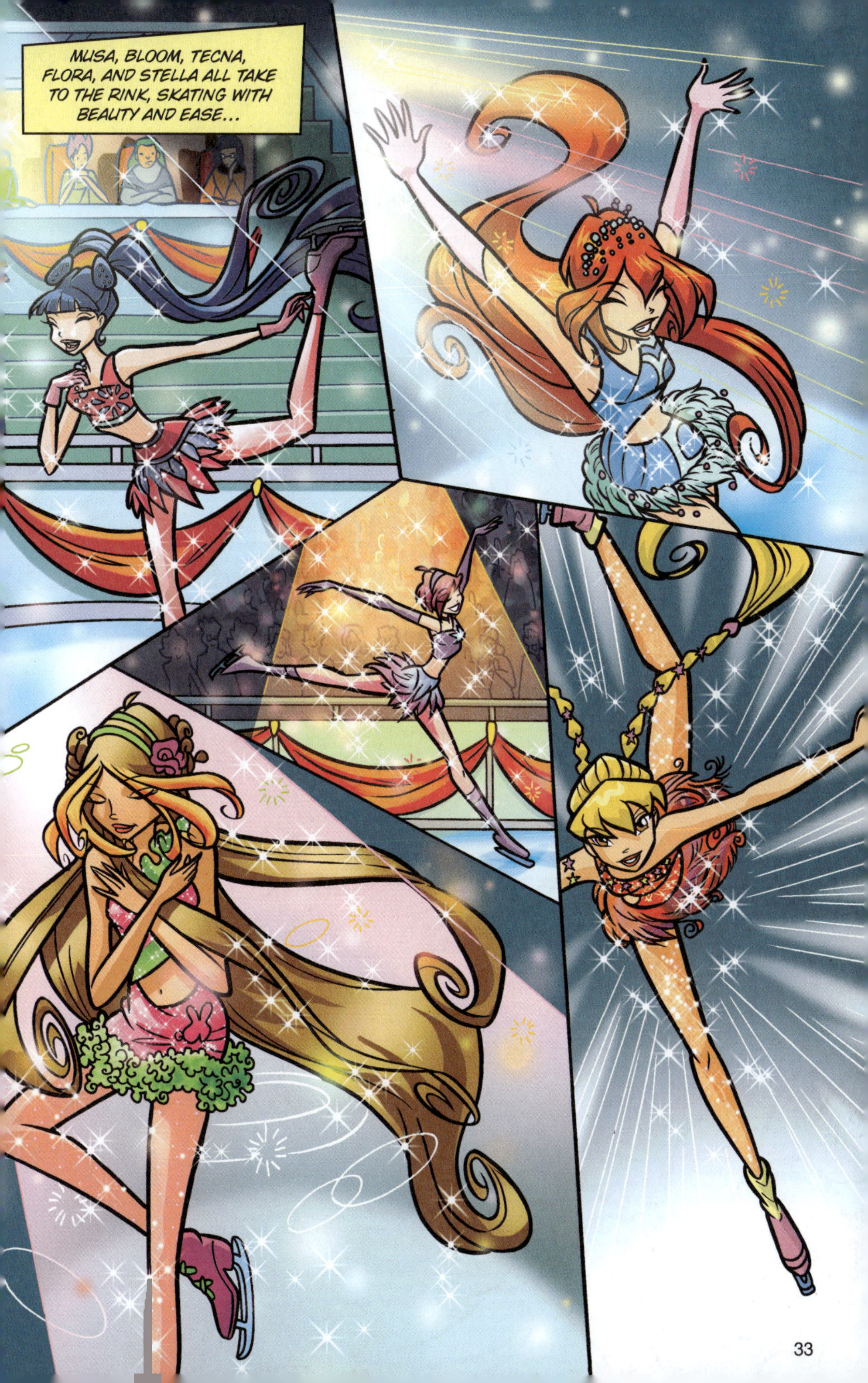
MUSA, BLOOM, TECNA, FLORA, AND STELLA ALL TAKE TO THE RINK, SKATING WITH BEAUTY AND EASE...

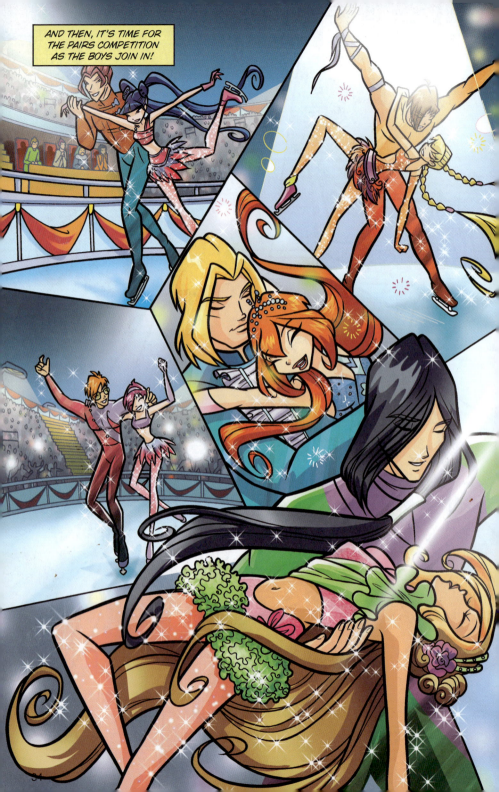

AND THEN, IT'S TIME FOR THE PAIRS COMPETITION AS THE BOYS JOIN IN!

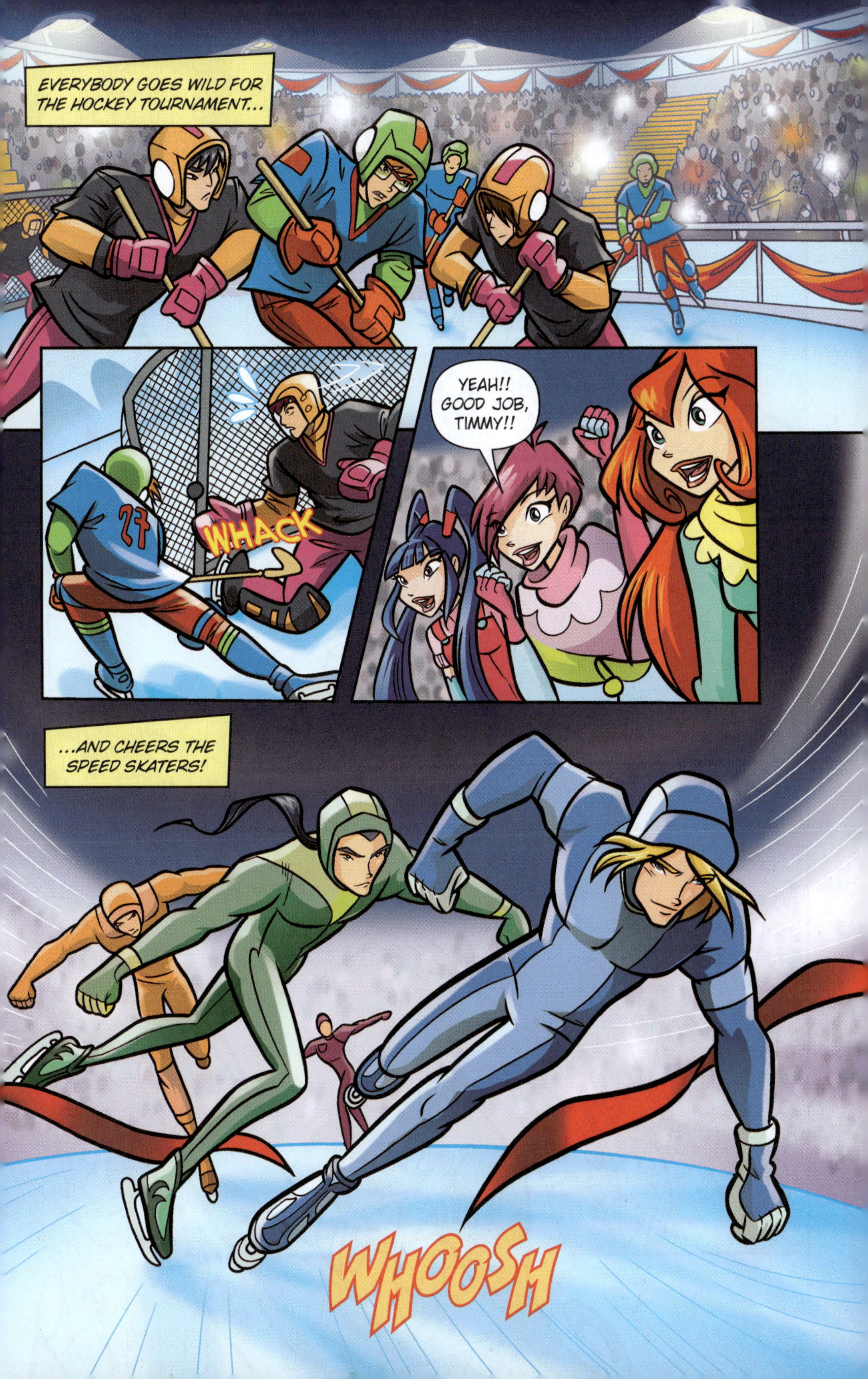
EVERYBODY GOES WILD FOR THE HOCKEY TOURNAMENT...
WHACK
YEAH!! GOOD JOB, TIMMY!!
...AND CHEERS THE SPEED SKATERS!
WHOOSH

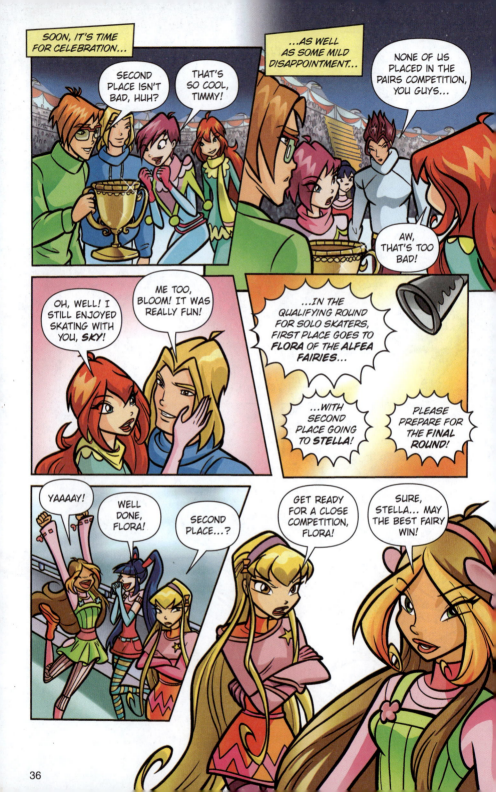

SOON, IT'S TIME FOR CELEBRATION...

SECOND PLACE ISN'T BAD, HUH?

THAT'S SO COOL, TIMMY!

...AS WELL AS SOME MILD DISAPPOINTMENT...

NONE OF US PLACED IN THE PAIRS COMPETITION, YOU GUYS...

AW, THAT'S TOO BAD!

OH, WELL! I STILL ENJOYED SKATING WITH YOU, *SKY*!

ME TOO, BLOOM! IT WAS REALLY FUN!

...IN THE QUALIFYING ROUND FOR SOLO SKATERS, FIRST PLACE GOES TO *FLORA* OF THE ALFEA FAIRIES...

...WITH SECOND PLACE GOING TO *STELLA*!

PLEASE PREPARE FOR THE FINAL ROUND!

YAAAAY!

WELL DONE, FLORA!

SECOND PLACE...?

GET READY FOR A CLOSE COMPETITION, FLORA!

SURE, STELLA... MAY THE BEST FAIRY WIN!

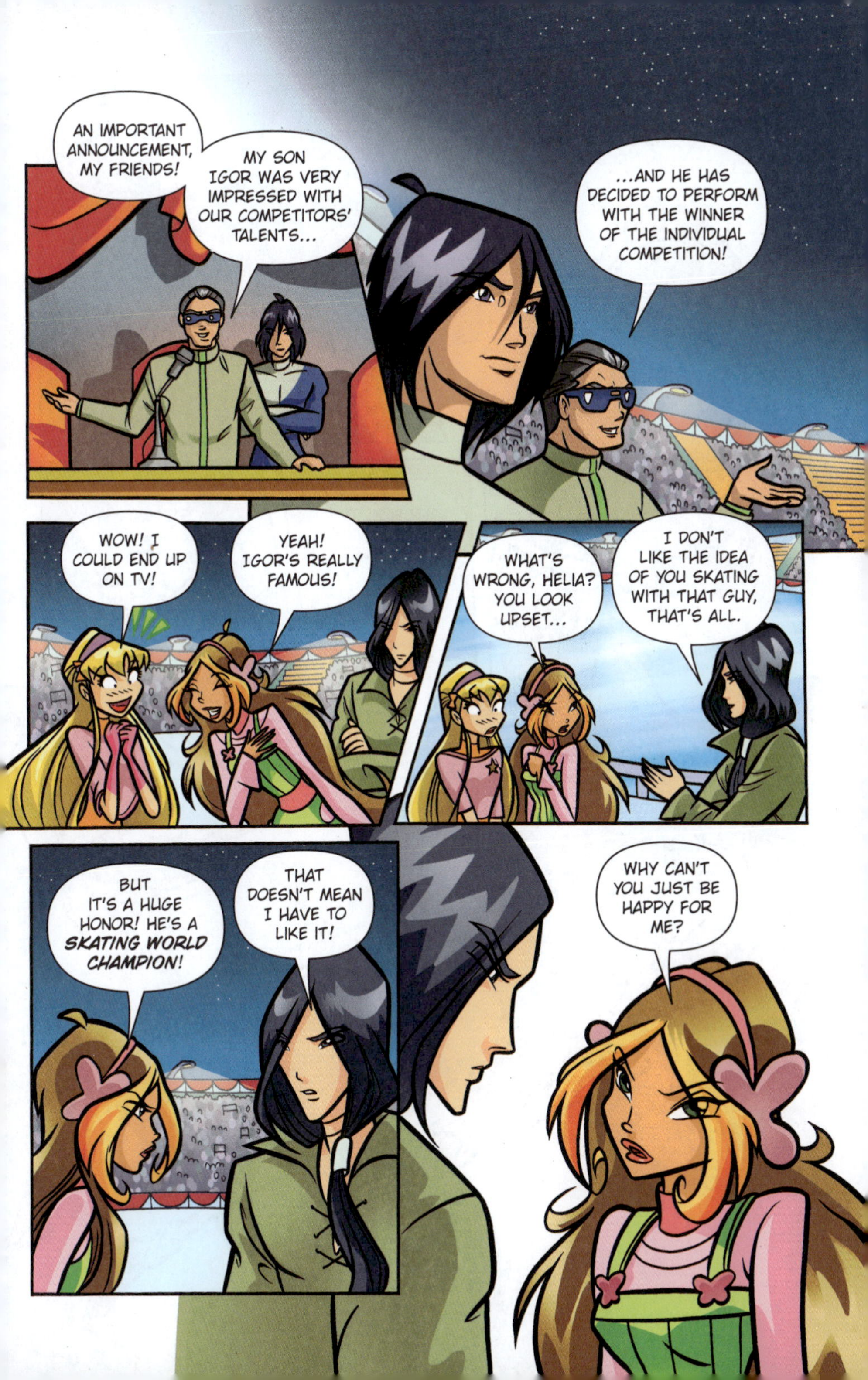
AN IMPORTANT ANNOUNCEMENT, MY FRIENDS!
MY SON IGOR WAS VERY IMPRESSED WITH OUR COMPETITORS' TALENTS...
...AND HE HAS DECIDED TO PERFORM WITH THE WINNER OF THE INDIVIDUAL COMPETITION!
WOW! I COULD END UP ON TV!
YEAH! IGOR'S REALLY FAMOUS!
WHAT'S WRONG, HELIA? YOU LOOK UPSET...
I DON'T LIKE THE IDEA OF YOU SKATING WITH THAT GUY, THAT'S ALL.
BUT IT'S A HUGE HONOR! HE'S A ***SKATING WORLD CHAMPION!***
THAT DOESN'T MEAN I HAVE TO LIKE IT!
WHY CAN'T YOU JUST BE HAPPY FOR ME?

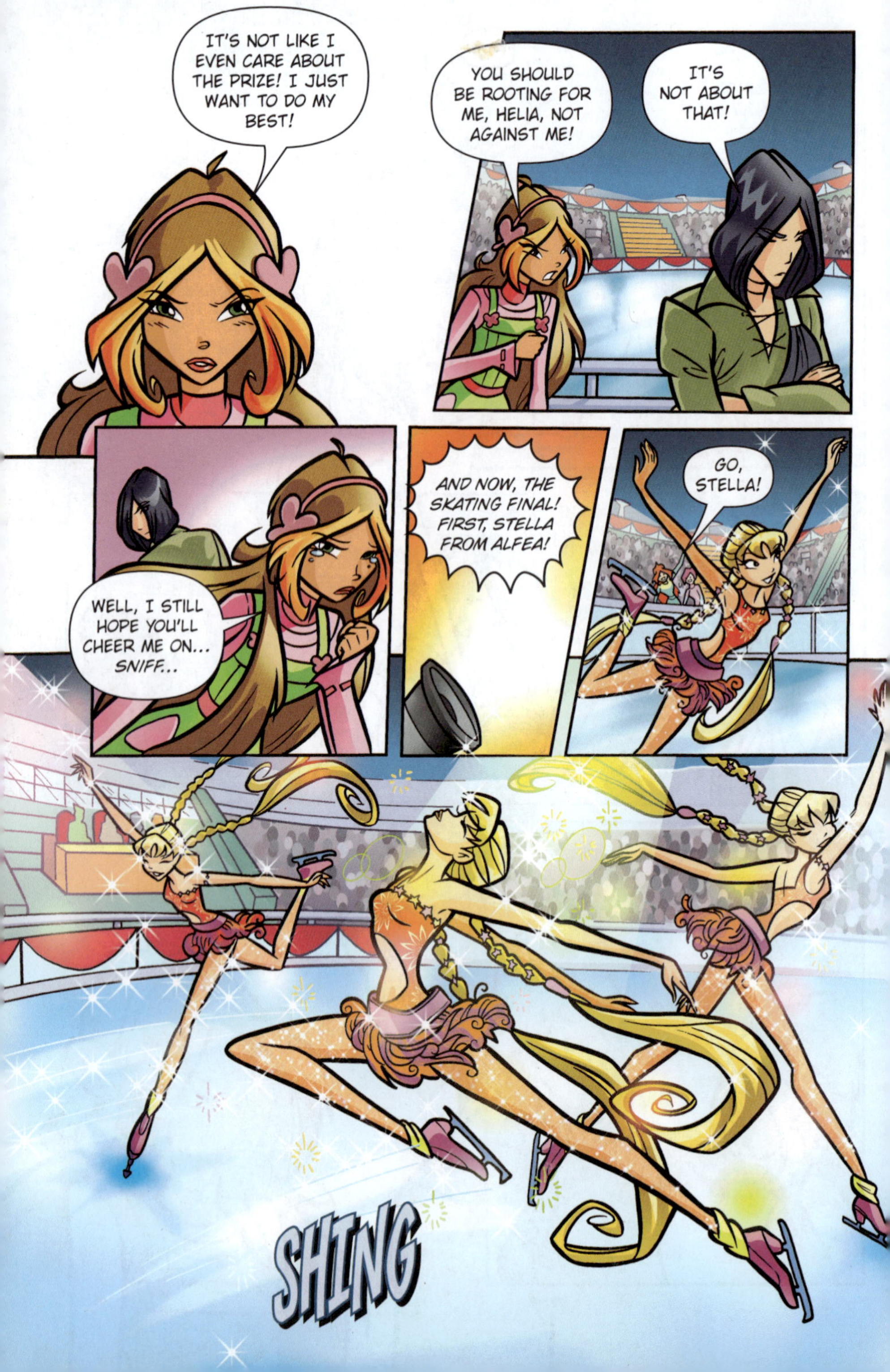
IT'S NOT LIKE I EVEN CARE ABOUT THE PRIZE! I JUST WANT TO DO MY BEST!
YOU SHOULD BE ROOTING FOR ME, HELIA, NOT AGAINST ME!
IT'S NOT ABOUT THAT!
WELL, I STILL HOPE YOU'LL CHEER ME ON... SNIFF...
AND NOW, THE SKATING FINAL! FIRST, STELLA FROM ALFEA!
GO, STELLA!
SHING

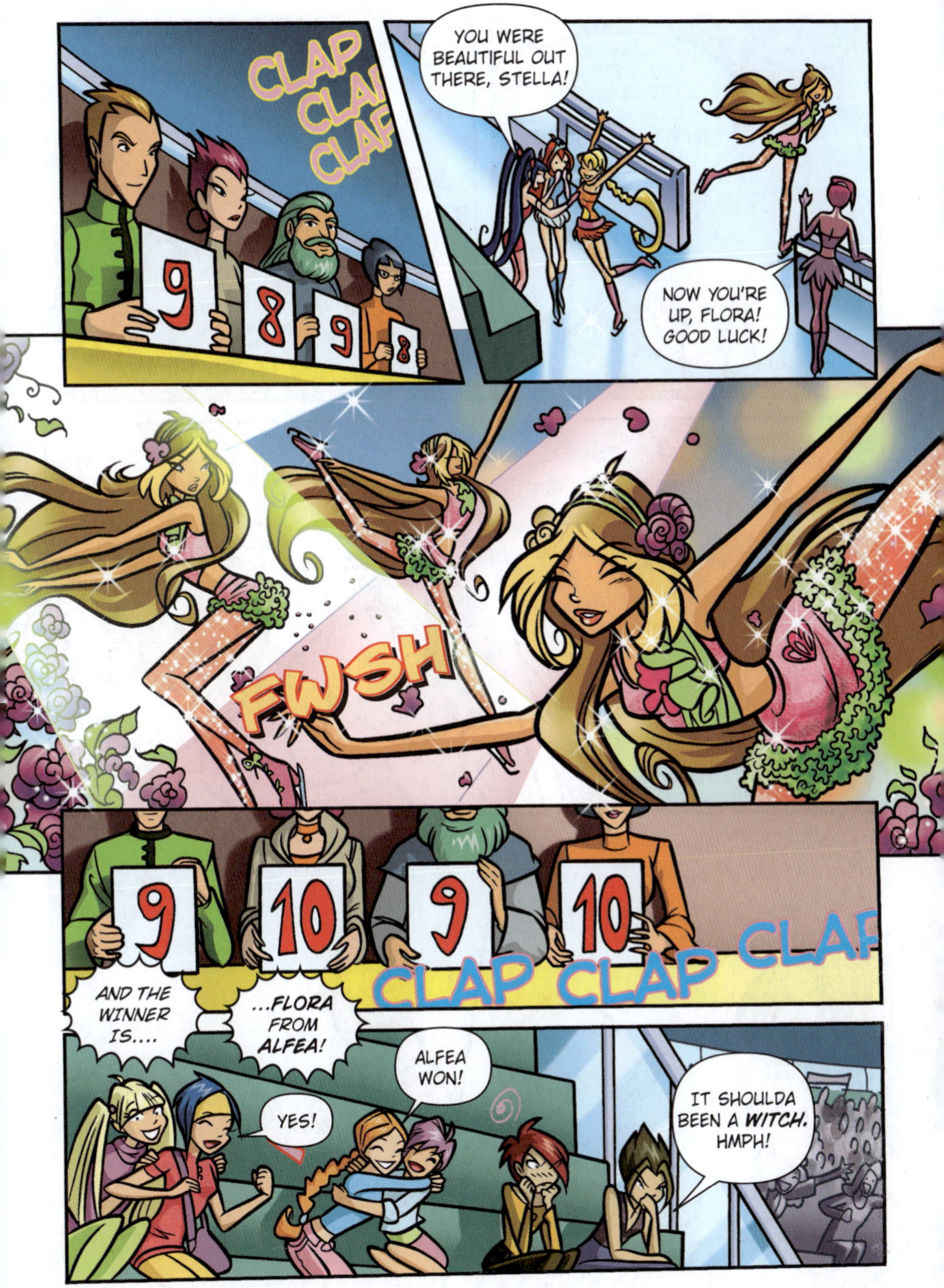
CLAP CLAP CLAP
9
8
9
8
YOU WERE BEAUTIFUL OUT THERE, STELLA!
NOW YOU'RE UP, FLORA! GOOD LUCK!
FWSH
9
10
9
10
CLAP CLAP CLAP
AND THE WINNER IS....
...FLORA FROM ALFEA!
YES!
ALFEA WON!
IT SHOULDA BEEN A WITCH. HMPH!

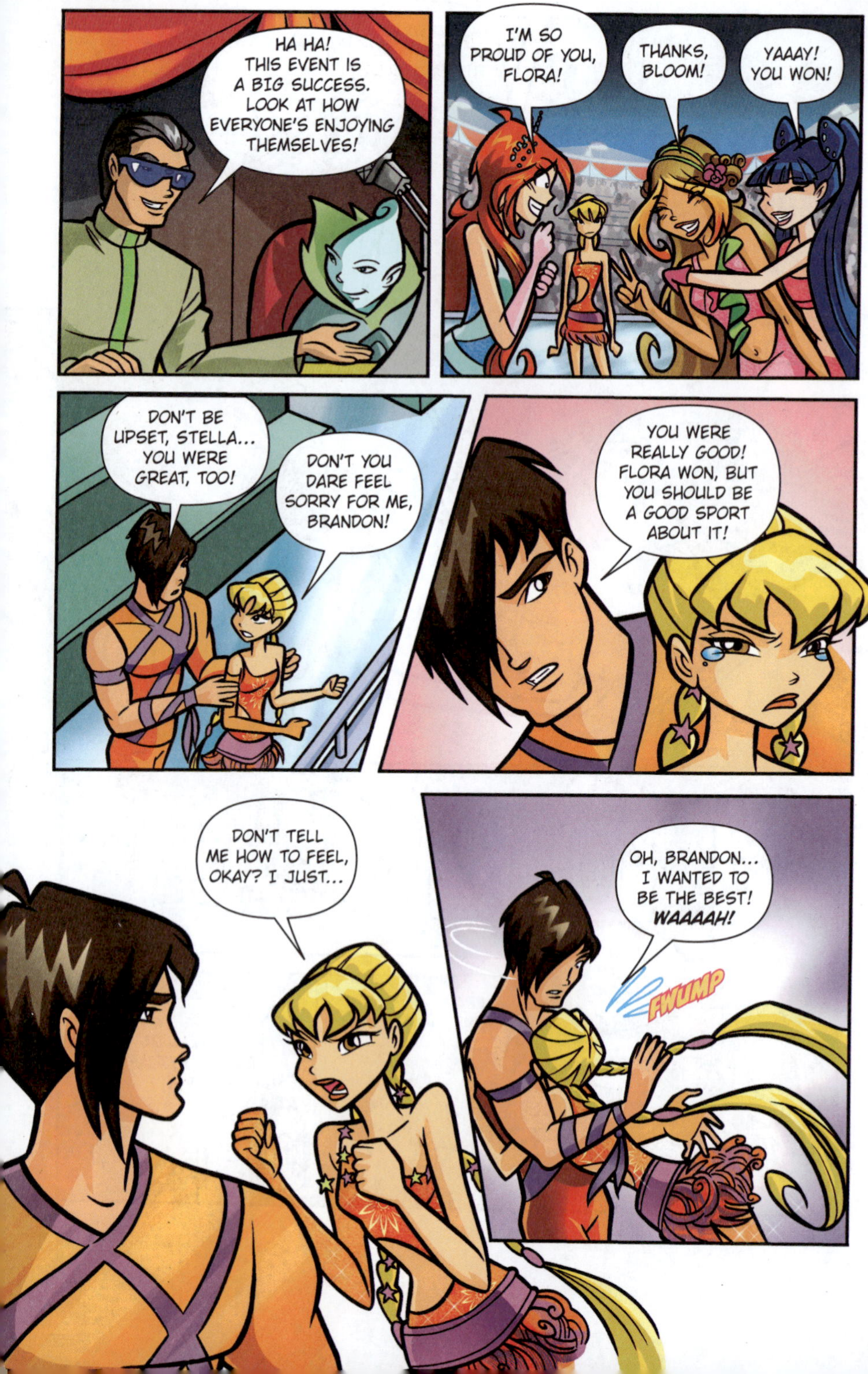
HA HA! THIS EVENT IS A BIG SUCCESS. LOOK AT HOW EVERYONE'S ENJOYING THEMSELVES!
I'M SO PROUD OF YOU, FLORA!
THANKS, BLOOM!
YAAAY! YOU WON!
DON'T BE UPSET, STELLA... YOU WERE GREAT, TOO!
DON'T YOU DARE FEEL SORRY FOR ME, BRANDON!
YOU WERE REALLY GOOD! FLORA WON, BUT YOU SHOULD BE A GOOD SPORT ABOUT IT!
DON'T TELL ME HOW TO FEEL, OKAY? I JUST...
OH, BRANDON... I WANTED TO BE THE BEST! ***WAAAAH!***
FWUMP

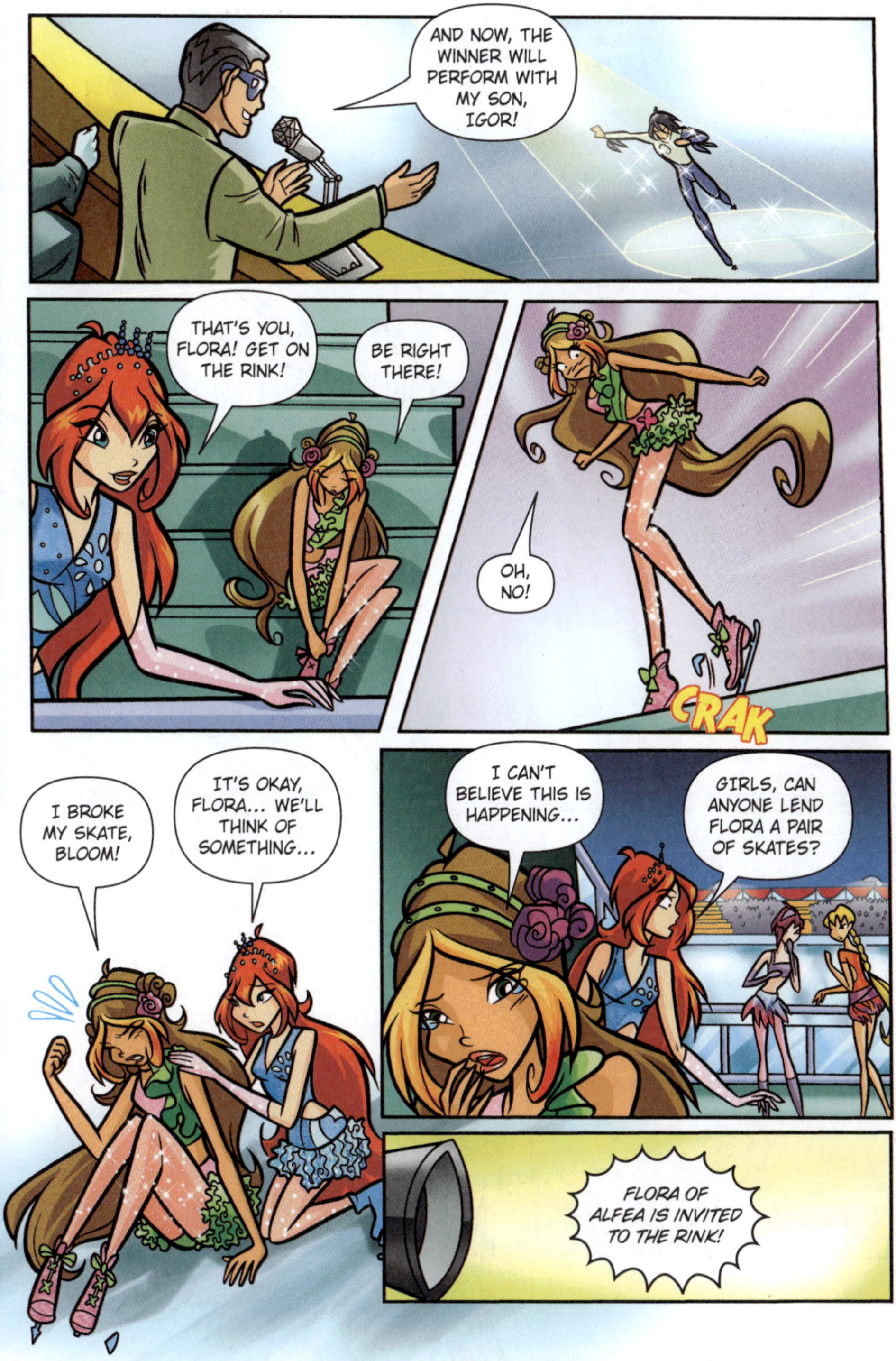

AND NOW, THE WINNER WILL PERFORM WITH MY SON, IGOR!
THAT'S YOU, FLORA! GET ON THE RINK!
BE RIGHT THERE!
OH, NO!
CRAK
I BROKE MY SKATE, BLOOM!
IT'S OKAY, FLORA... WE'LL THINK OF SOMETHING...
I CAN'T BELIEVE THIS IS HAPPENING...
GIRLS, CAN ANYONE LEND FLORA A PAIR OF SKATES?
FLORA OF ALFEA IS INVITED TO THE RINK!

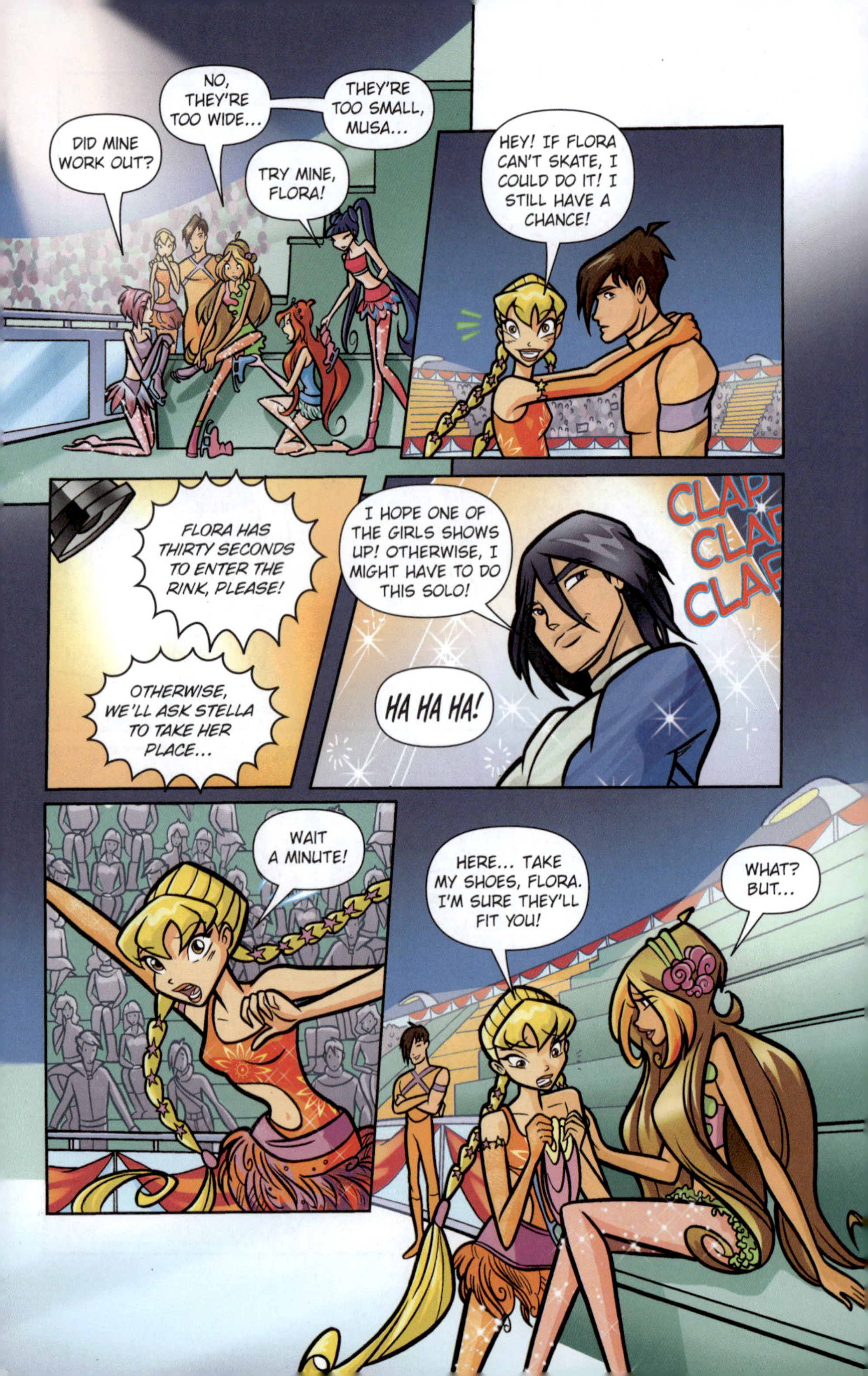
DID MINE WORK OUT?
NO, THEY'RE TOO WIDE...
THEY'RE TOO SMALL, MUSA...
TRY MINE, FLORA!
HEY! IF FLORA CAN'T SKATE, I COULD DO IT! I STILL HAVE A CHANCE!
FLORA HAS THIRTY SECONDS TO ENTER THE RINK, PLEASE!
OTHERWISE, WE'LL ASK STELLA TO TAKE HER PLACE...
I HOPE ONE OF THE GIRLS SHOWS UP! OTHERWISE, I MIGHT HAVE TO DO THIS SOLO!
HA HA HA!
WAIT A MINUTE!
HERE... TAKE MY SHOES, FLORA. I'M SURE THEY'LL FIT YOU!
WHAT? BUT...

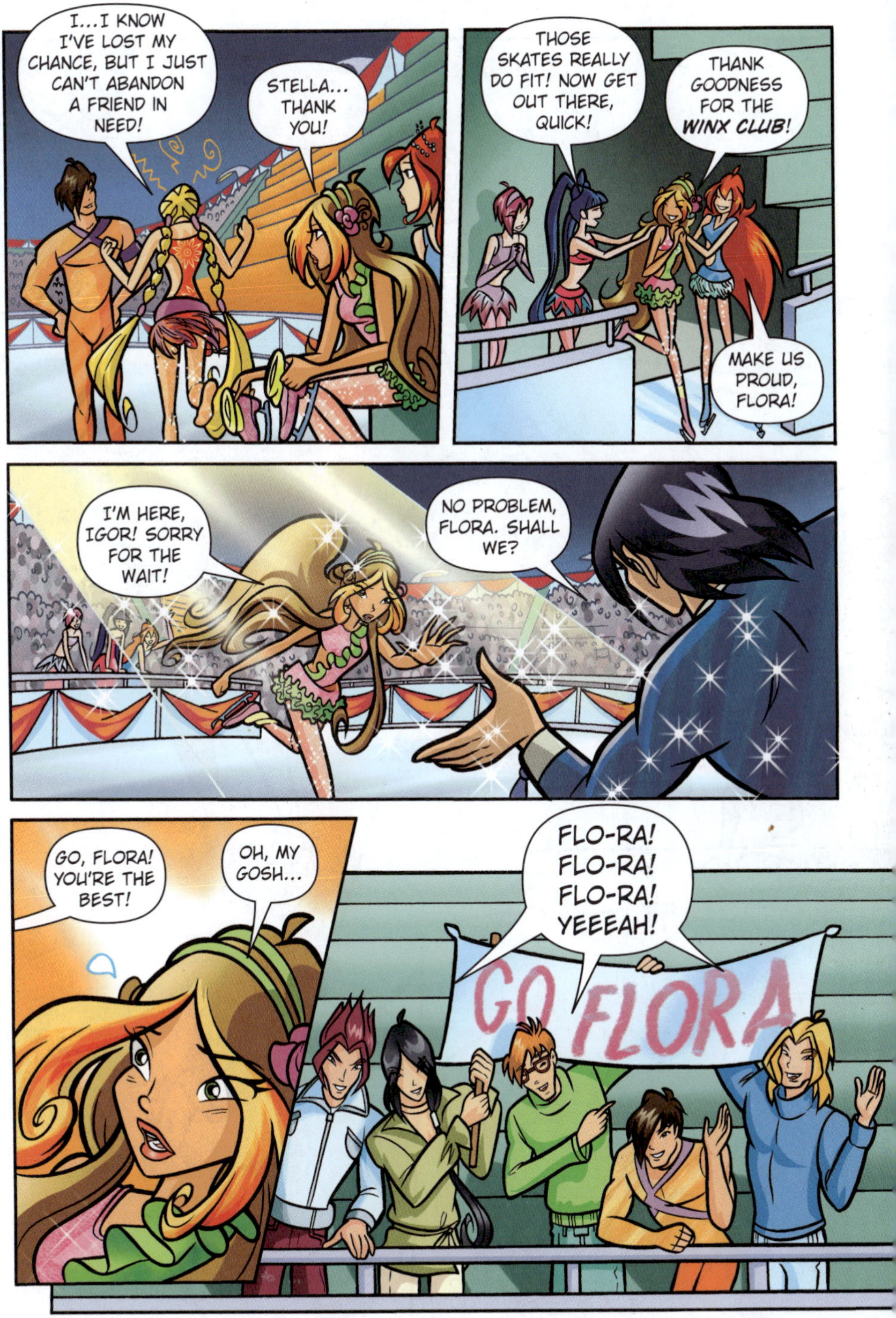
I...I KNOW I'VE LOST MY CHANCE, BUT I JUST CAN'T ABANDON A FRIEND IN NEED!
STELLA... THANK YOU!
THOSE SKATES REALLY DO FIT! NOW GET OUT THERE, QUICK!
THANK GOODNESS FOR THE WINX CLUB!
MAKE US PROUD, FLORA!
I'M HERE, IGOR! SORRY FOR THE WAIT!
NO PROBLEM, FLORA. SHALL WE?
GO, FLORA! YOU'RE THE BEST!
OH, MY GOSH...
FLO-RA! FLO-RA! FLO-RA! YEEEAH!
GO FLORA

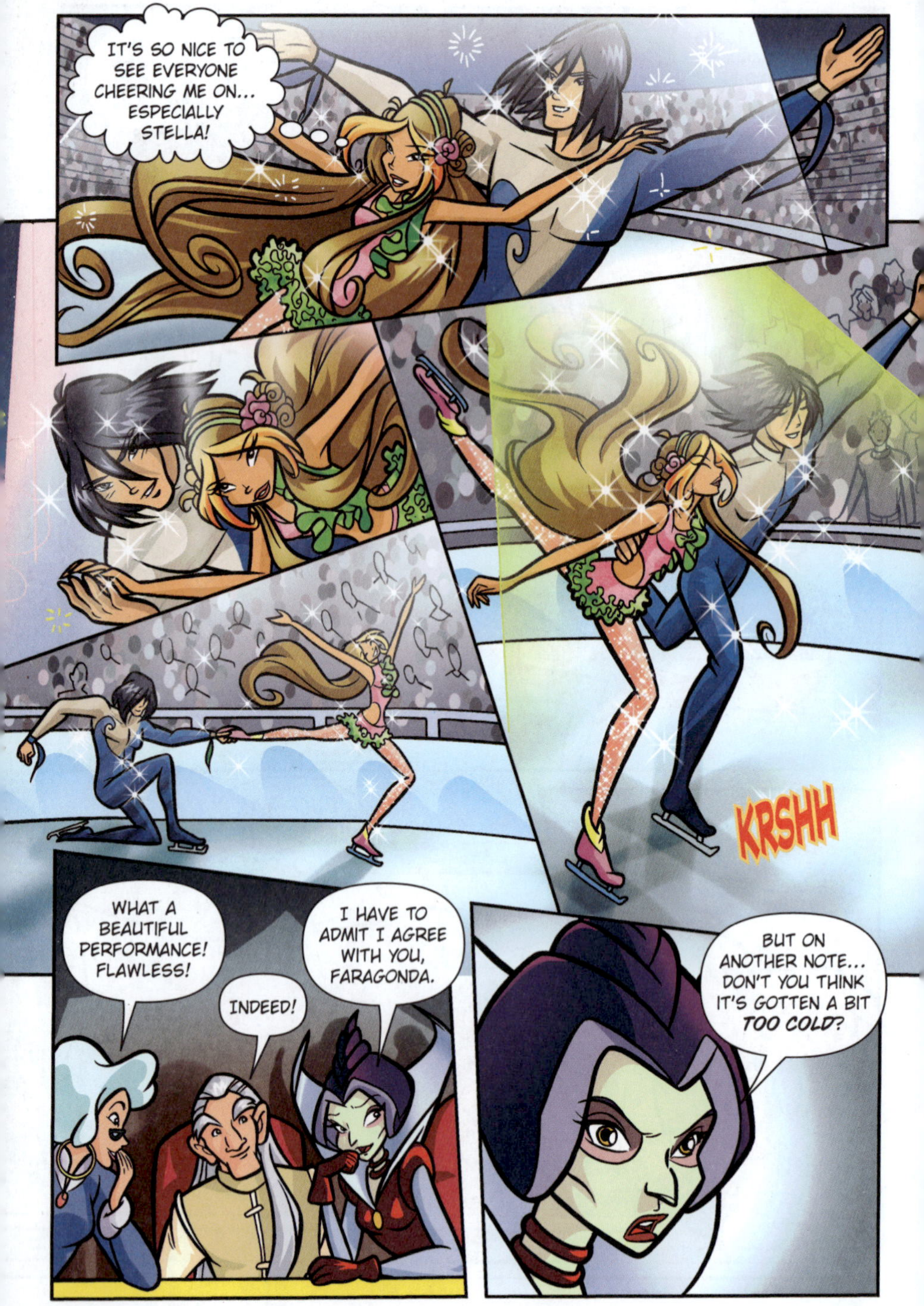
IT'S SO NICE TO SEE EVERYONE CHEERING ME ON... ESPECIALLY STELLA!
KRSHH
WHAT A BEAUTIFUL PERFORMANCE! FLAWLESS!
INDEED!
I HAVE TO ADMIT I AGREE WITH YOU, FARAGONDA.
BUT ON ANOTHER NOTE... DON'T YOU THINK IT'S GOTTEN A BIT *TOO COLD*?

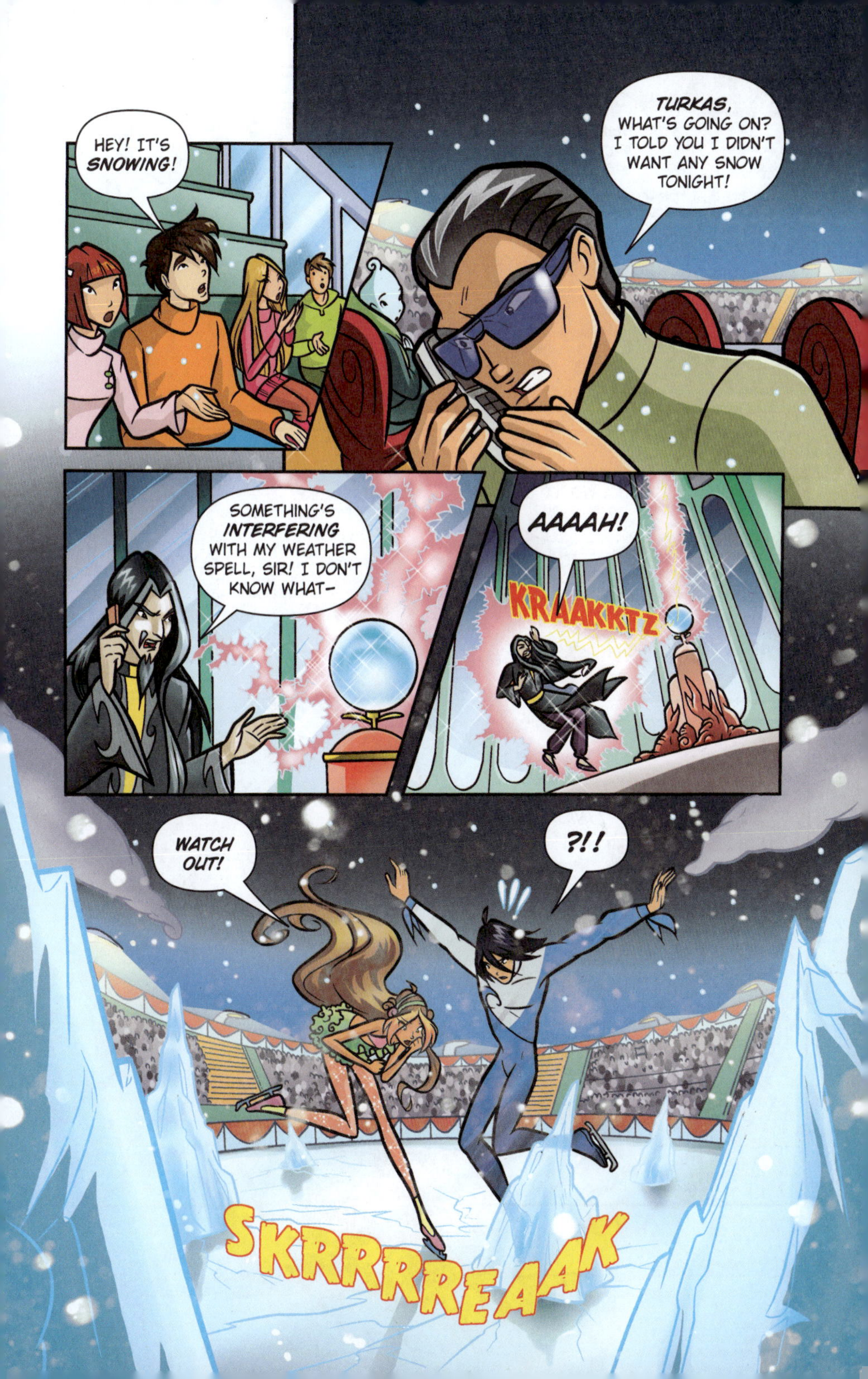
HEY! IT'S SNOWING!
TURKAS, WHAT'S GOING ON? I TOLD YOU I DIDN'T WANT ANY SNOW TONIGHT!
SOMETHING'S INTERFERING WITH MY WEATHER SPELL, SIR! I DON'T KNOW WHAT-
AAAAH!
KRAAKKTZ
WATCH OUT!
?!!
SKRRRREAAK

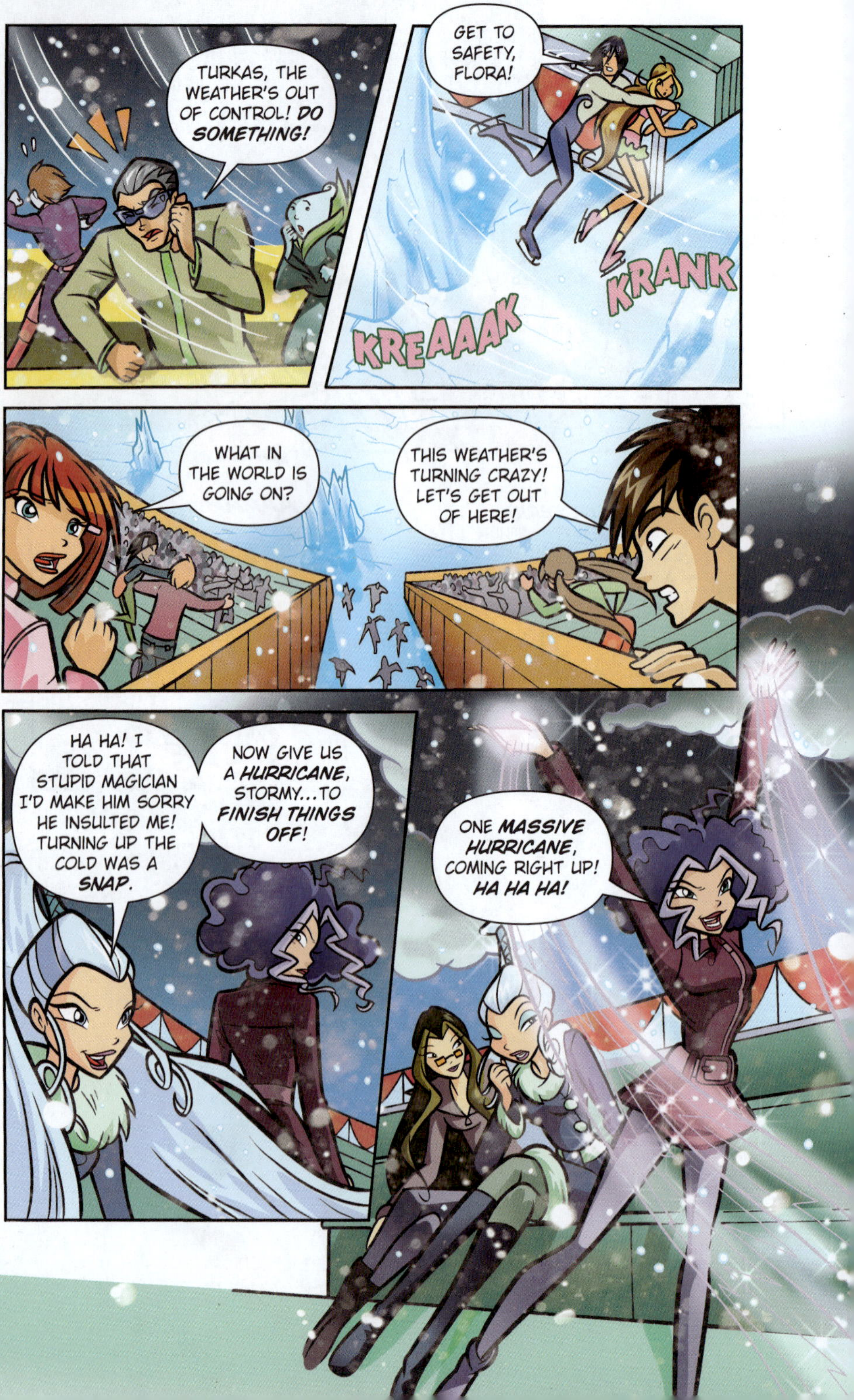
TURKAS, THE WEATHER'S OUT OF CONTROL! DO SOMETHING!
GET TO SAFETY, FLORA!
KREAAAK
KRANK
WHAT IN THE WORLD IS GOING ON?
THIS WEATHER'S TURNING CRAZY! LET'S GET OUT OF HERE!
HA HA! I TOLD THAT STUPID MAGICIAN I'D MAKE HIM SORRY HE INSULTED ME! TURNING UP THE COLD WAS A SNAP.
NOW GIVE US A HURRICANE, STORMY...TO FINISH THINGS OFF!
ONE MASSIVE HURRICANE, COMING RIGHT UP! HA HA HA!

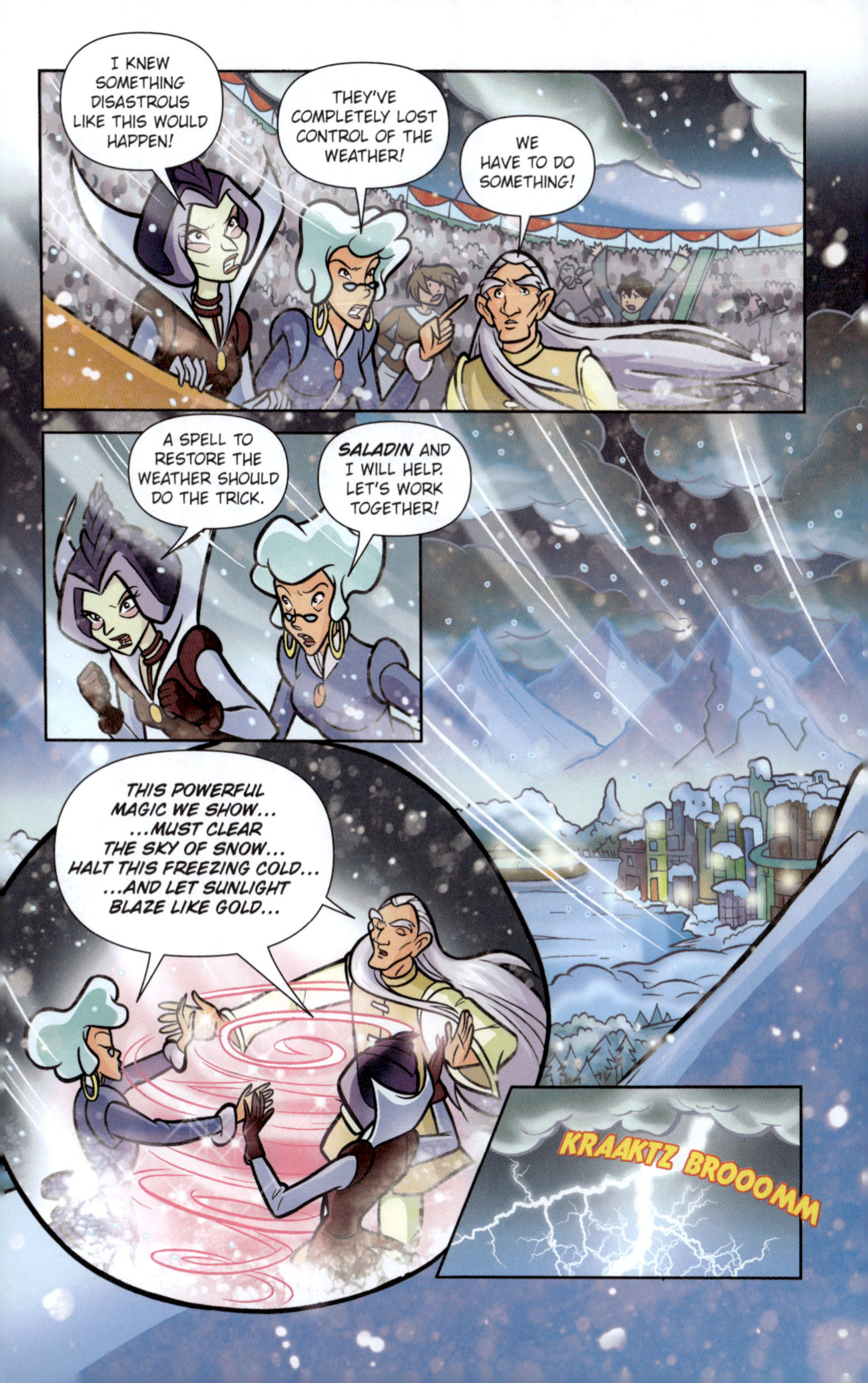
I KNEW SOMETHING DISASTROUS LIKE THIS WOULD HAPPEN!
THEY'VE COMPLETELY LOST CONTROL OF THE WEATHER!
WE HAVE TO DO SOMETHING!
A SPELL TO RESTORE THE WEATHER SHOULD DO THE TRICK.
SALADIN AND I WILL HELP. LET'S WORK TOGETHER!
THIS POWERFUL MAGIC WE SHOW... ...MUST CLEAR THE SKY OF SNOW... HALT THIS FREEZING COLD... ...AND LET SUNLIGHT BLAZE LIKE GOLD...
KRAAKTZ BROOOMM

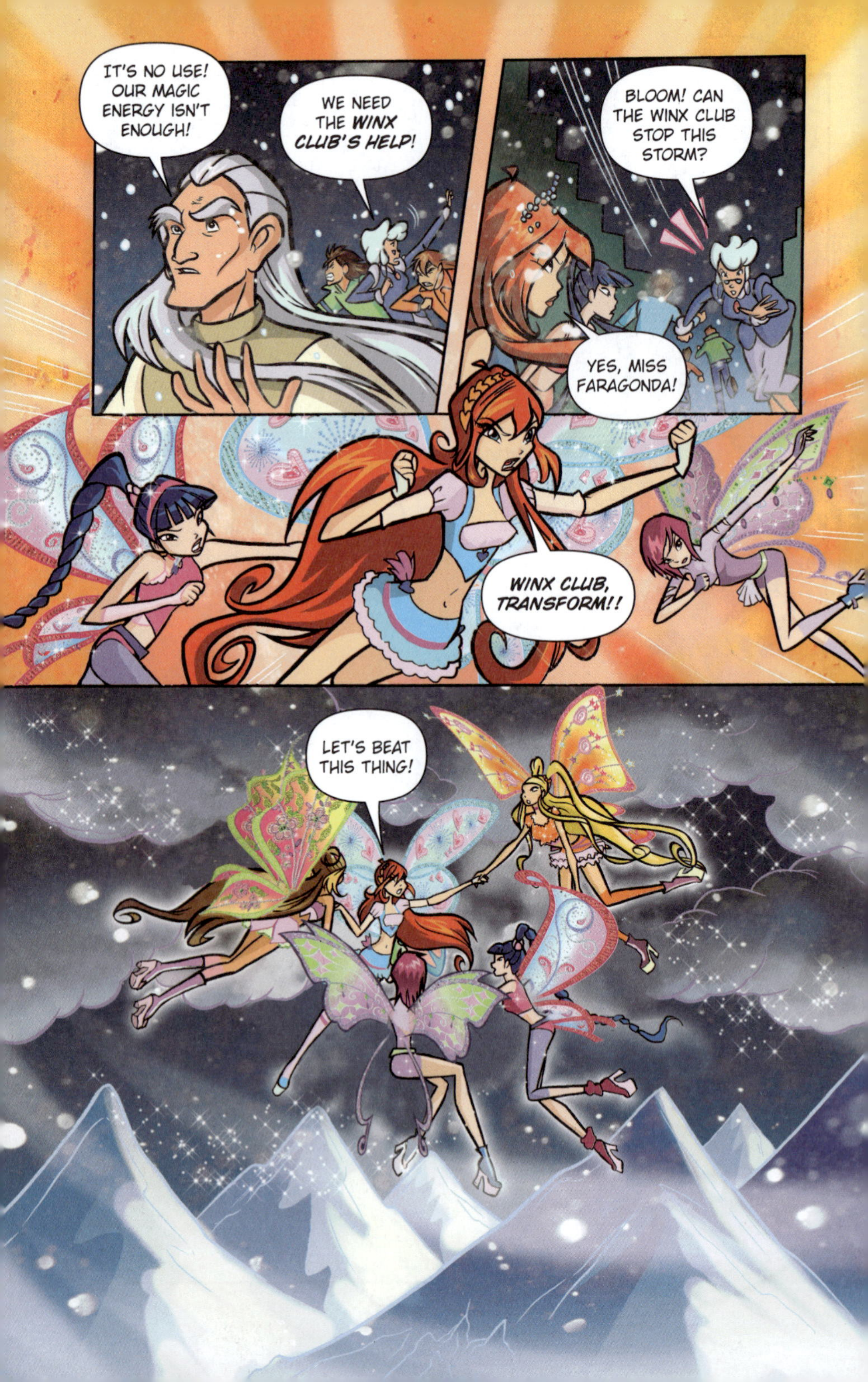
IT'S NO USE! OUR MAGIC ENERGY ISN'T ENOUGH!
WE NEED THE WINX CLUB'S HELP!
BLOOM! CAN THE WINX CLUB STOP THIS STORM?
YES, MISS FARAGONDA!
WINX CLUB, TRANSFORM!!
LET'S BEAT THIS THING!

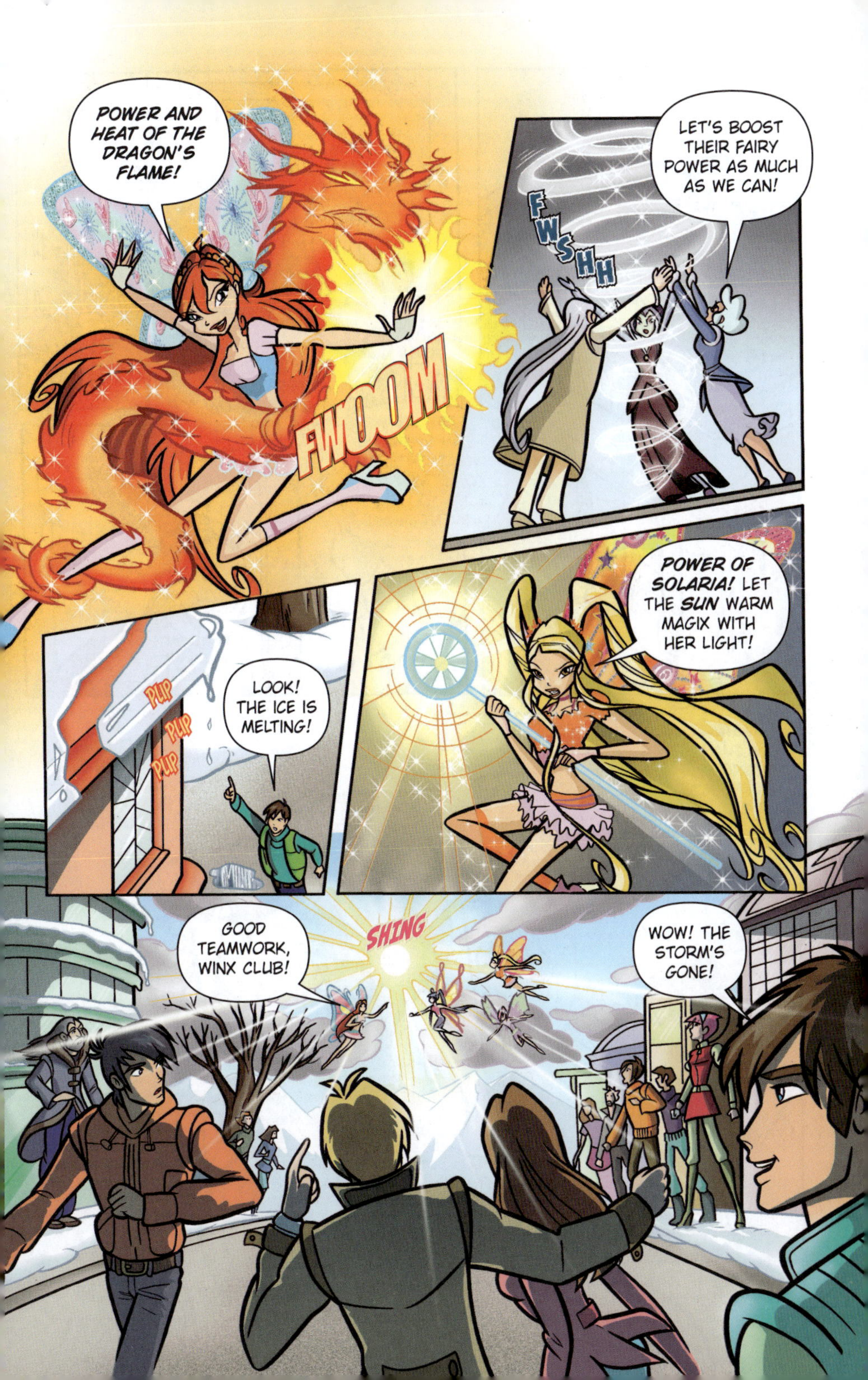
POWER AND HEAT OF THE DRAGON'S FLAME!
FWOOM
LET'S BOOST THEIR FAIRY POWER AS MUCH AS WE CAN!
FWSHH
POWER OF SOLARIA! LET THE SUN WARM MAGIX WITH HER LIGHT!
PLIP
PLIP
PLIP
LOOK! THE ICE IS MELTING!
GOOD TEAMWORK, WINX CLUB!
SHING
WOW! THE STORM'S GONE!

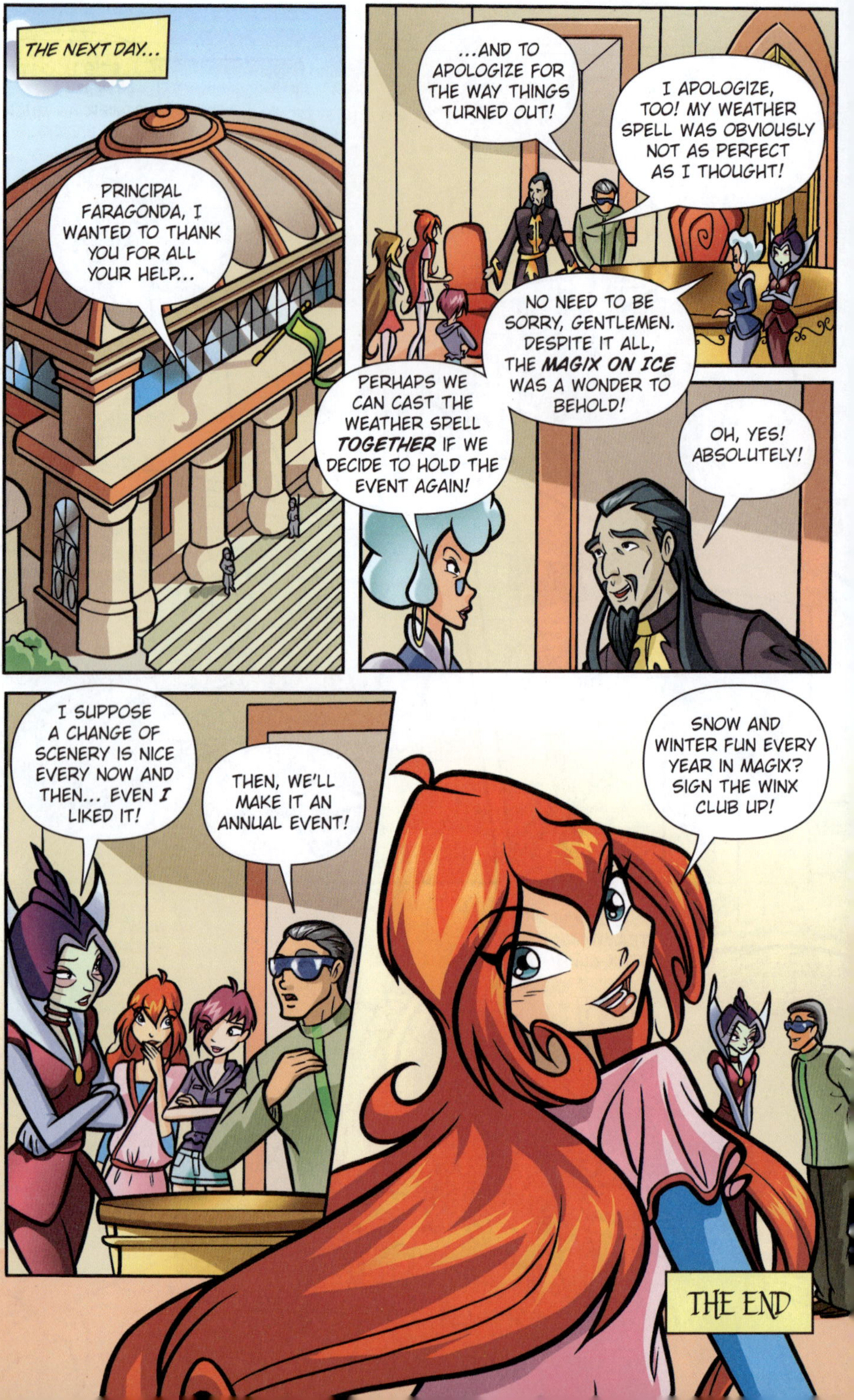
THE NEXT DAY...
PRINCIPAL FARAGONDA, I WANTED TO THANK YOU FOR ALL YOUR HELP...
...AND TO APOLOGIZE FOR THE WAY THINGS TURNED OUT!
I APOLOGIZE, TOO! MY WEATHER SPELL WAS OBVIOUSLY NOT AS PERFECT AS I THOUGHT!
NO NEED TO BE SORRY, GENTLEMEN. DESPITE IT ALL, THE *MAGIX ON ICE* WAS A WONDER TO BEHOLD!
PERHAPS WE CAN CAST THE WEATHER SPELL *TOGETHER* IF WE DECIDE TO HOLD THE EVENT AGAIN!
OH, YES! ABSOLUTELY!
I SUPPOSE A CHANGE OF SCENERY IS NICE EVERY NOW AND THEN... EVEN *I* LIKED IT!
THEN, WE'LL MAKE IT AN ANNUAL EVENT!
SNOW AND WINTER FUN EVERY YEAR IN MAGIX? SIGN THE WINX CLUB UP!
THE END

Time for Magic

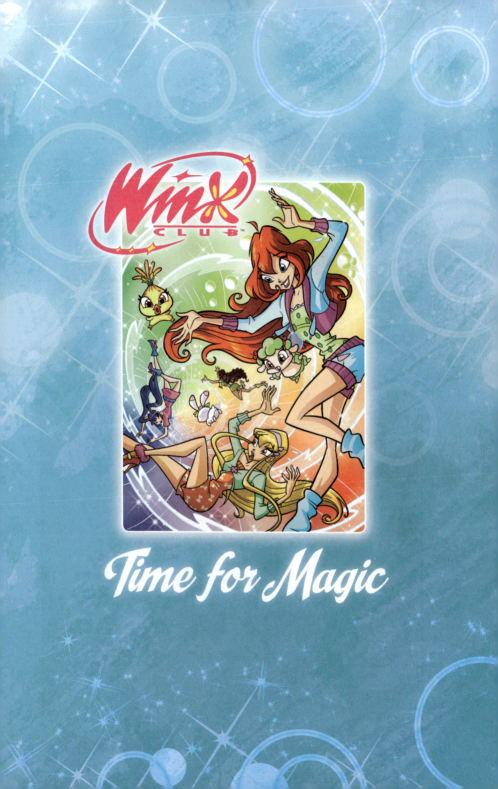

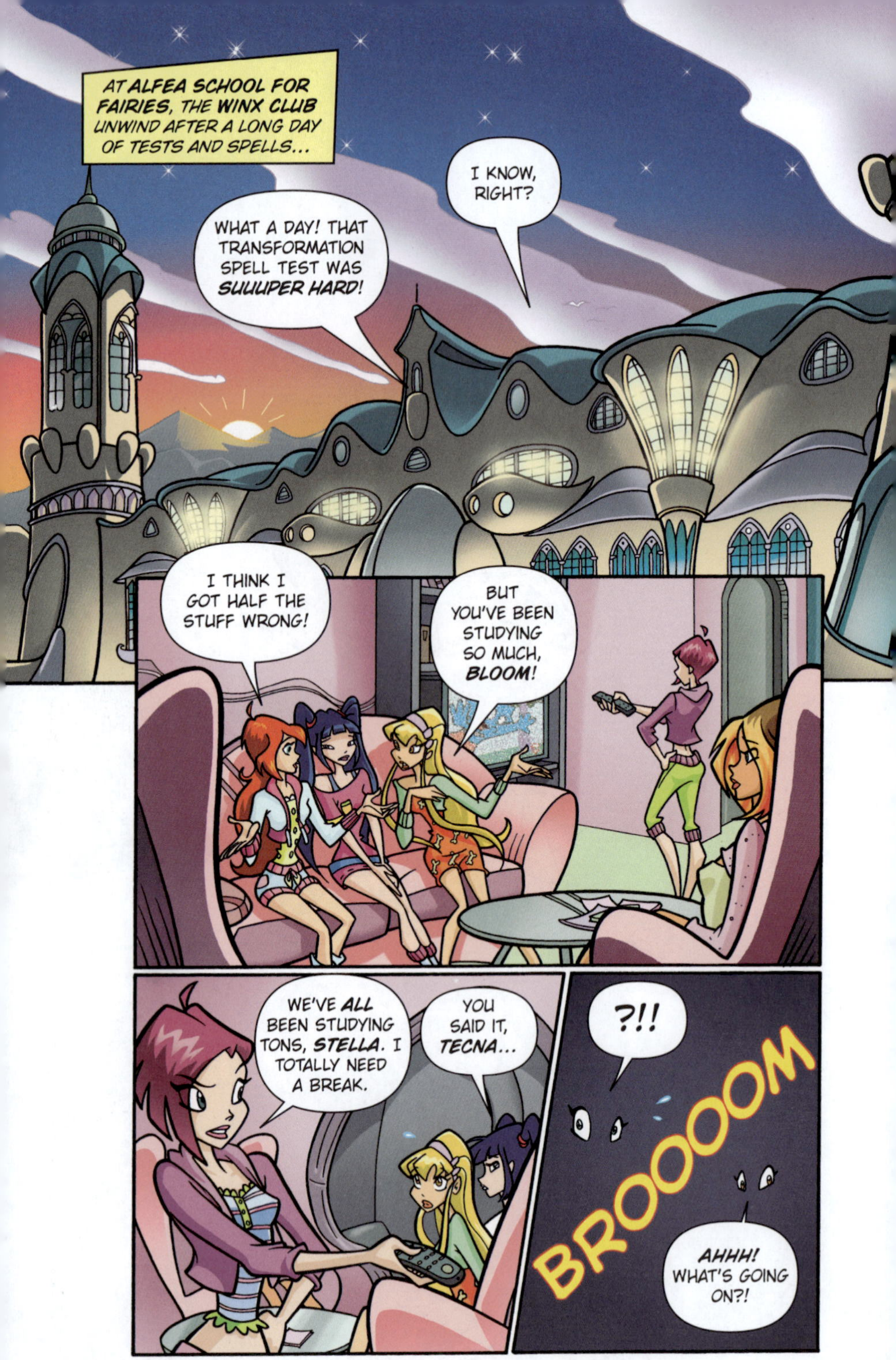
AT ALFEA SCHOOL FOR FAIRIES, THE WINX CLUB UNWIND AFTER A LONG DAY OF TESTS AND SPELLS...
WHAT A DAY! THAT TRANSFORMATION SPELL TEST WAS SUUUPER HARD!
I KNOW, RIGHT?
I THINK I GOT HALF THE STUFF WRONG!
BUT YOU'VE BEEN STUDYING SO MUCH, BLOOM!
WE'VE ALL BEEN STUDYING TONS, STELLA. I TOTALLY NEED A BREAK.
YOU SAID IT, TECNA...
?!!
BROOOOM
AHHH! WHAT'S GOING ON?!

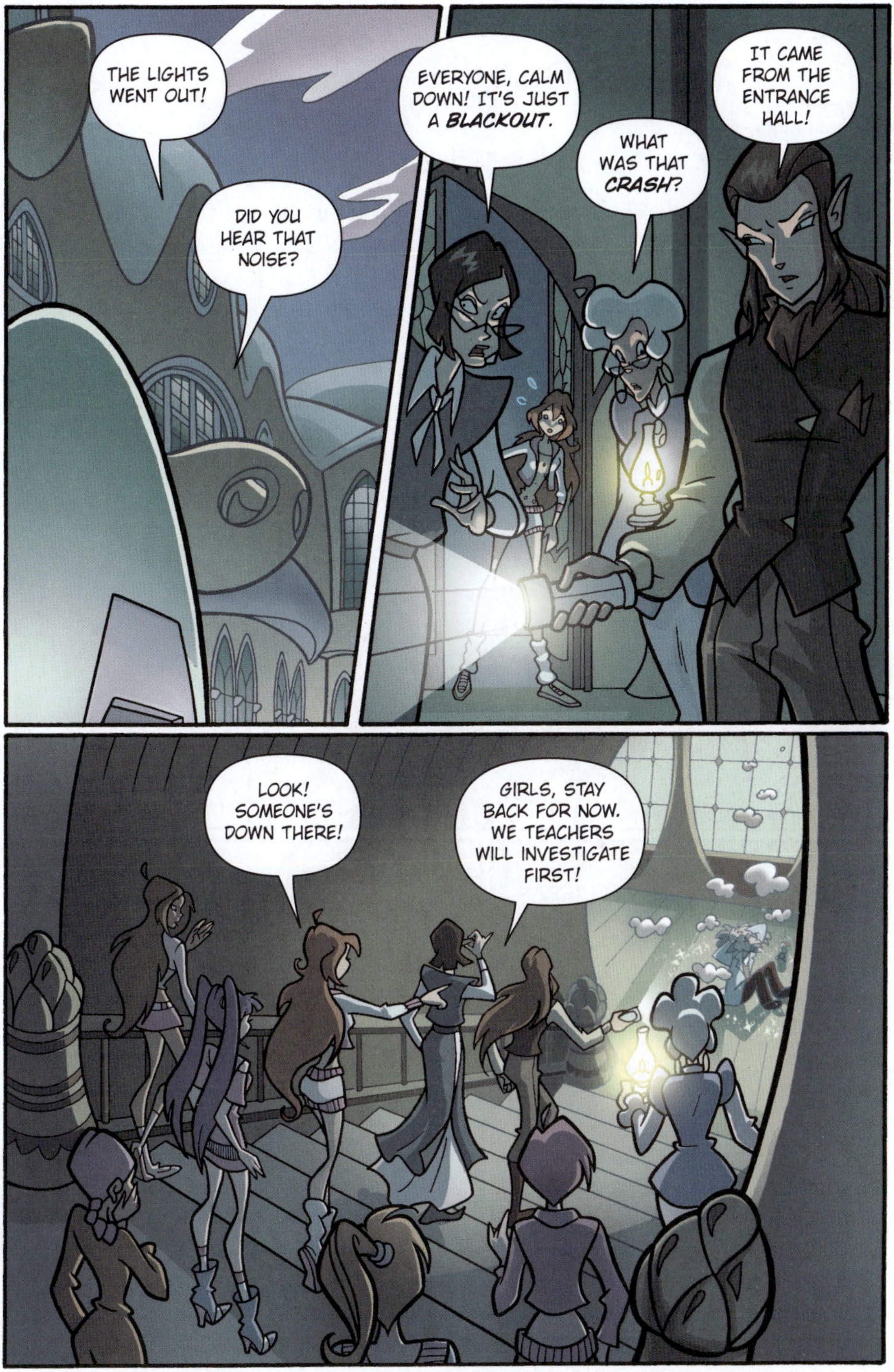
THE LIGHTS WENT OUT!
DID YOU HEAR THAT NOISE?
EVERYONE, CALM DOWN! IT'S JUST A **BLACKOUT**.
WHAT WAS THAT **CRASH**?
IT CAME FROM THE ENTRANCE HALL!
LOOK! SOMEONE'S DOWN THERE!
GIRLS, STAY BACK FOR NOW. WE TEACHERS WILL INVESTIGATE FIRST!

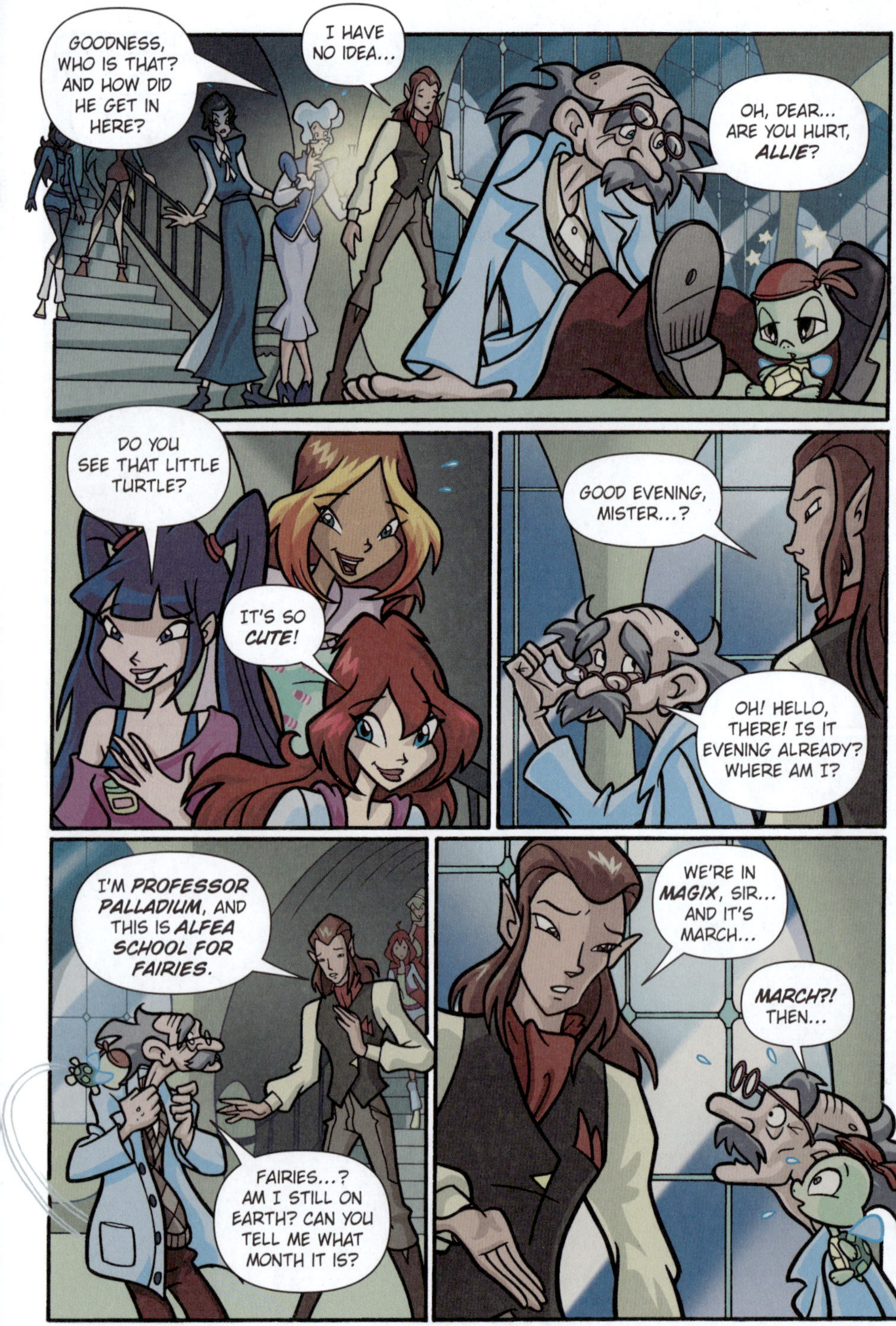

GOODNESS, WHO IS THAT? AND HOW DID HE GET IN HERE?
I HAVE NO IDEA...
OH, DEAR... ARE YOU HURT, ALLIE?
DO YOU SEE THAT LITTLE TURTLE?
IT'S SO CUTE!
GOOD EVENING, MISTER...?
OH! HELLO, THERE! IS IT EVENING ALREADY? WHERE AM I?
I'M PROFESSOR PALLADIUM, AND THIS IS ALFEA SCHOOL FOR FAIRIES.
FAIRIES...? AM I STILL ON EARTH? CAN YOU TELL ME WHAT MONTH IT IS?
WE'RE IN MAGIX, SIR... AND IT'S MARCH...
MARCH?! THEN...

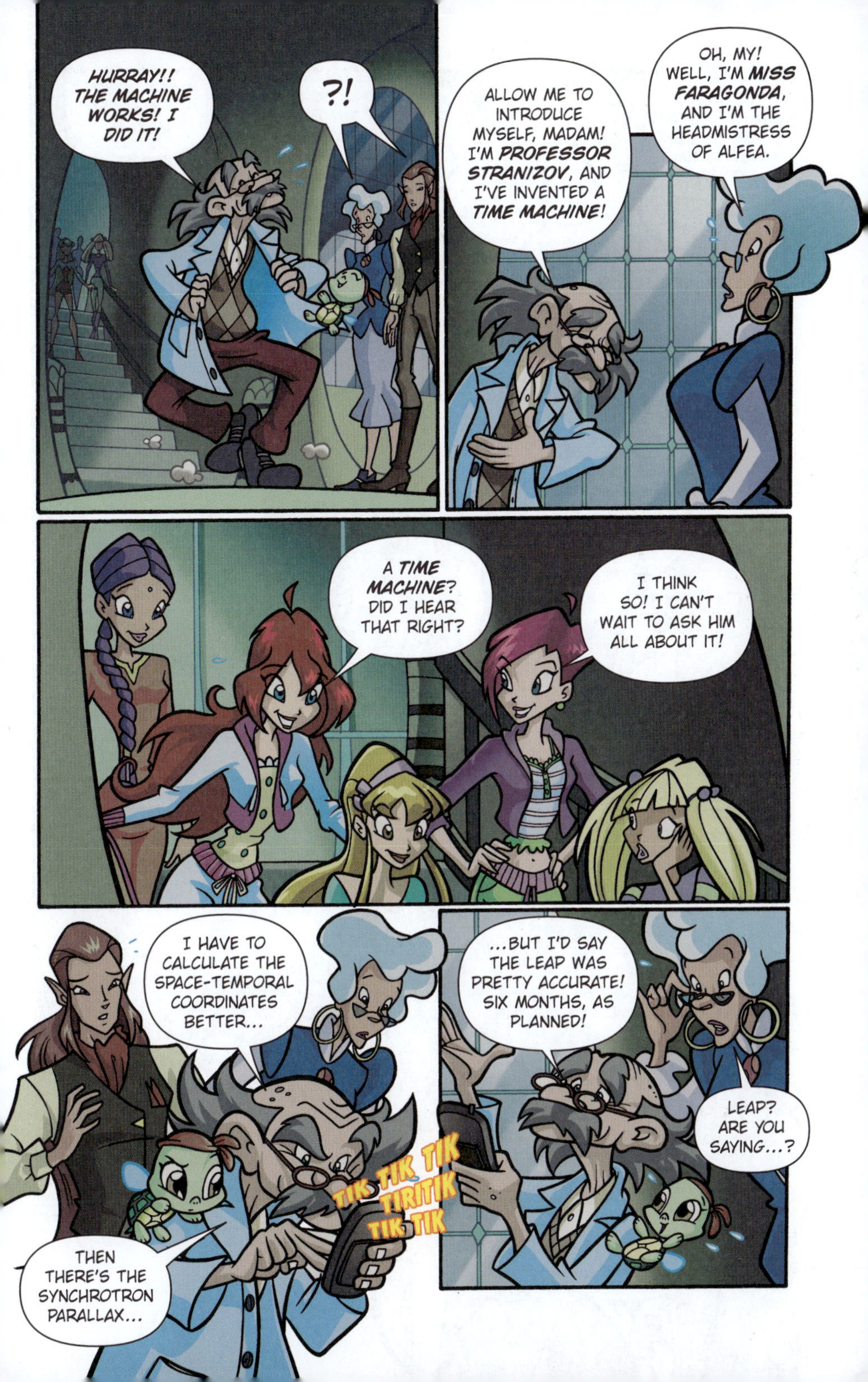
HURRAY!! THE MACHINE WORKS! I DID IT!
?!
ALLOW ME TO INTRODUCE MYSELF, MADAM! I'M PROFESSOR STRANIZOV, AND I'VE INVENTED A TIME MACHINE!
OH, MY! WELL, I'M MISS FARAGONDA, AND I'M THE HEADMISTRESS OF ALFEA.
A TIME MACHINE? DID I HEAR THAT RIGHT?
I THINK SO! I CAN'T WAIT TO ASK HIM ALL ABOUT IT!
I HAVE TO CALCULATE THE SPACE-TEMPORAL COORDINATES BETTER...
TIK TIK TIK TIRITIK TIK TIK
THEN THERE'S THE SYNCHROTRON PARALLAX...
...BUT I'D SAY THE LEAP WAS PRETTY ACCURATE! SIX MONTHS, AS PLANNED!
LEAP? ARE YOU SAYING...?

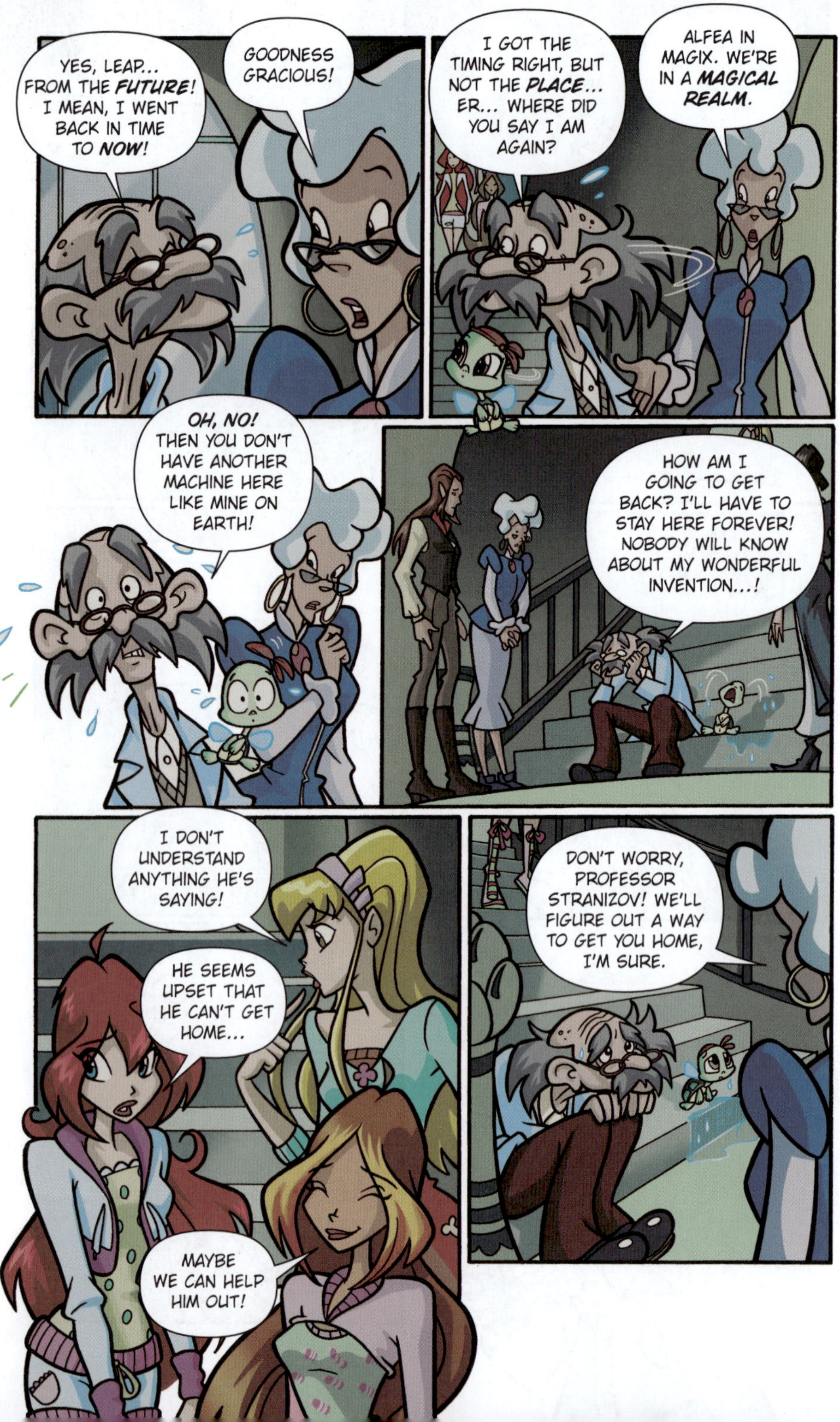
YES, LEAP... FROM THE FUTURE! I MEAN, I WENT BACK IN TIME TO NOW!
GOODNESS GRACIOUS!
I GOT THE TIMING RIGHT, BUT NOT THE PLACE... ER... WHERE DID YOU SAY I AM AGAIN?
ALFEA IN MAGIX. WE'RE IN A MAGICAL REALM.
OH, NO! THEN YOU DON'T HAVE ANOTHER MACHINE HERE LIKE MINE ON EARTH!
HOW AM I GOING TO GET BACK? I'LL HAVE TO STAY HERE FOREVER! NOBODY WILL KNOW ABOUT MY WONDERFUL INVENTION...!
I DON'T UNDERSTAND ANYTHING HE'S SAYING!
HE SEEMS UPSET THAT HE CAN'T GET HOME...
MAYBE WE CAN HELP HIM OUT!
DON'T WORRY, PROFESSOR STRANIZOV! WE'LL FIGURE OUT A WAY TO GET YOU HOME, I'M SURE.

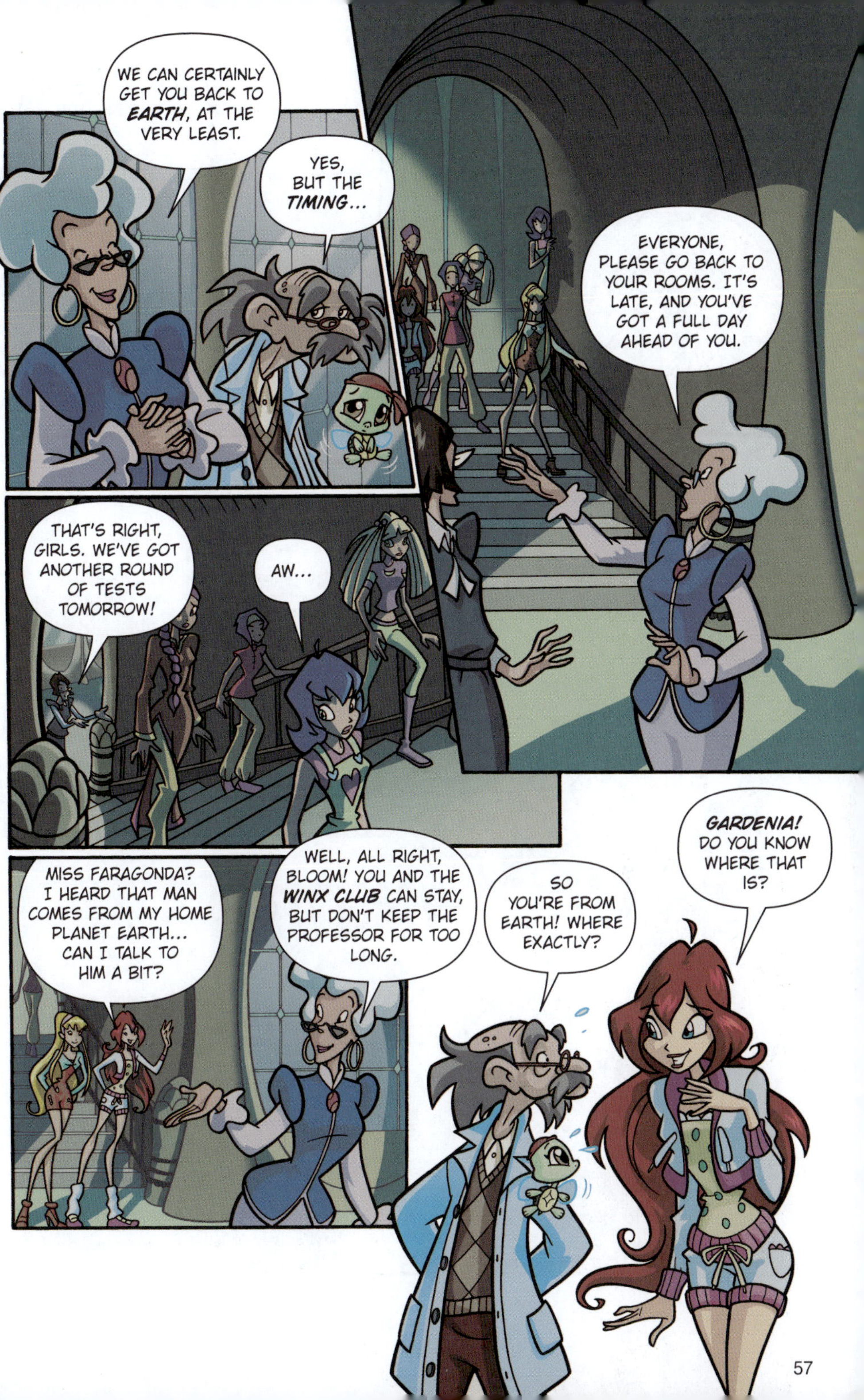
WE CAN CERTAINLY GET YOU BACK TO EARTH, AT THE VERY LEAST.
YES, BUT THE TIMING...
EVERYONE, PLEASE GO BACK TO YOUR ROOMS. IT'S LATE, AND YOU'VE GOT A FULL DAY AHEAD OF YOU.
THAT'S RIGHT, GIRLS. WE'VE GOT ANOTHER ROUND OF TESTS TOMORROW!
AW...
MISS FARAGONDA? I HEARD THAT MAN COMES FROM MY HOME PLANET EARTH... CAN I TALK TO HIM A BIT?
WELL, ALL RIGHT, BLOOM! YOU AND THE WINX CLUB CAN STAY, BUT DON'T KEEP THE PROFESSOR FOR TOO LONG.
SO YOU'RE FROM EARTH! WHERE EXACTLY?
GARDENIA! DO YOU KNOW WHERE THAT IS?

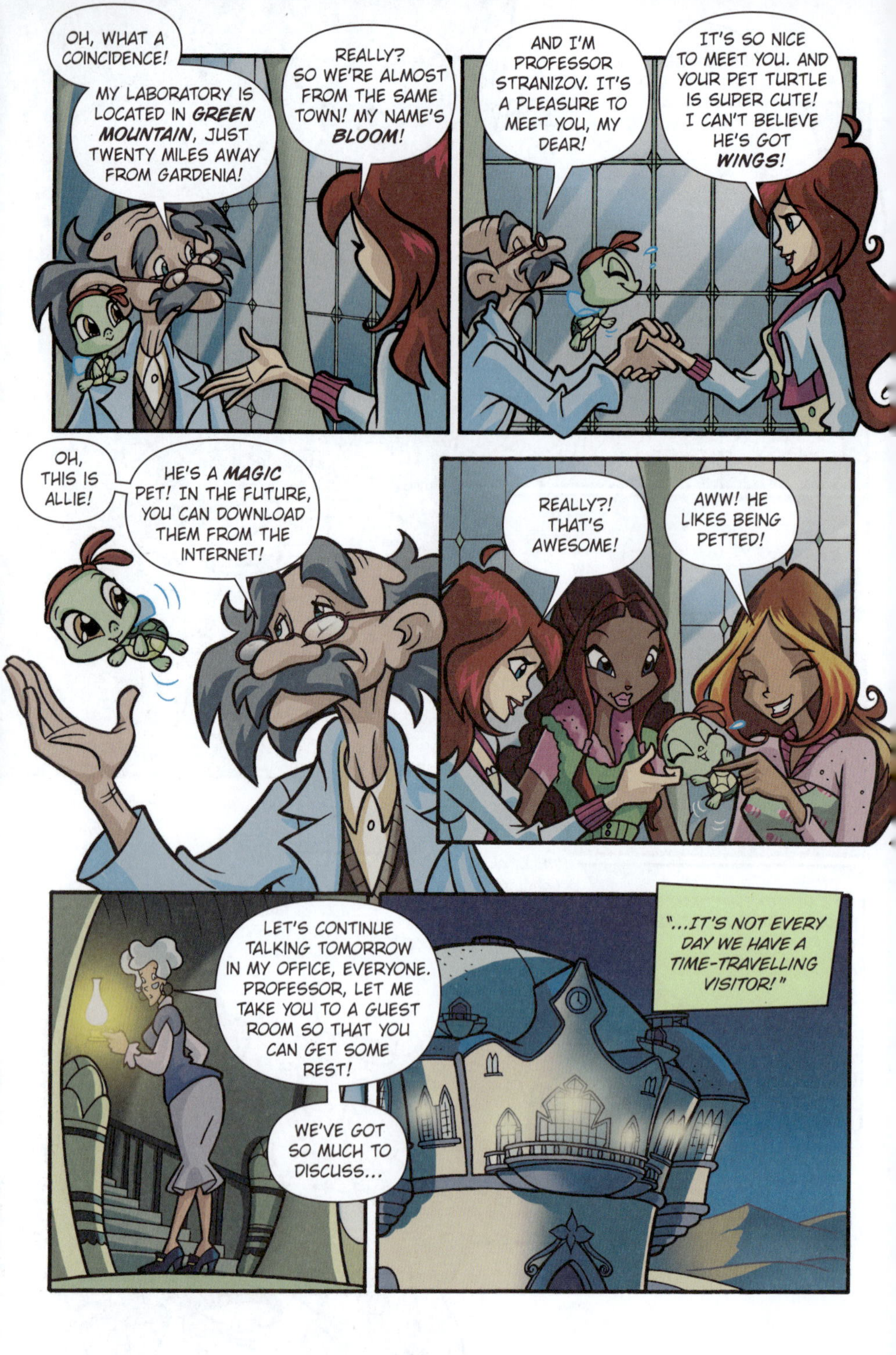
OH, WHAT A COINCIDENCE!
MY LABORATORY IS LOCATED IN GREEN MOUNTAIN, JUST TWENTY MILES AWAY FROM GARDENIA!
REALLY? SO WE'RE ALMOST FROM THE SAME TOWN! MY NAME'S BLOOM!
AND I'M PROFESSOR STRANIZOV. IT'S A PLEASURE TO MEET YOU, MY DEAR!
IT'S SO NICE TO MEET YOU. AND YOUR PET TURTLE IS SUPER CUTE! I CAN'T BELIEVE HE'S GOT WINGS!
OH, THIS IS ALLIE!
HE'S A MAGIC PET! IN THE FUTURE, YOU CAN DOWNLOAD THEM FROM THE INTERNET!
REALLY?! THAT'S AWESOME!
AWW! HE LIKES BEING PETTED!
LET'S CONTINUE TALKING TOMORROW IN MY OFFICE, EVERYONE. PROFESSOR, LET ME TAKE YOU TO A GUEST ROOM SO THAT YOU CAN GET SOME REST!
WE'VE GOT SO MUCH TO DISCUSS...
"...IT'S NOT EVERY DAY WE HAVE A TIME-TRAVELLING VISITOR!"

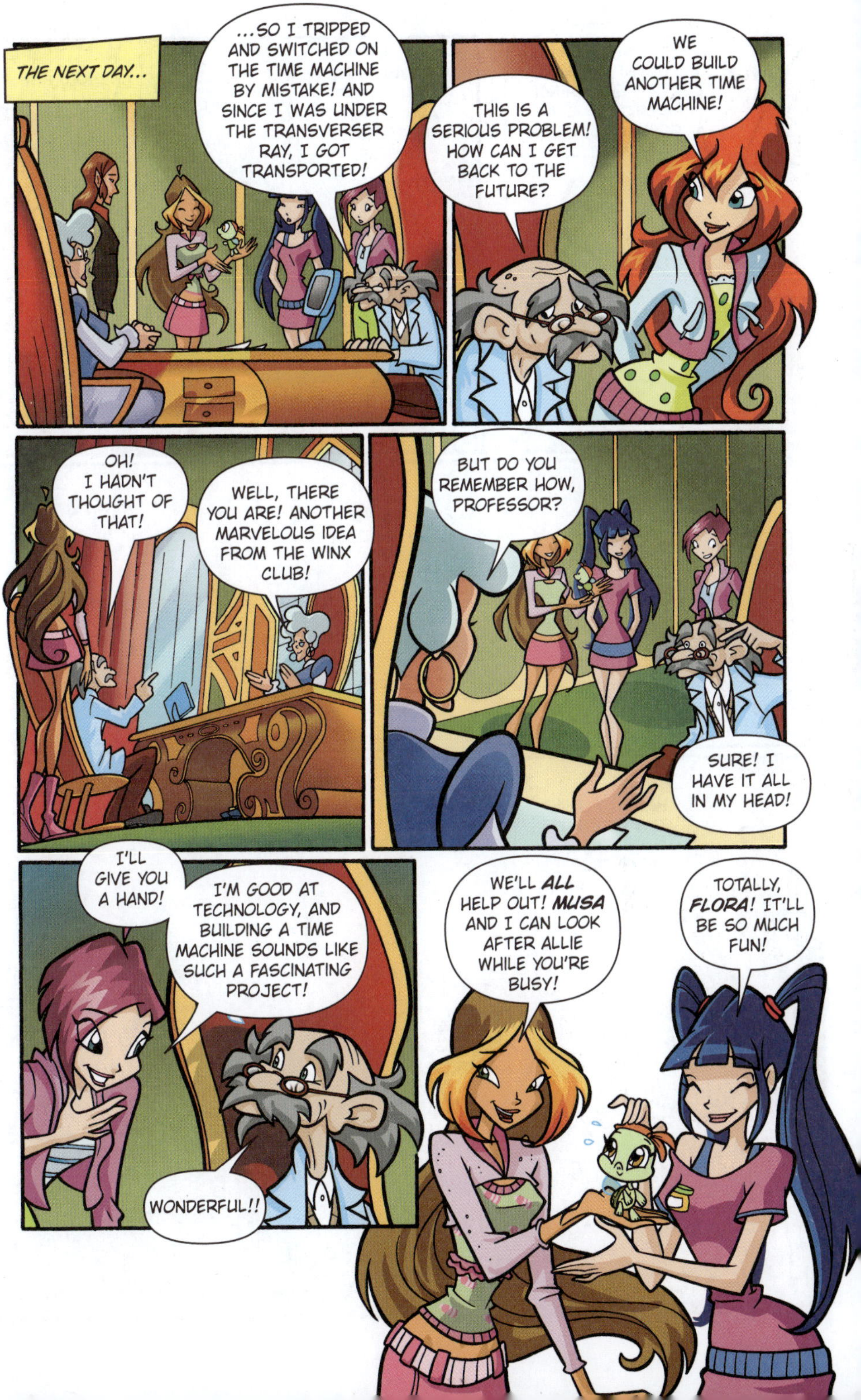
THE NEXT DAY...
...SO I TRIPPED AND SWITCHED ON THE TIME MACHINE BY MISTAKE! AND SINCE I WAS UNDER THE TRANSVERSER RAY, I GOT TRANSPORTED!
THIS IS A SERIOUS PROBLEM! HOW CAN I GET BACK TO THE FUTURE?
WE COULD BUILD ANOTHER TIME MACHINE!
OH! I HADN'T THOUGHT OF THAT!
WELL, THERE YOU ARE! ANOTHER MARVELOUS IDEA FROM THE WINX CLUB!
BUT DO YOU REMEMBER HOW, PROFESSOR?
SURE! I HAVE IT ALL IN MY HEAD!
I'LL GIVE YOU A HAND!
I'M GOOD AT TECHNOLOGY, AND BUILDING A TIME MACHINE SOUNDS LIKE SUCH A FASCINATING PROJECT!
WONDERFUL!!
WE'LL **ALL** HELP OUT! **MUSA** AND I CAN LOOK AFTER ALLIE WHILE YOU'RE BUSY!
TOTALLY, **FLORA**! IT'LL BE SO MUCH FUN!

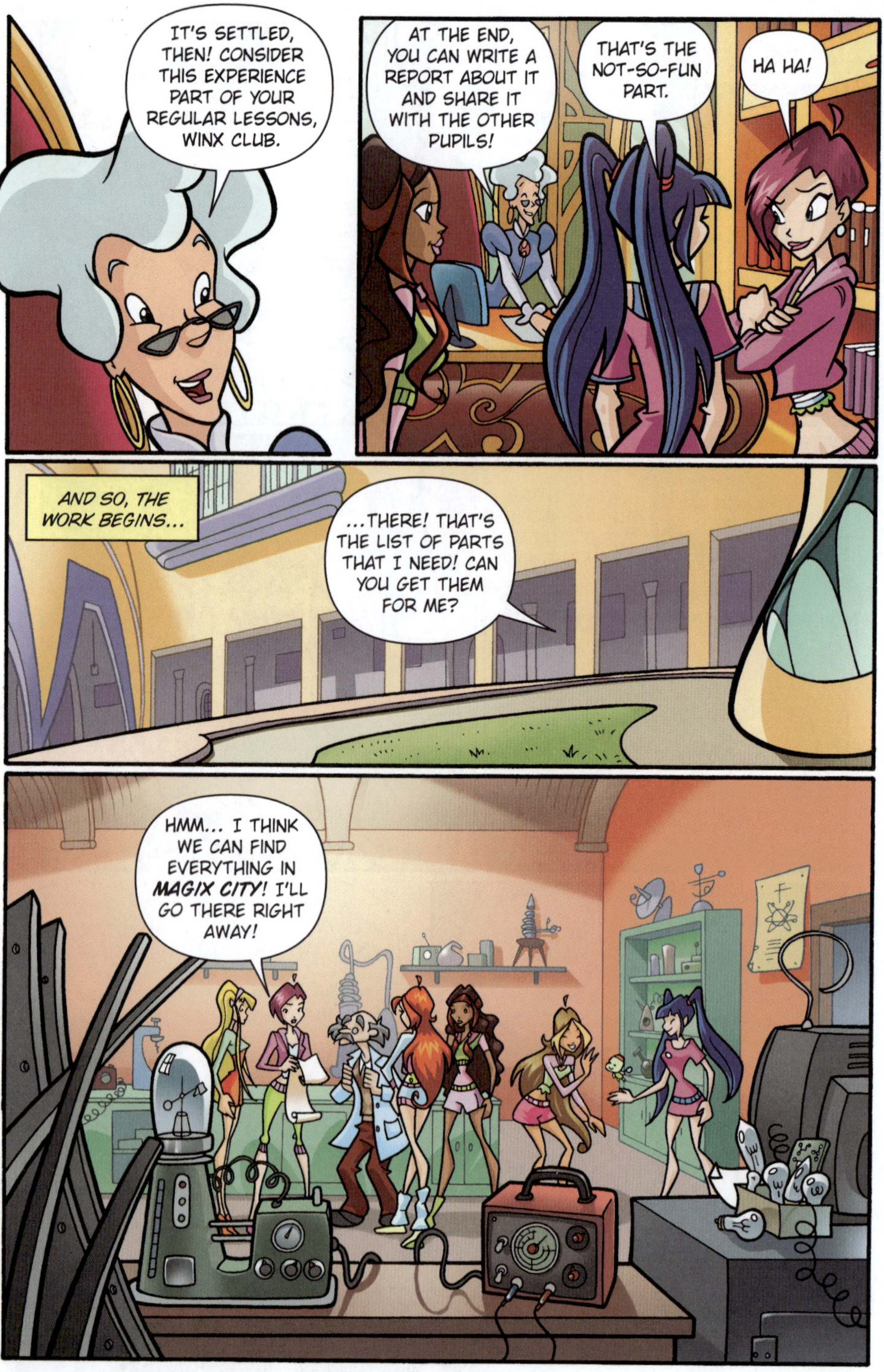
IT'S SETTLED, THEN! CONSIDER THIS EXPERIENCE PART OF YOUR REGULAR LESSONS, WINX CLUB.
AT THE END, YOU CAN WRITE A REPORT ABOUT IT AND SHARE IT WITH THE OTHER PUPILS!
THAT'S THE NOT-SO-FUN PART.
HA HA!
AND SO, THE WORK BEGINS...
...THERE! THAT'S THE LIST OF PARTS THAT I NEED! CAN YOU GET THEM FOR ME?
HMM... I THINK WE CAN FIND EVERYTHING IN MAGIX CITY! I'LL GO THERE RIGHT AWAY!

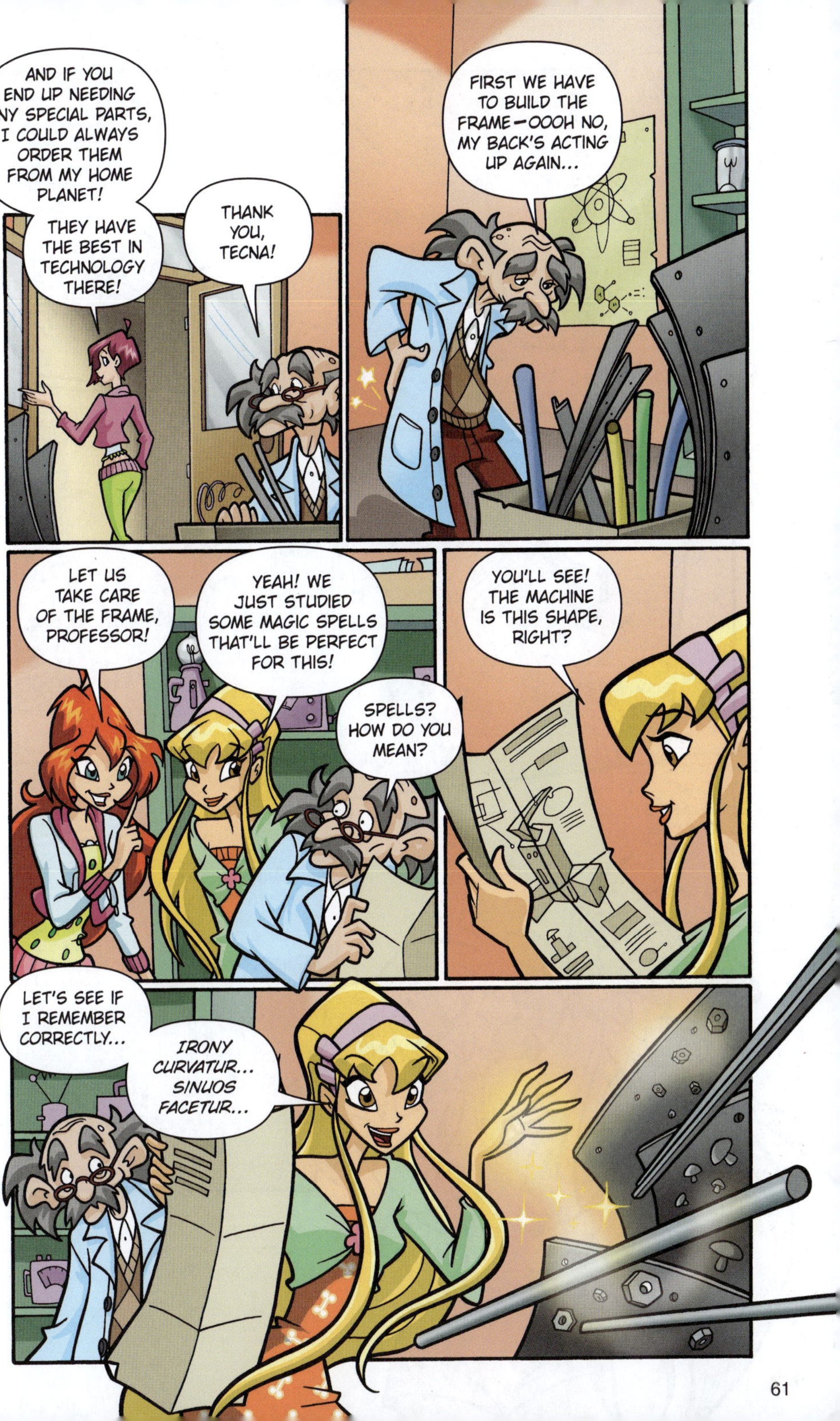
AND IF YOU END UP NEEDING ANY SPECIAL PARTS, I COULD ALWAYS ORDER THEM FROM MY HOME PLANET!
THEY HAVE THE BEST IN TECHNOLOGY THERE!
THANK YOU, TECNA!
FIRST WE HAVE TO BUILD THE FRAME—OOOH NO, MY BACK'S ACTING UP AGAIN...
LET US TAKE CARE OF THE FRAME, PROFESSOR!
YEAH! WE JUST STUDIED SOME MAGIC SPELLS THAT'LL BE PERFECT FOR THIS!
SPELLS? HOW DO YOU MEAN?
YOU'LL SEE! THE MACHINE IS THIS SHAPE, RIGHT?
LET'S SEE IF I REMEMBER CORRECTLY...
IRONY CURVATUR... SINUOS FACETUR...

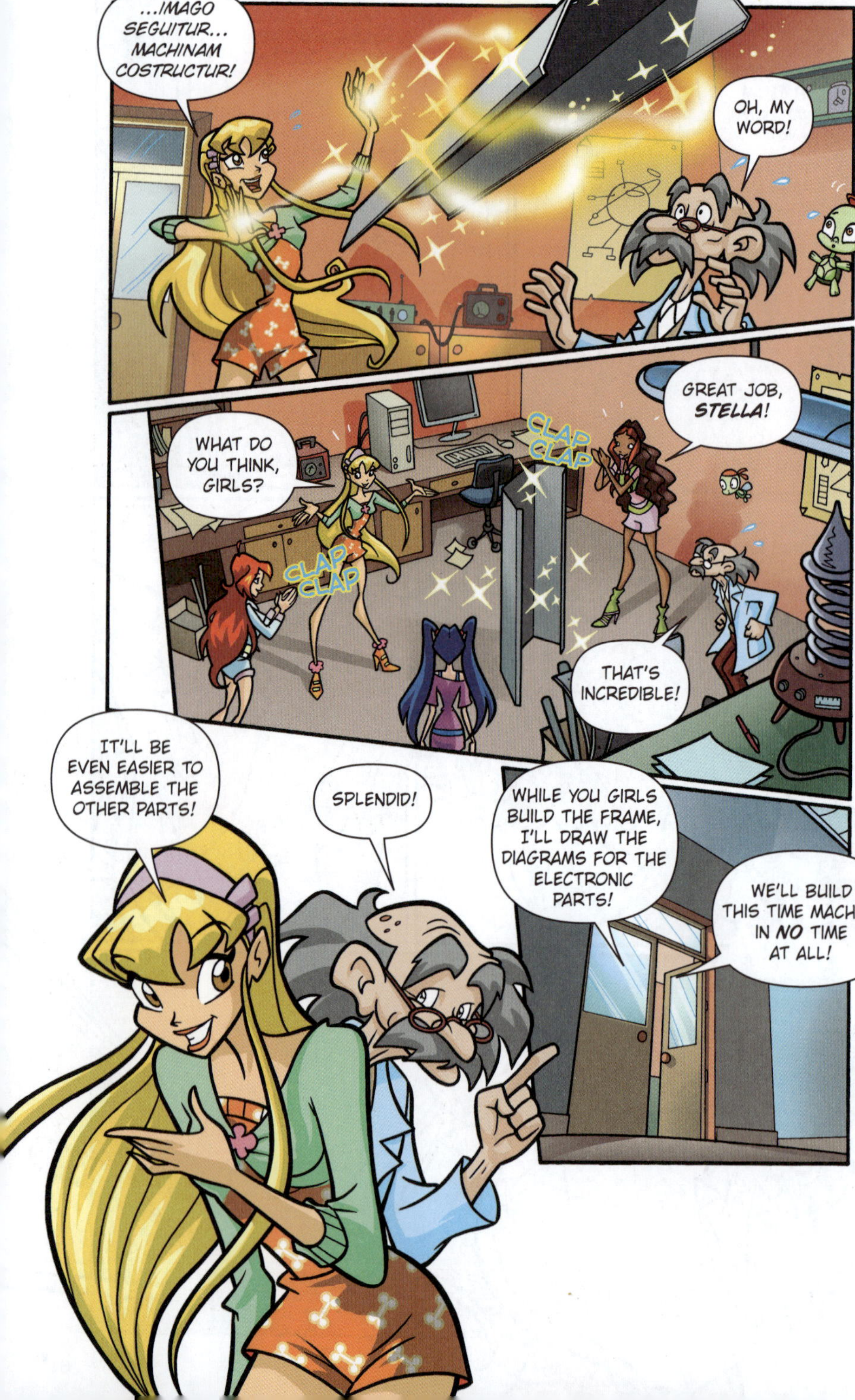
...IMAGO SEGUITUR... MACHINAM COSTRUCTUR!
OH, MY WORD!
WHAT DO YOU THINK, GIRLS?
CLAP CLAP
CLAP CLAP
GREAT JOB, **STELLA**!
THAT'S INCREDIBLE!
IT'LL BE EVEN EASIER TO ASSEMBLE THE OTHER PARTS!
SPLENDID!
WHILE YOU GIRLS BUILD THE FRAME, I'LL DRAW THE DIAGRAMS FOR THE ELECTRONIC PARTS!
WE'LL BUILD THIS TIME MACHINE IN **NO** TIME AT ALL!

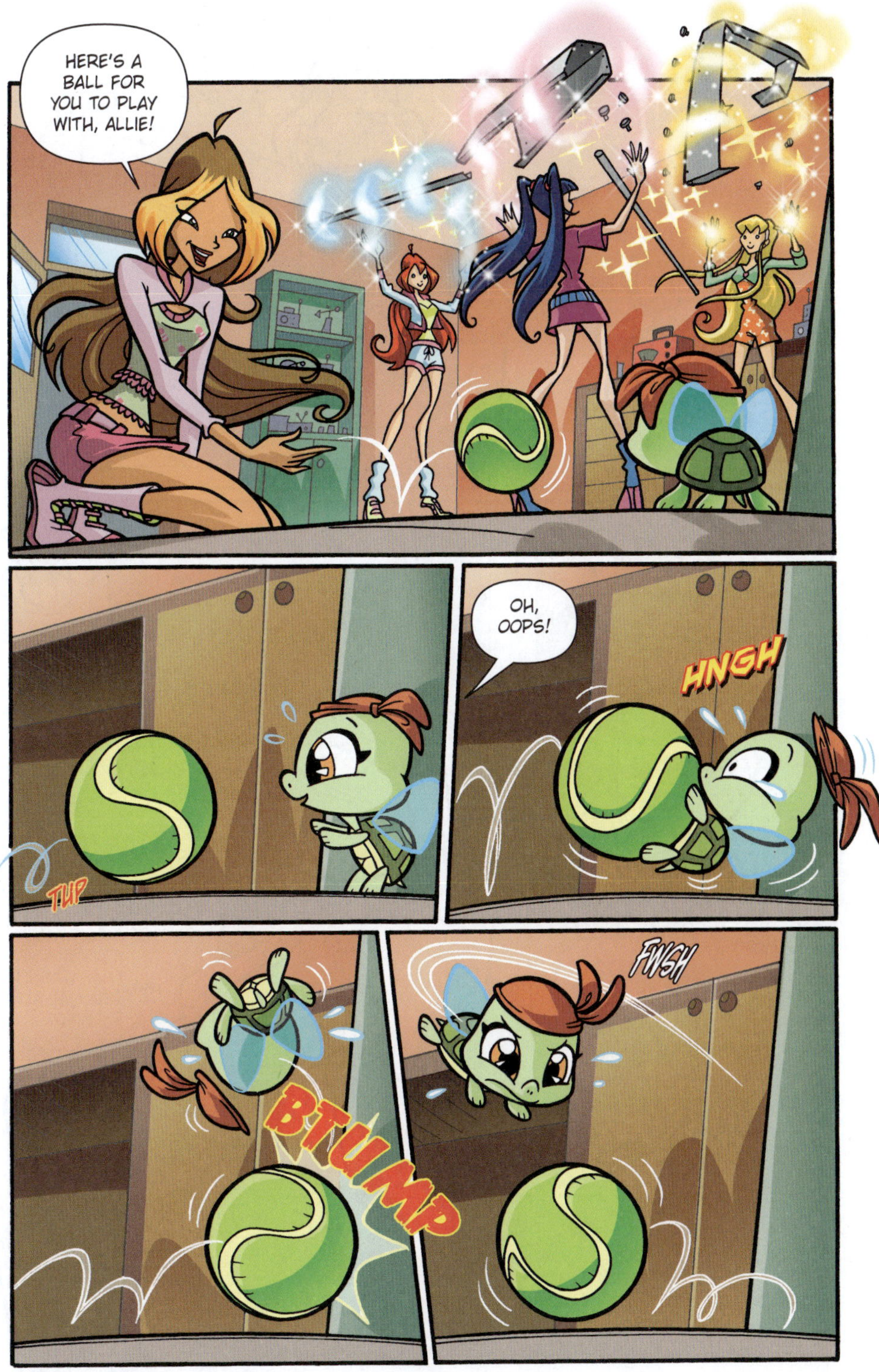
HERE'S A BALL FOR YOU TO PLAY WITH, ALLIE!
TUP
OH, OOPS!
HNGH
BTUMP
FWSH

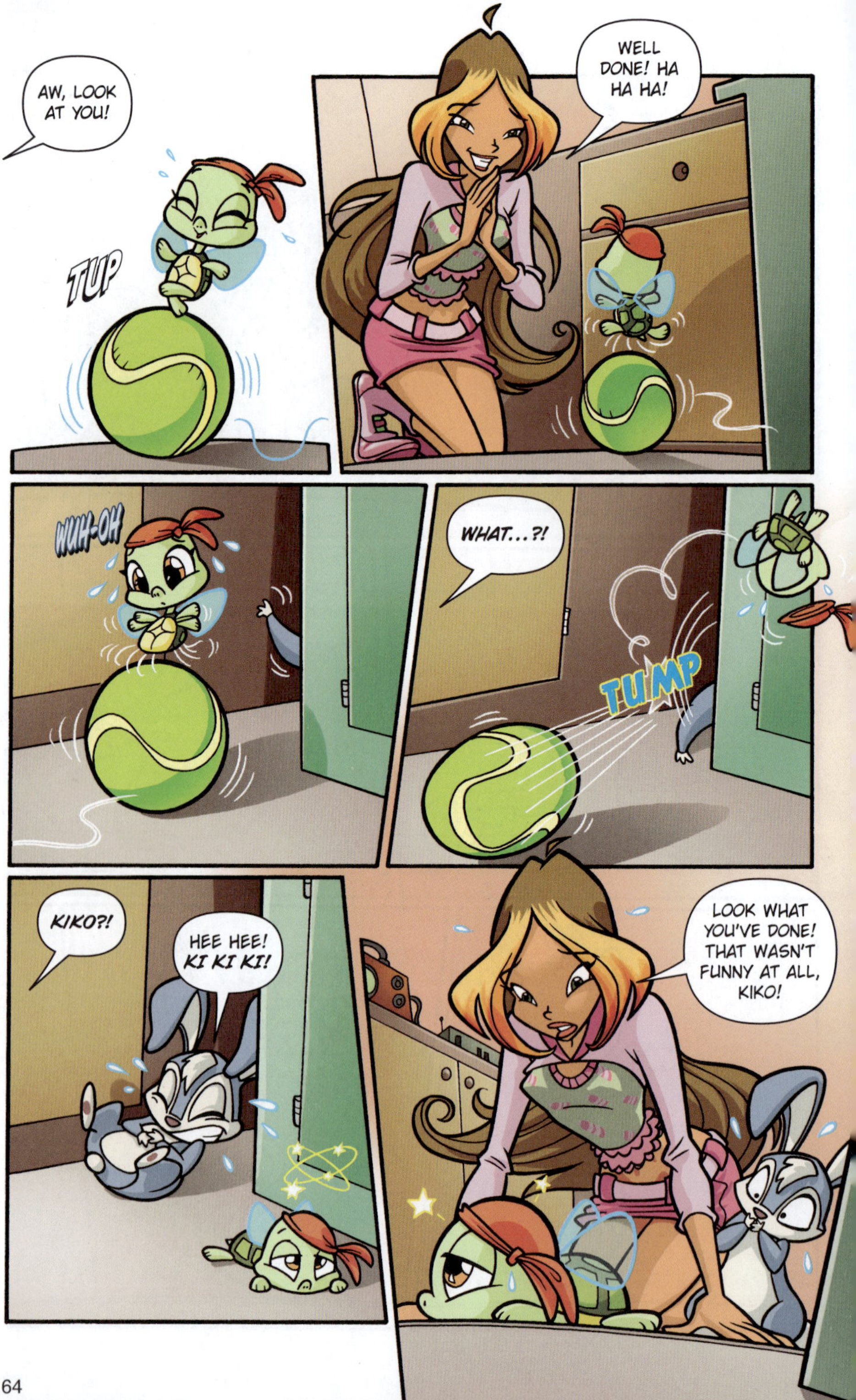
AW, LOOK AT YOU!
TUP
WELL DONE! HA HA HA!
WUH-OH
WHAT...?!
TUMP
KIKO?!
HEE HEE! KI KI KI!
LOOK WHAT YOU'VE DONE! THAT WASN'T FUNNY AT ALL, KIKO!

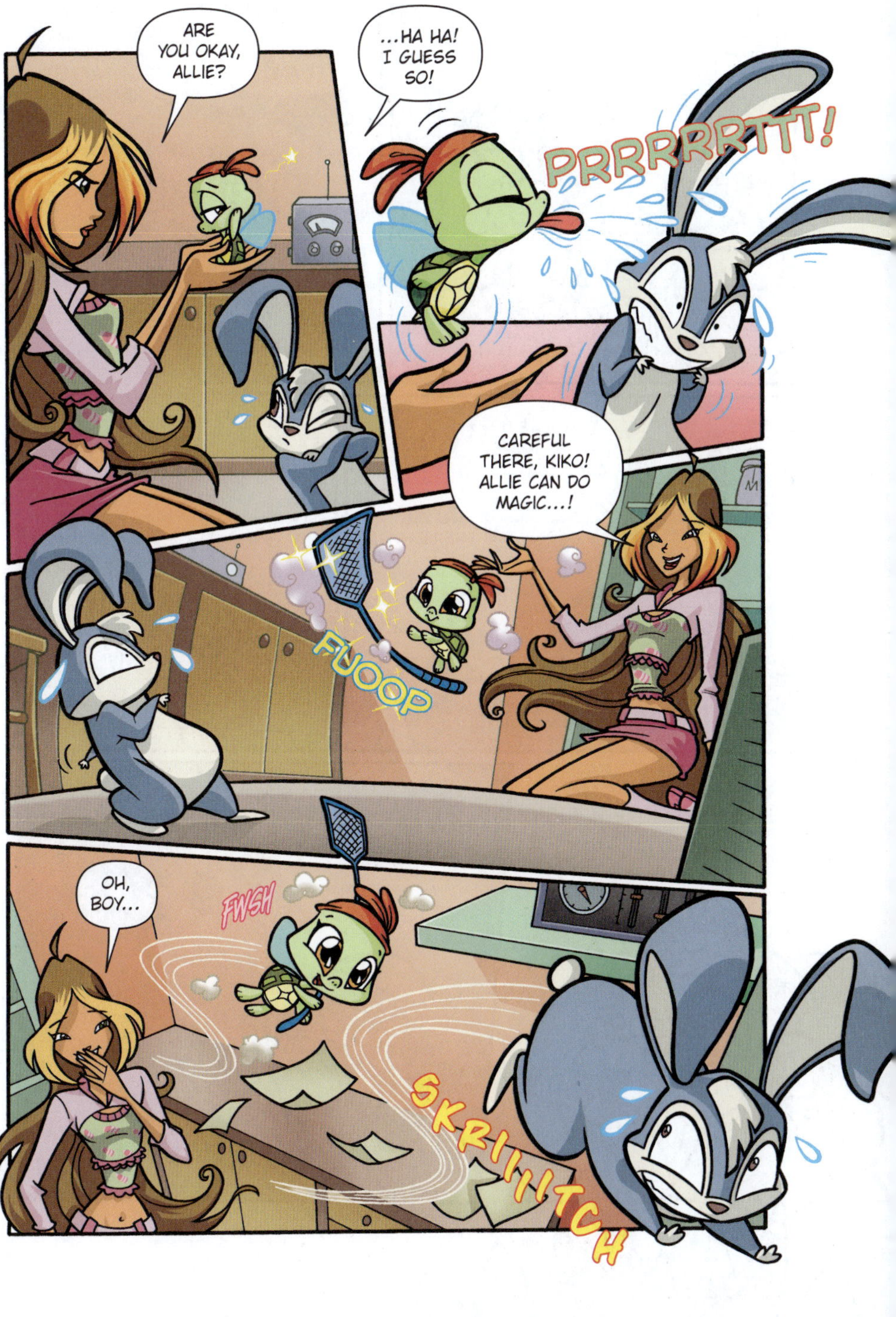
ARE YOU OKAY, ALLIE?
...HA HA! I GUESS SO!
PRRRRRTTT!
CAREFUL THERE, KIKO! ALLIE CAN DO MAGIC...!
FUOOP
OH, BOY...
FWSH
SKRIIIITCH

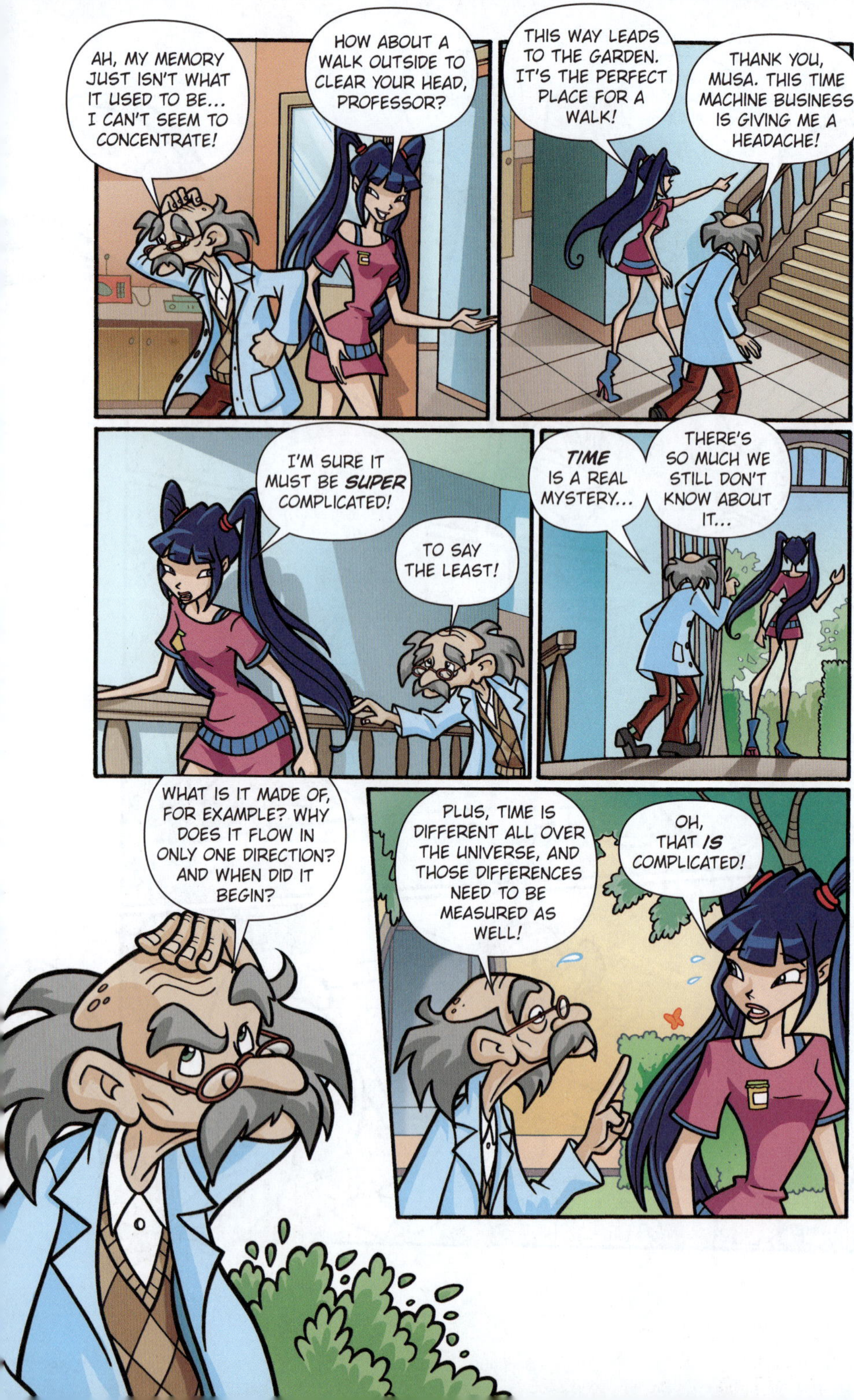
AH, MY MEMORY JUST ISN'T WHAT IT USED TO BE... I CAN'T SEEM TO CONCENTRATE!
HOW ABOUT A WALK OUTSIDE TO CLEAR YOUR HEAD, PROFESSOR?
THIS WAY LEADS TO THE GARDEN. IT'S THE PERFECT PLACE FOR A WALK!
THANK YOU, MUSA. THIS TIME MACHINE BUSINESS IS GIVING ME A HEADACHE!
I'M SURE IT MUST BE ***SUPER*** COMPLICATED!
TO SAY THE LEAST!
TIME IS A REAL MYSTERY...
THERE'S SO MUCH WE STILL DON'T KNOW ABOUT IT...
WHAT IS IT MADE OF, FOR EXAMPLE? WHY DOES IT FLOW IN ONLY ONE DIRECTION? AND WHEN DID IT BEGIN?
PLUS, TIME IS DIFFERENT ALL OVER THE UNIVERSE, AND THOSE DIFFERENCES NEED TO BE MEASURED AS WELL!
OH, THAT ***IS*** COMPLICATED!

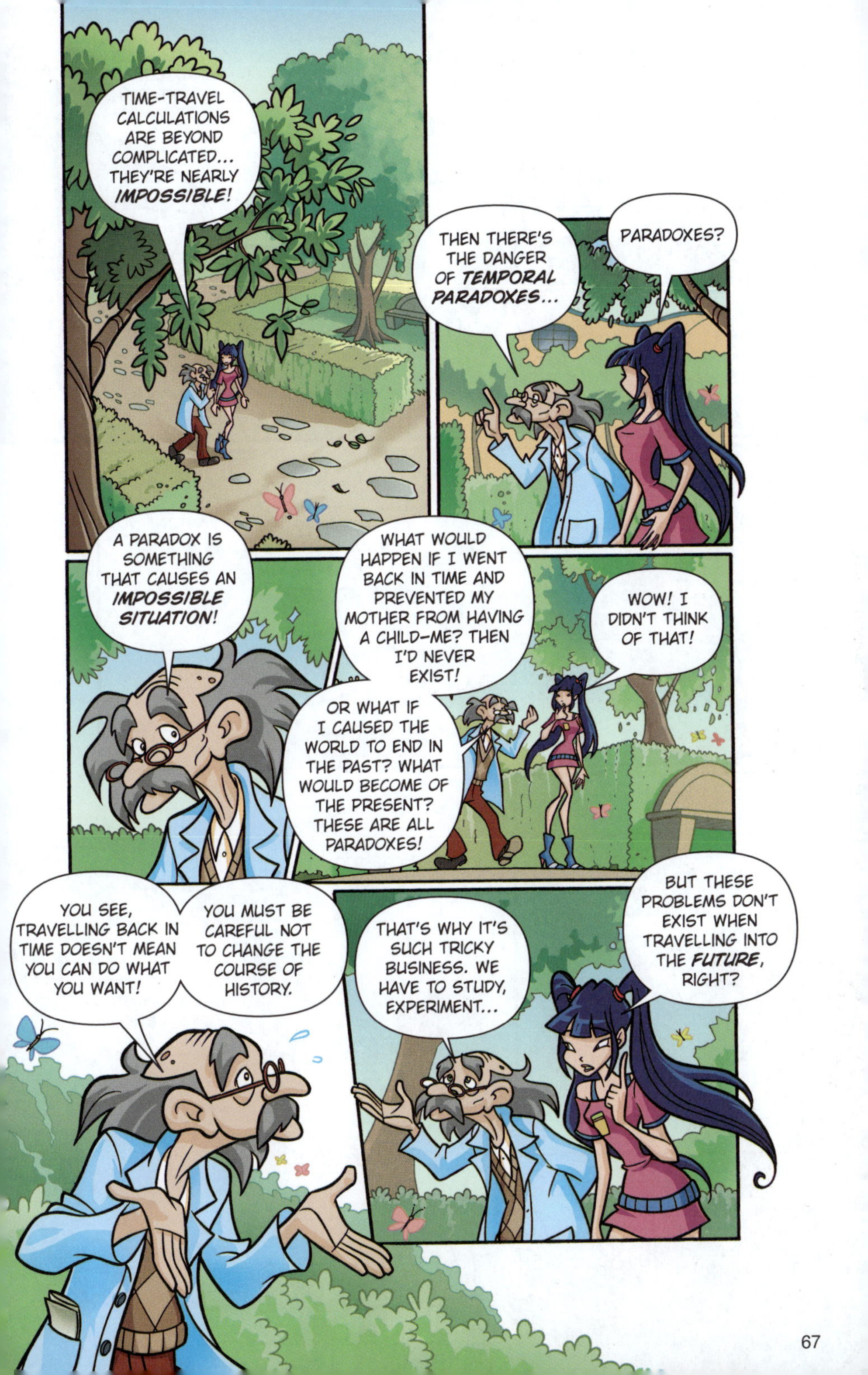

TIME-TRAVEL CALCULATIONS ARE BEYOND COMPLICATED... THEY'RE NEARLY *IMPOSSIBLE*!
THEN THERE'S THE DANGER OF *TEMPORAL PARADOXES*...
PARADOXES?
A PARADOX IS SOMETHING THAT CAUSES AN *IMPOSSIBLE SITUATION*!
WHAT WOULD HAPPEN IF I WENT BACK IN TIME AND PREVENTED MY MOTHER FROM HAVING A CHILD—ME? THEN I'D NEVER EXIST!
OR WHAT IF I CAUSED THE WORLD TO END IN THE PAST? WHAT WOULD BECOME OF THE PRESENT? THESE ARE ALL PARADOXES!
WOW! I DIDN'T THINK OF THAT!
YOU SEE, TRAVELLING BACK IN TIME DOESN'T MEAN YOU CAN DO WHAT YOU WANT!
YOU MUST BE CAREFUL NOT TO CHANGE THE COURSE OF HISTORY.
THAT'S WHY IT'S SUCH TRICKY BUSINESS. WE HAVE TO STUDY, EXPERIMENT...
BUT THESE PROBLEMS DON'T EXIST WHEN TRAVELLING INTO THE *FUTURE*, RIGHT?

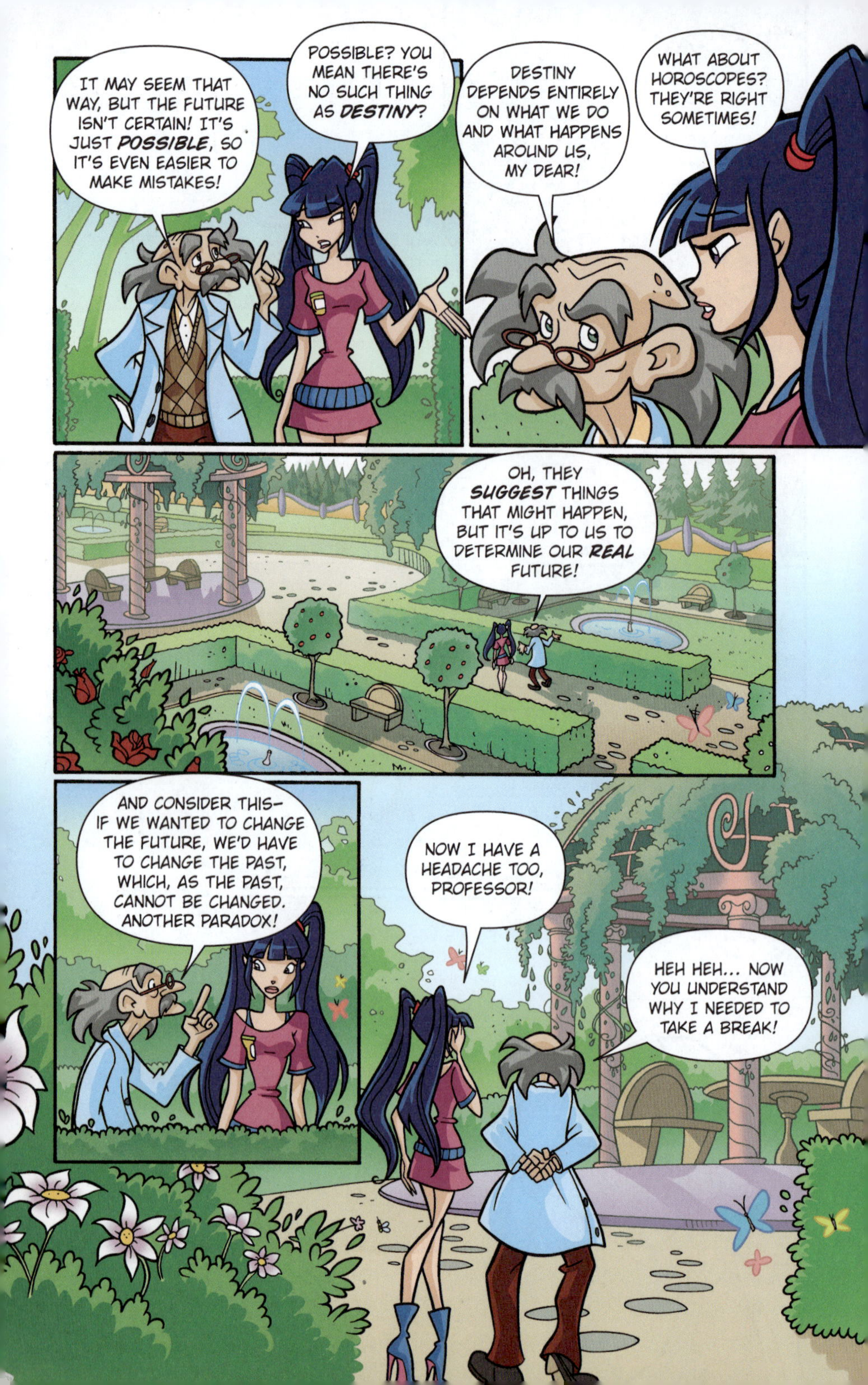
IT MAY SEEM THAT WAY, BUT THE FUTURE ISN'T CERTAIN! IT'S JUST POSSIBLE, SO IT'S EVEN EASIER TO MAKE MISTAKES!
POSSIBLE? YOU MEAN THERE'S NO SUCH THING AS DESTINY?
DESTINY DEPENDS ENTIRELY ON WHAT WE DO AND WHAT HAPPENS AROUND US, MY DEAR!
WHAT ABOUT HOROSCOPES? THEY'RE RIGHT SOMETIMES!
OH, THEY SUGGEST THINGS THAT MIGHT HAPPEN, BUT IT'S UP TO US TO DETERMINE OUR REAL FUTURE!
AND CONSIDER THIS- IF WE WANTED TO CHANGE THE FUTURE, WE'D HAVE TO CHANGE THE PAST, WHICH, AS THE PAST, CANNOT BE CHANGED. ANOTHER PARADOX!
NOW I HAVE A HEADACHE TOO, PROFESSOR!
HEH HEH... NOW YOU UNDERSTAND WHY I NEEDED TO TAKE A BREAK!

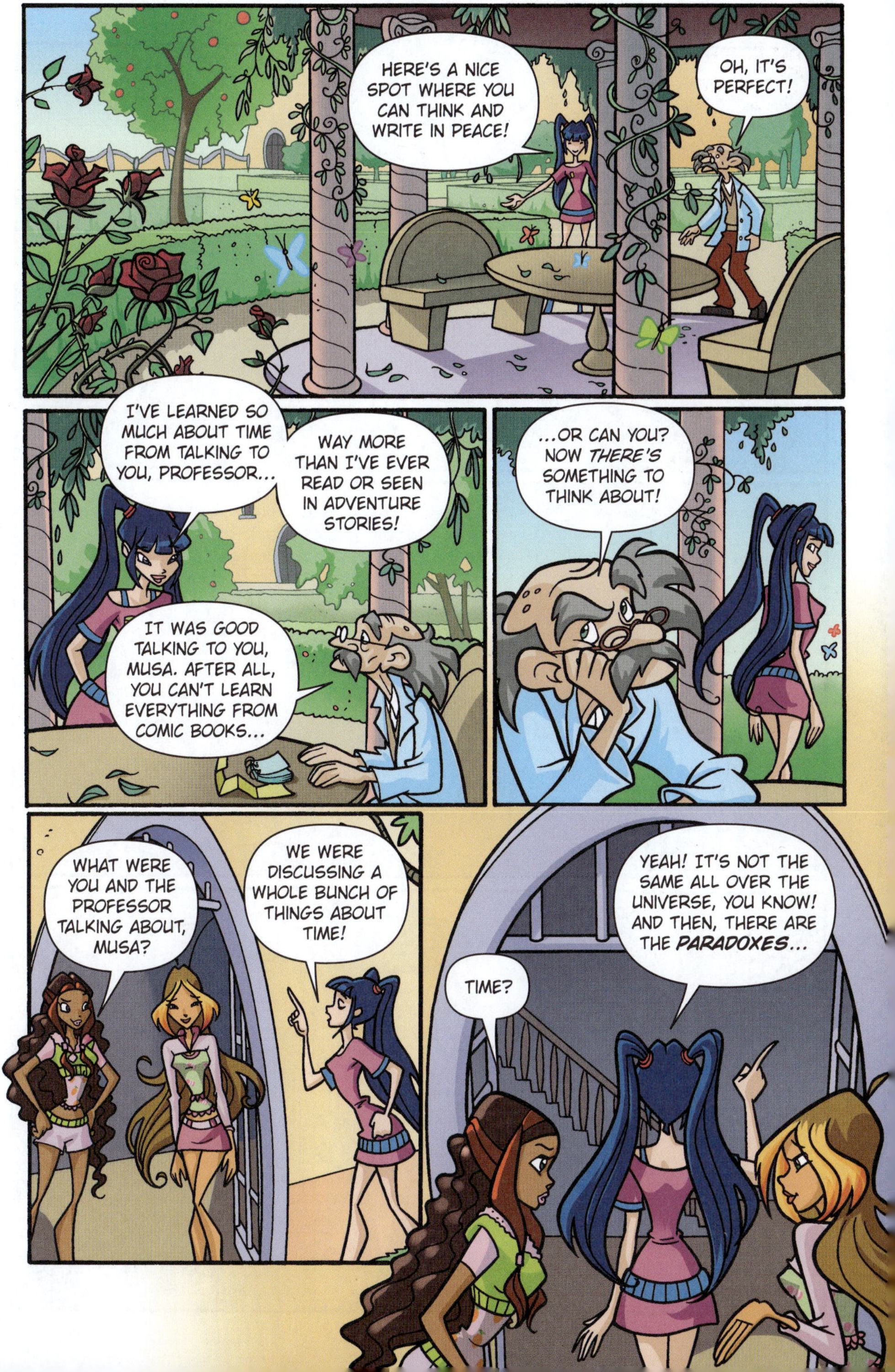
HERE'S A NICE SPOT WHERE YOU CAN THINK AND WRITE IN PEACE!
OH, IT'S PERFECT!
I'VE LEARNED SO MUCH ABOUT TIME FROM TALKING TO YOU, PROFESSOR...
WAY MORE THAN I'VE EVER READ OR SEEN IN ADVENTURE STORIES!
IT WAS GOOD TALKING TO YOU, MUSA. AFTER ALL, YOU CAN'T LEARN EVERYTHING FROM COMIC BOOKS...
...OR CAN YOU? NOW *THERE'S* SOMETHING TO THINK ABOUT!
WHAT WERE YOU AND THE PROFESSOR TALKING ABOUT, MUSA?
WE WERE DISCUSSING A WHOLE BUNCH OF THINGS ABOUT TIME!
TIME?
YEAH! IT'S NOT THE SAME ALL OVER THE UNIVERSE, YOU KNOW! AND THEN, THERE ARE THE ***PARADOXES***...

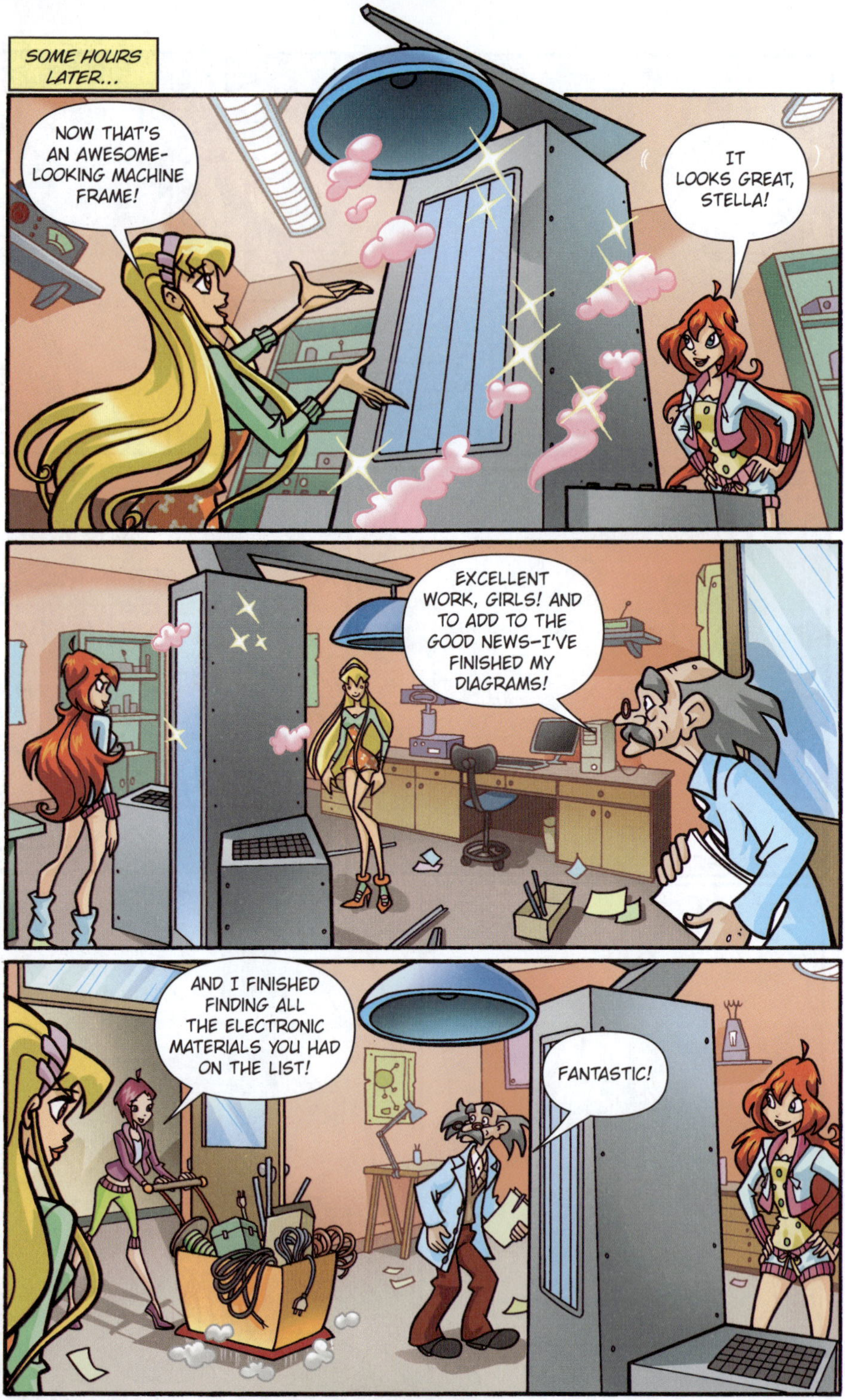
SOME HOURS LATER...
NOW THAT'S AN AWESOME-LOOKING MACHINE FRAME!
IT LOOKS GREAT, STELLA!
EXCELLENT WORK, GIRLS! AND TO ADD TO THE GOOD NEWS–I'VE FINISHED MY DIAGRAMS!
AND I FINISHED FINDING ALL THE ELECTRONIC MATERIALS YOU HAD ON THE LIST!
FANTASTIC!

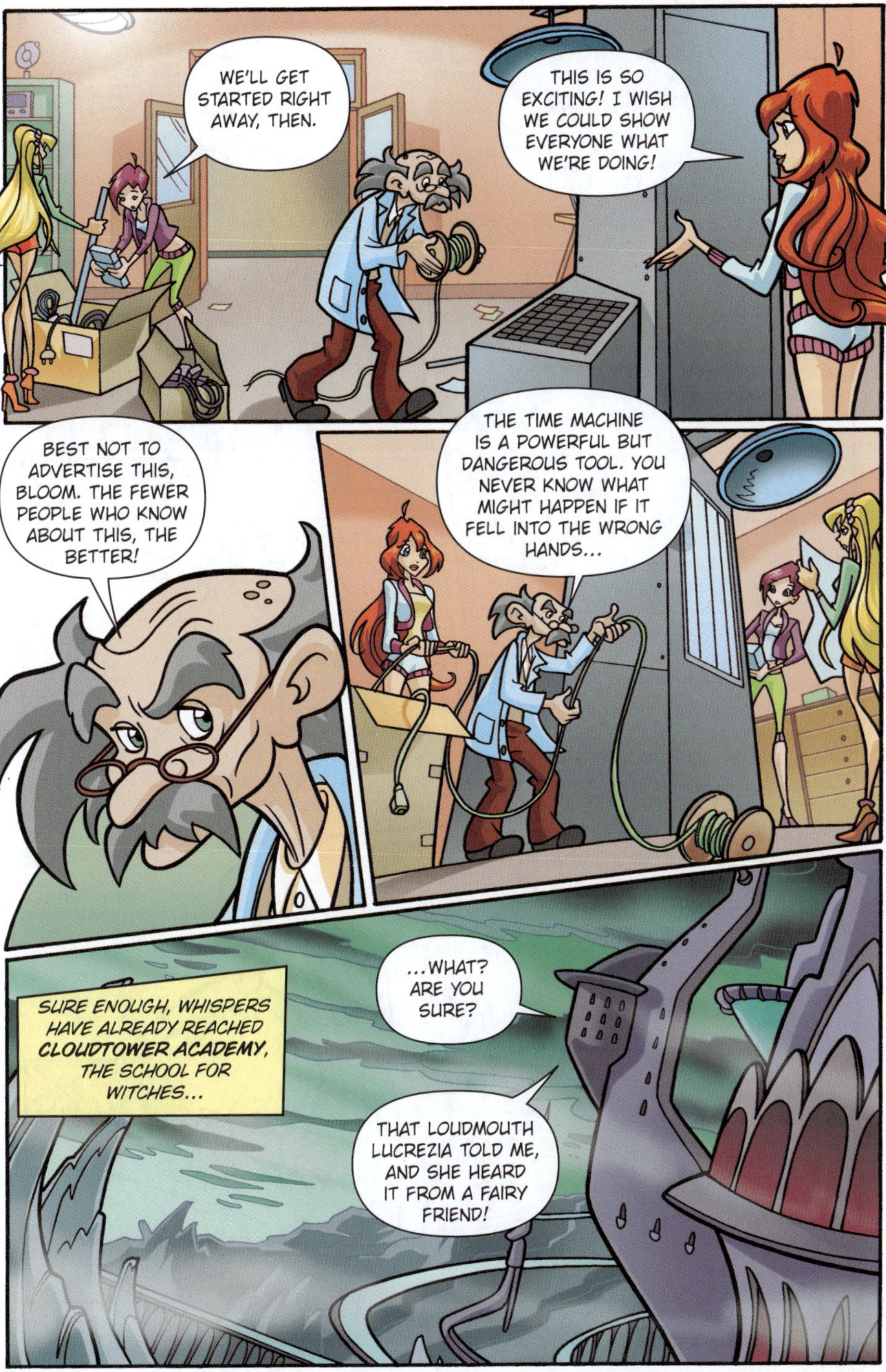
WE'LL GET STARTED RIGHT AWAY, THEN.
THIS IS SO EXCITING! I WISH WE COULD SHOW EVERYONE WHAT WE'RE DOING!
BEST NOT TO ADVERTISE THIS, BLOOM. THE FEWER PEOPLE WHO KNOW ABOUT THIS, THE BETTER!
THE TIME MACHINE IS A POWERFUL BUT DANGEROUS TOOL. YOU NEVER KNOW WHAT MIGHT HAPPEN IF IT FELL INTO THE WRONG HANDS...
SURE ENOUGH, WHISPERS HAVE ALREADY REACHED **CLOUDTOWER ACADEMY**, THE SCHOOL FOR WITCHES...
...WHAT? ARE YOU SURE?
THAT LOUDMOUTH LUCREZIA TOLD ME, AND SHE HEARD IT FROM A FAIRY FRIEND!

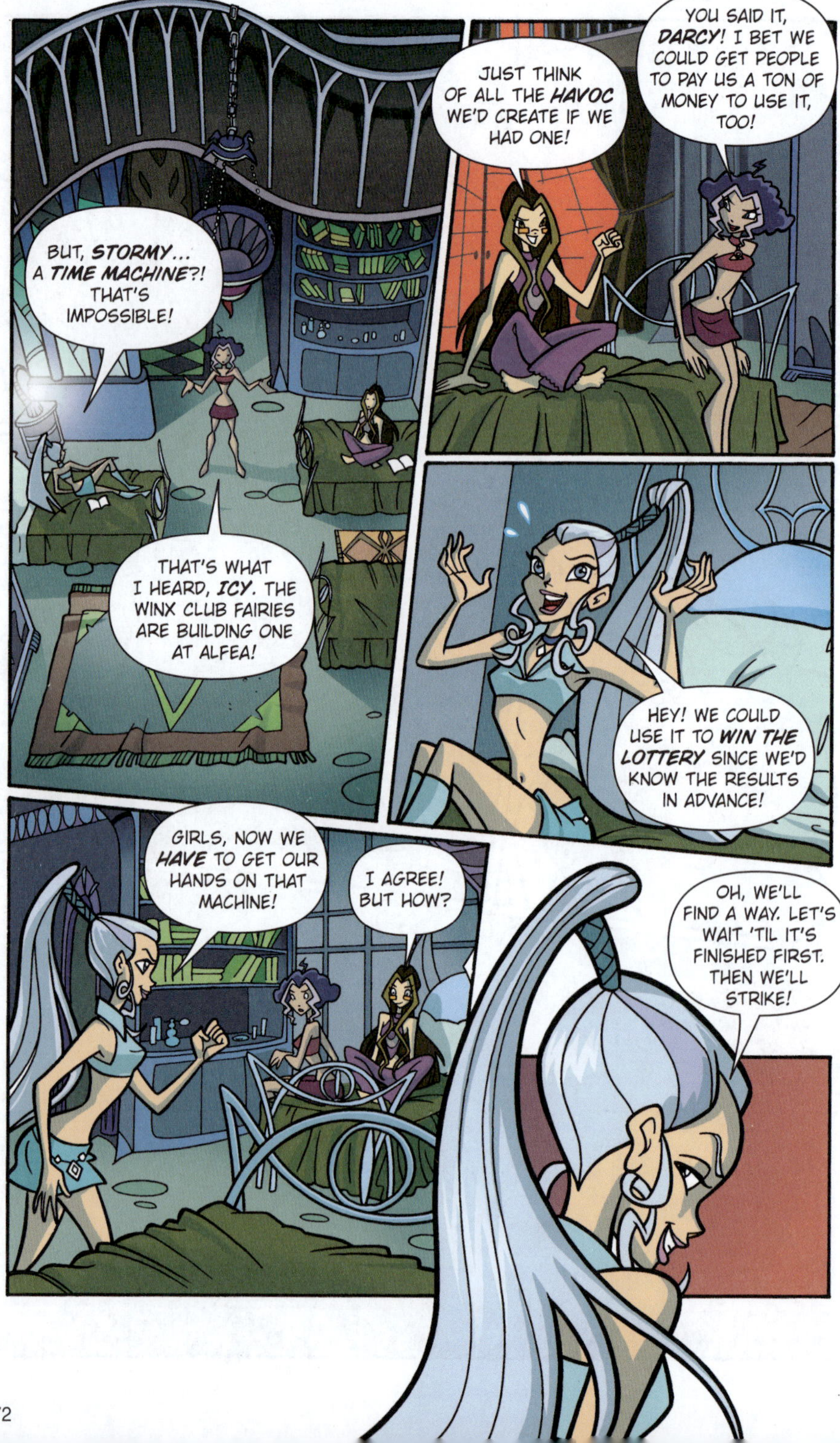
BUT, STORMY... A TIME MACHINE?! THAT'S IMPOSSIBLE!
THAT'S WHAT I HEARD, ICY. THE WINX CLUB FAIRIES ARE BUILDING ONE AT ALFEA!
JUST THINK OF ALL THE HAVOC WE'D CREATE IF WE HAD ONE!
YOU SAID IT, DARCY! I BET WE COULD GET PEOPLE TO PAY US A TON OF MONEY TO USE IT, TOO!
HEY! WE COULD USE IT TO WIN THE LOTTERY SINCE WE'D KNOW THE RESULTS IN ADVANCE!
GIRLS, NOW WE HAVE TO GET OUR HANDS ON THAT MACHINE!
I AGREE! BUT HOW?
OH, WE'LL FIND A WAY. LET'S WAIT 'TIL IT'S FINISHED FIRST. THEN WE'LL STRIKE!

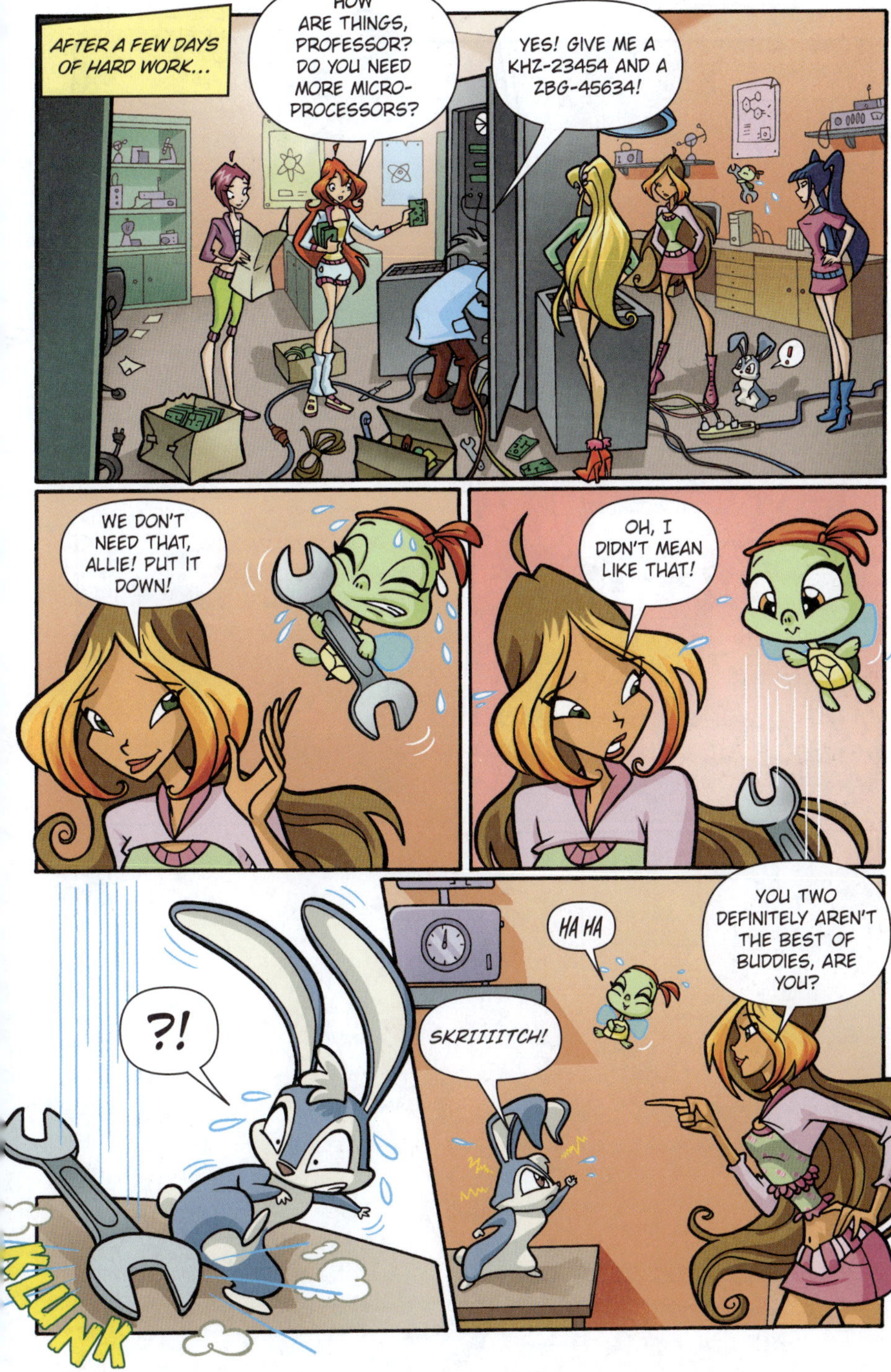
AFTER A FEW DAYS OF HARD WORK...
HOW ARE THINGS, PROFESSOR? DO YOU NEED MORE MICRO-PROCESSORS?
YES! GIVE ME A KHZ-23454 AND A ZBG-45634!
WE DON'T NEED THAT, ALLIE! PUT IT DOWN!
OH, I DIDN'T MEAN LIKE THAT!
?!
KLUNK
HA HA
SKRIIIITCH!
YOU TWO DEFINITELY AREN'T THE BEST OF BUDDIES, ARE YOU?

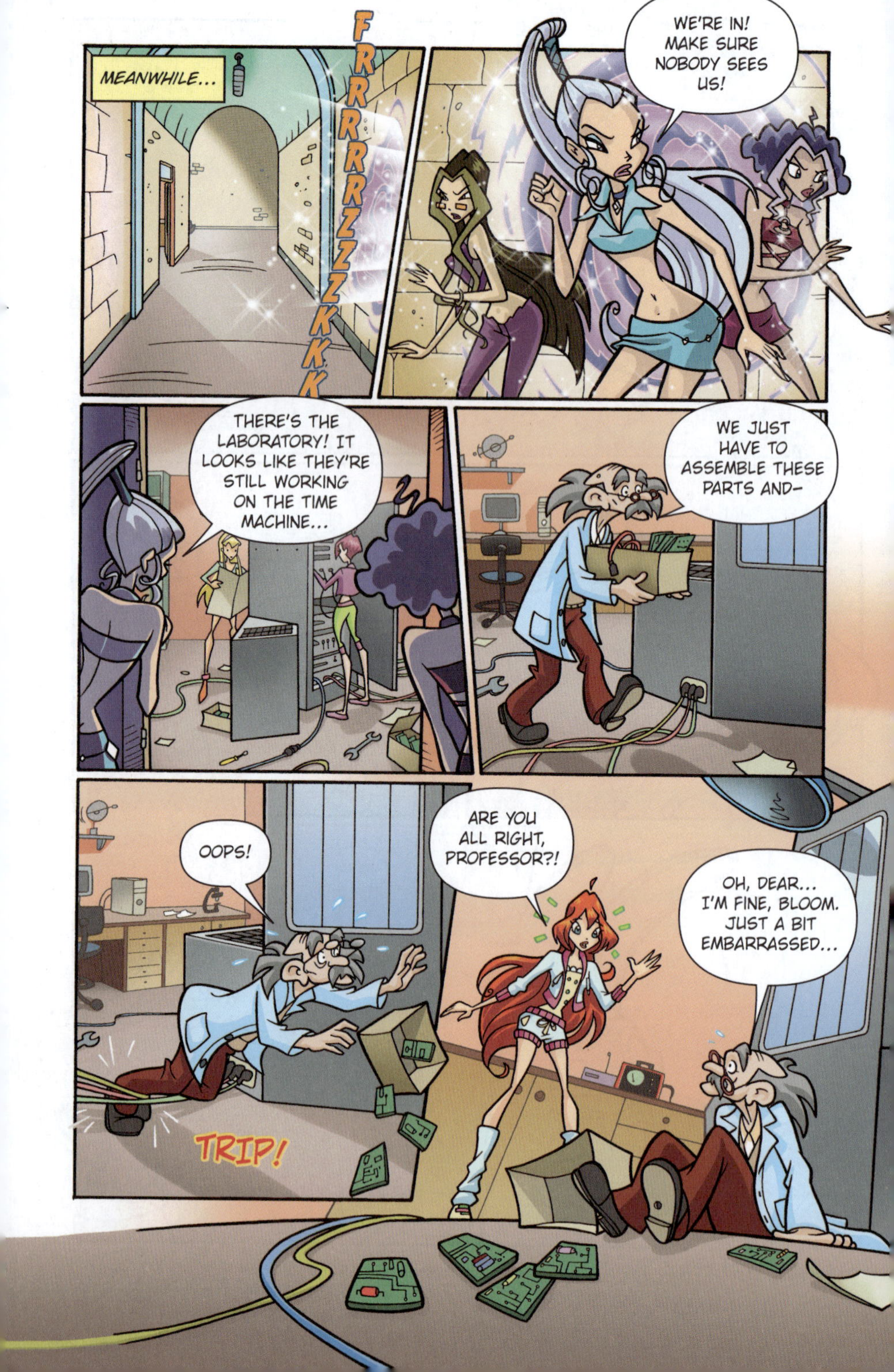
MEANWHILE...
FRRRRRZZZZKKK
WE'RE IN! MAKE SURE NOBODY SEES US!
THERE'S THE LABORATORY! IT LOOKS LIKE THEY'RE STILL WORKING ON THE TIME MACHINE...
WE JUST HAVE TO ASSEMBLE THESE PARTS AND—
OOPS!
TRIP!
ARE YOU ALL RIGHT, PROFESSOR?!
OH, DEAR... I'M FINE, BLOOM. JUST A BIT EMBARRASSED...

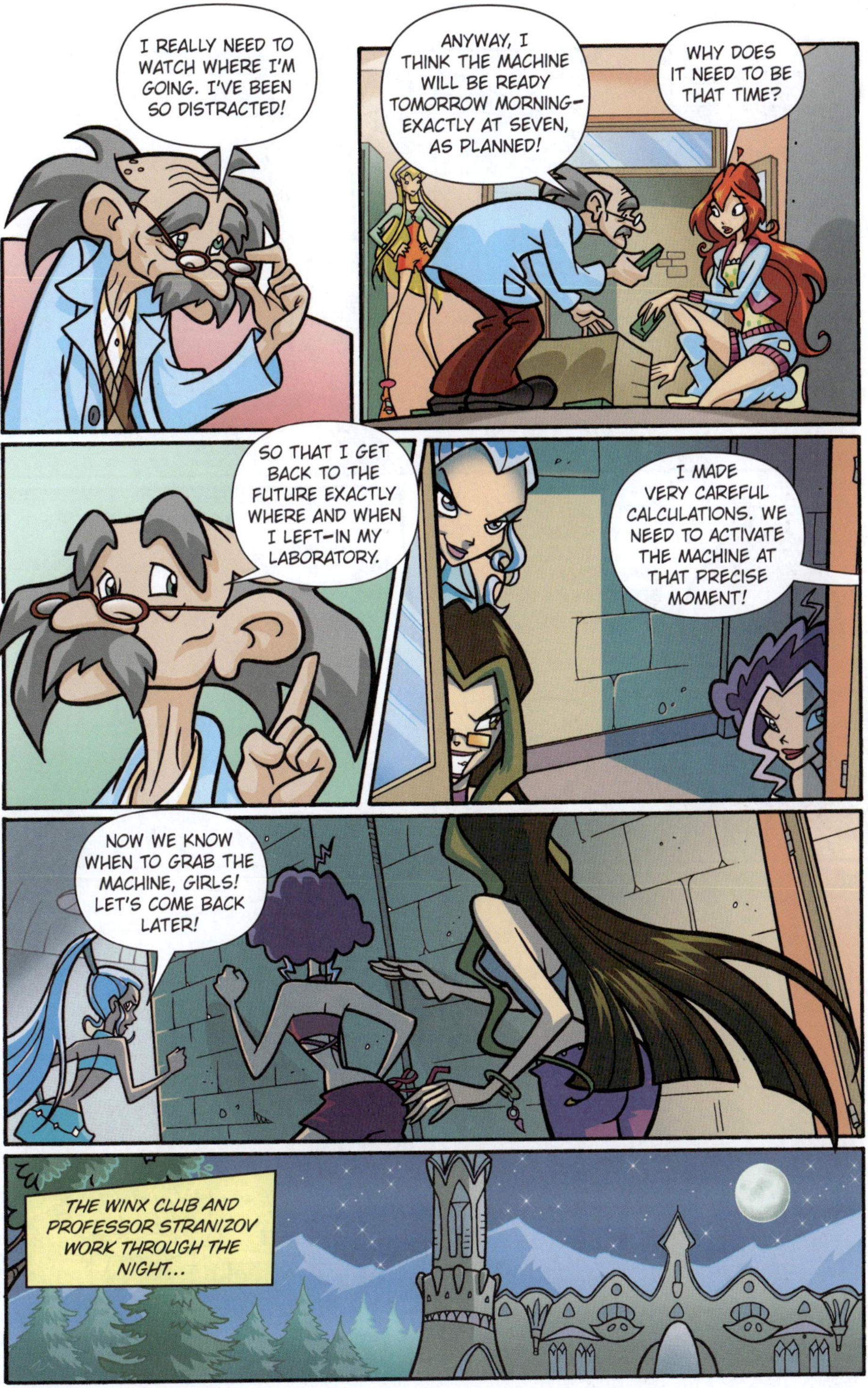
I REALLY NEED TO WATCH WHERE I'M GOING. I'VE BEEN SO DISTRACTED!
ANYWAY, I THINK THE MACHINE WILL BE READY TOMORROW MORNING-EXACTLY AT SEVEN, AS PLANNED!
WHY DOES IT NEED TO BE THAT TIME?
SO THAT I GET BACK TO THE FUTURE EXACTLY WHERE AND WHEN I LEFT-IN MY LABORATORY.
I MADE VERY CAREFUL CALCULATIONS. WE NEED TO ACTIVATE THE MACHINE AT THAT PRECISE MOMENT!
NOW WE KNOW WHEN TO GRAB THE MACHINE, GIRLS! LET'S COME BACK LATER!
THE WINX CLUB AND PROFESSOR STRANIZOV WORK THROUGH THE NIGHT...

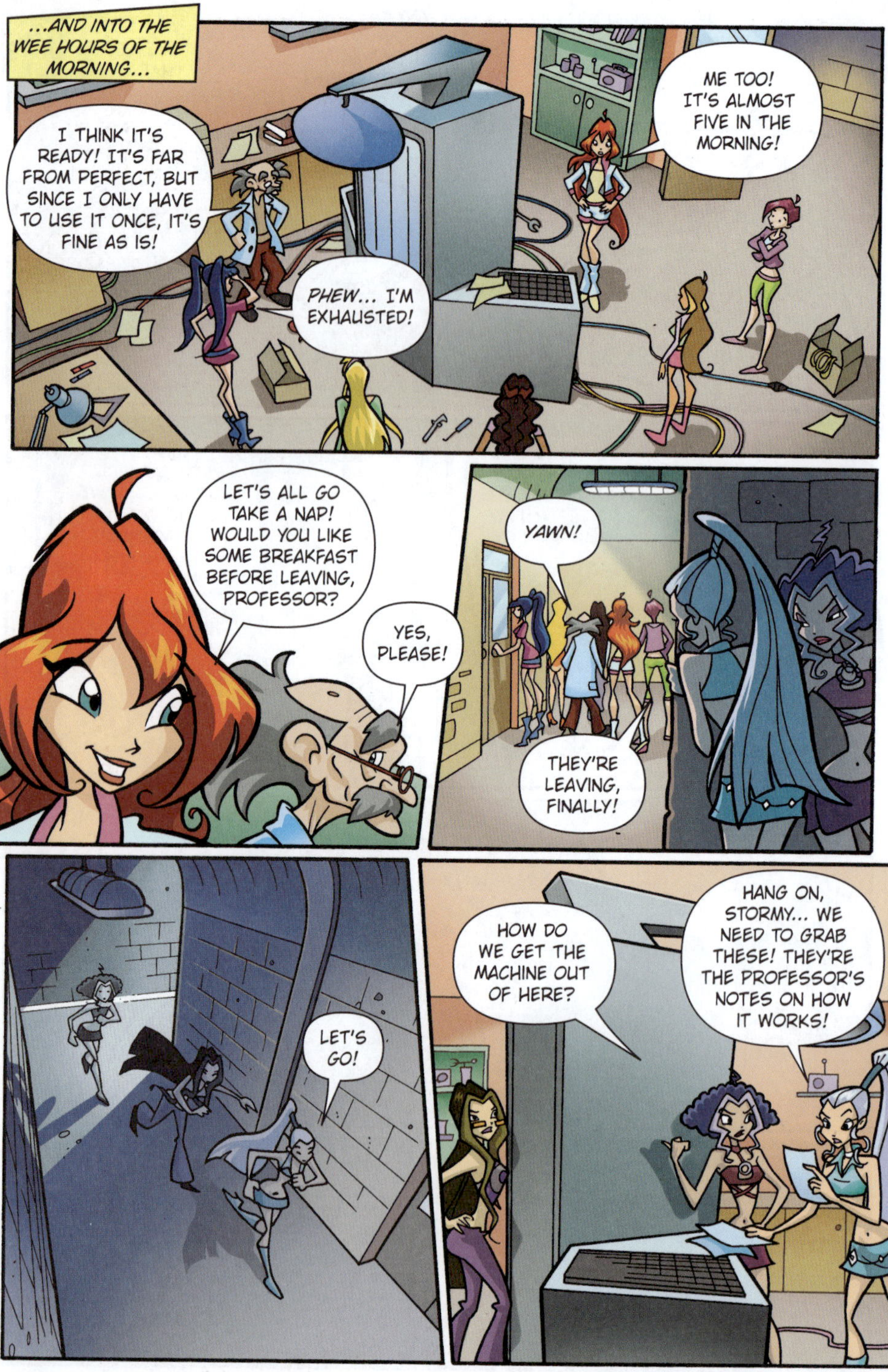
...AND INTO THE WEE HOURS OF THE MORNING...
I THINK IT'S READY! IT'S FAR FROM PERFECT, BUT SINCE I ONLY HAVE TO USE IT ONCE, IT'S FINE AS IS!
PHEW... I'M EXHAUSTED!
ME TOO! IT'S ALMOST FIVE IN THE MORNING!
LET'S ALL GO TAKE A NAP! WOULD YOU LIKE SOME BREAKFAST BEFORE LEAVING, PROFESSOR?
YES, PLEASE!
YAWN!
THEY'RE LEAVING, FINALLY!
LET'S GO!
HOW DO WE GET THE MACHINE OUT OF HERE?
HANG ON, STORMY... WE NEED TO GRAB THESE! THEY'RE THE PROFESSOR'S NOTES ON HOW IT WORKS!

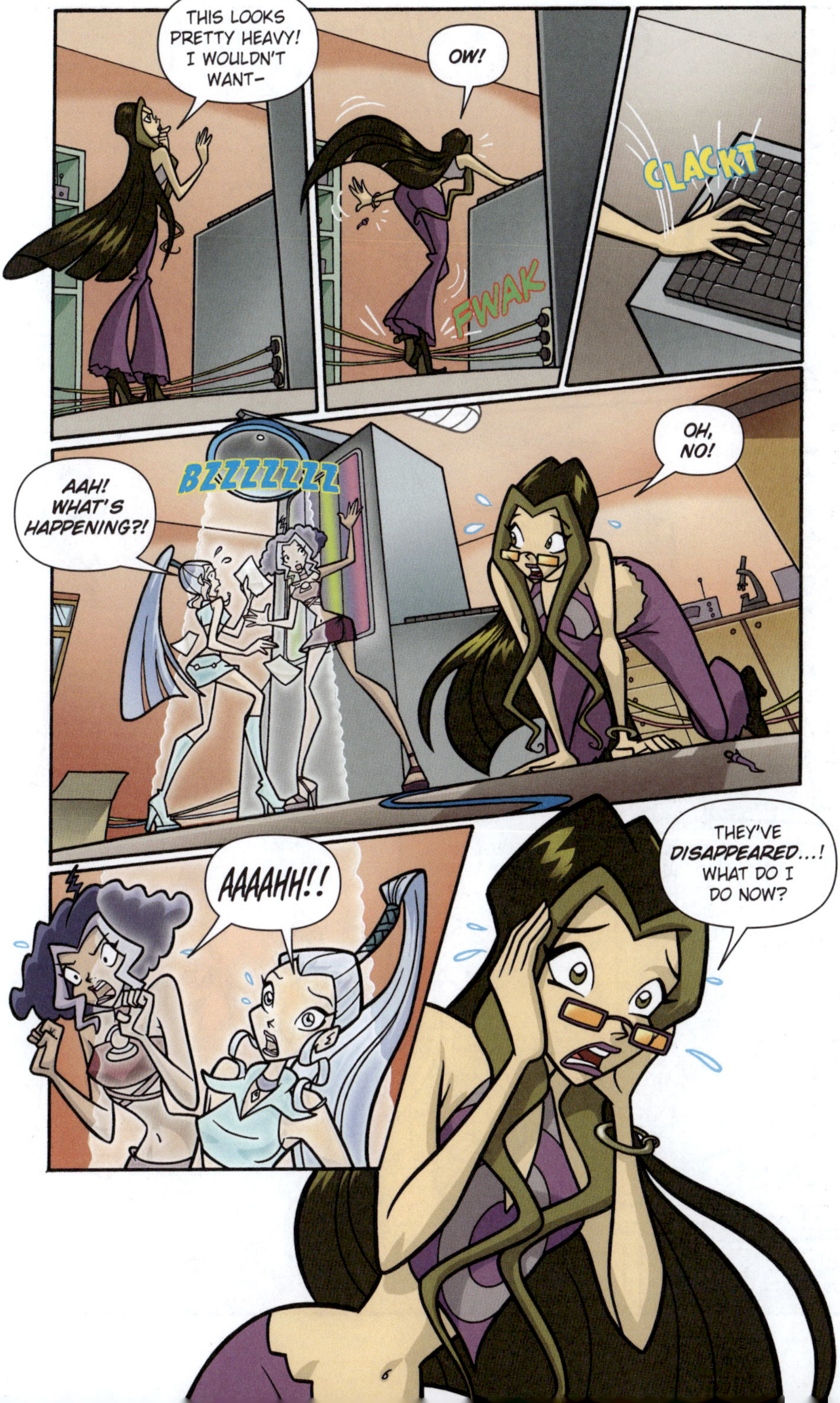
THIS LOOKS PRETTY HEAVY! I WOULDN'T WANT-
OW!
FWAK
CLACKT
BZZZZZZZ
OH, NO!
AAH! WHAT'S HAPPENING?!
AAAAHH!!
THEY'VE *DISAPPEARED*...! WHAT DO I DO NOW?

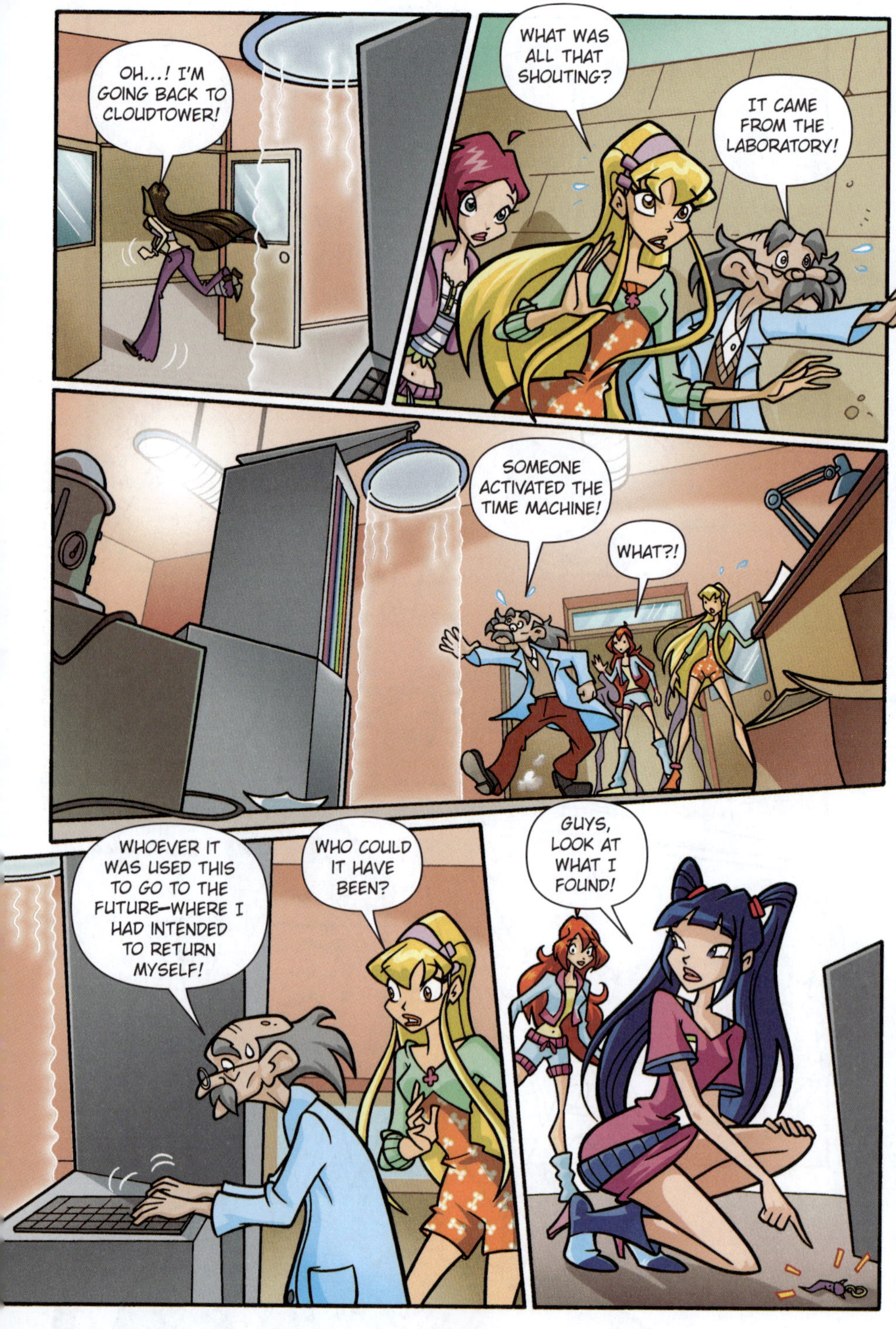
OH...! I'M GOING BACK TO CLOUDTOWER!
WHAT WAS ALL THAT SHOUTING?
IT CAME FROM THE LABORATORY!
SOMEONE ACTIVATED THE TIME MACHINE!
WHAT?!
WHOEVER IT WAS USED THIS TO GO TO THE FUTURE—WHERE I HAD INTENDED TO RETURN MYSELF!
WHO COULD IT HAVE BEEN?
GUYS, LOOK AT WHAT I FOUND!

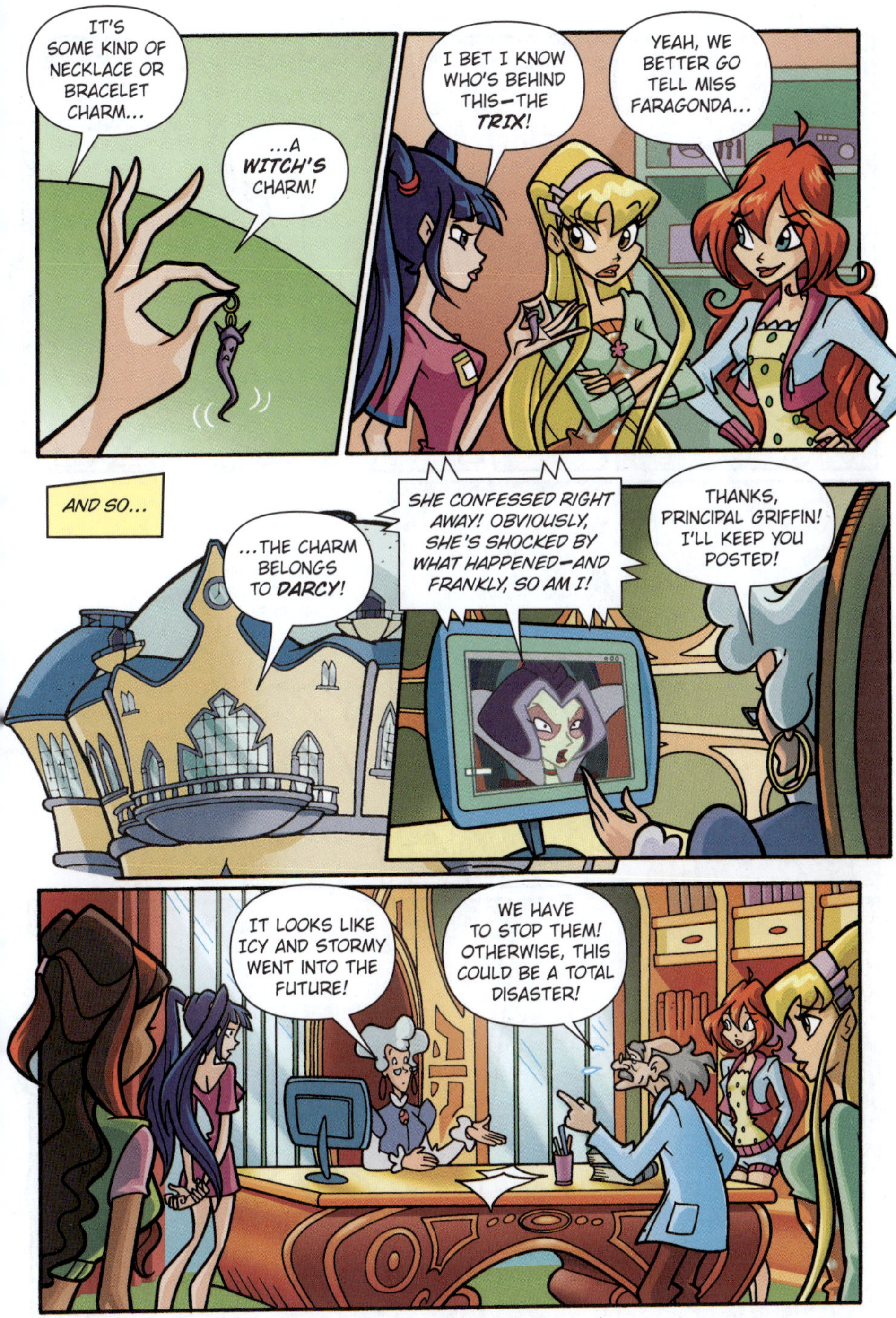
IT'S SOME KIND OF NECKLACE OR BRACELET CHARM...
...A WITCH'S CHARM!
I BET I KNOW WHO'S BEHIND THIS—THE TRIX!
YEAH, WE BETTER GO TELL MISS FARAGONDA...
AND SO...
...THE CHARM BELONGS TO DARCY!
SHE CONFESSED RIGHT AWAY! OBVIOUSLY, SHE'S SHOCKED BY WHAT HAPPENED—AND FRANKLY, SO AM I!
THANKS, PRINCIPAL GRIFFIN! I'LL KEEP YOU POSTED!
IT LOOKS LIKE ICY AND STORMY WENT INTO THE FUTURE!
WE HAVE TO STOP THEM! OTHERWISE, THIS COULD BE A TOTAL DISASTER!

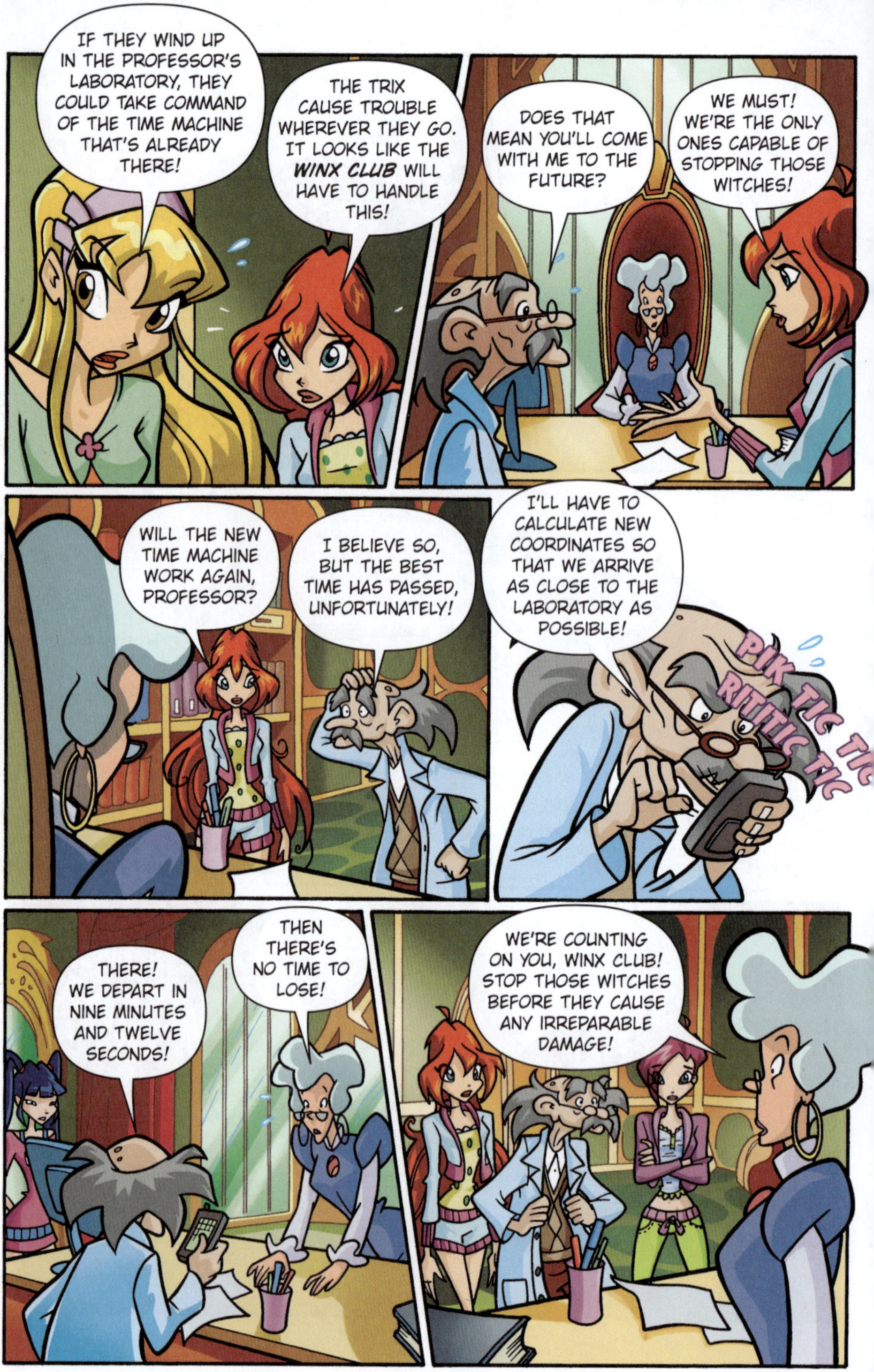
IF THEY WIND UP IN THE PROFESSOR'S LABORATORY, THEY COULD TAKE COMMAND OF THE TIME MACHINE THAT'S ALREADY THERE!
THE TRIX CAUSE TROUBLE WHEREVER THEY GO. IT LOOKS LIKE THE *WINX CLUB* WILL HAVE TO HANDLE THIS!
DOES THAT MEAN YOU'LL COME WITH ME TO THE FUTURE?
WE MUST! WE'RE THE ONLY ONES CAPABLE OF STOPPING THOSE WITCHES!
WILL THE NEW TIME MACHINE WORK AGAIN, PROFESSOR?
I BELIEVE SO, BUT THE BEST TIME HAS PASSED, UNFORTUNATELY!
I'LL HAVE TO CALCULATE NEW COORDINATES SO THAT WE ARRIVE AS CLOSE TO THE LABORATORY AS POSSIBLE!
PIK TIC TIC
RITITIC TIC
THERE! WE DEPART IN NINE MINUTES AND TWELVE SECONDS!
THEN THERE'S NO TIME TO LOSE!
WE'RE COUNTING ON YOU, WINX CLUB! STOP THOSE WITCHES BEFORE THEY CAUSE ANY IRREPARABLE DAMAGE!

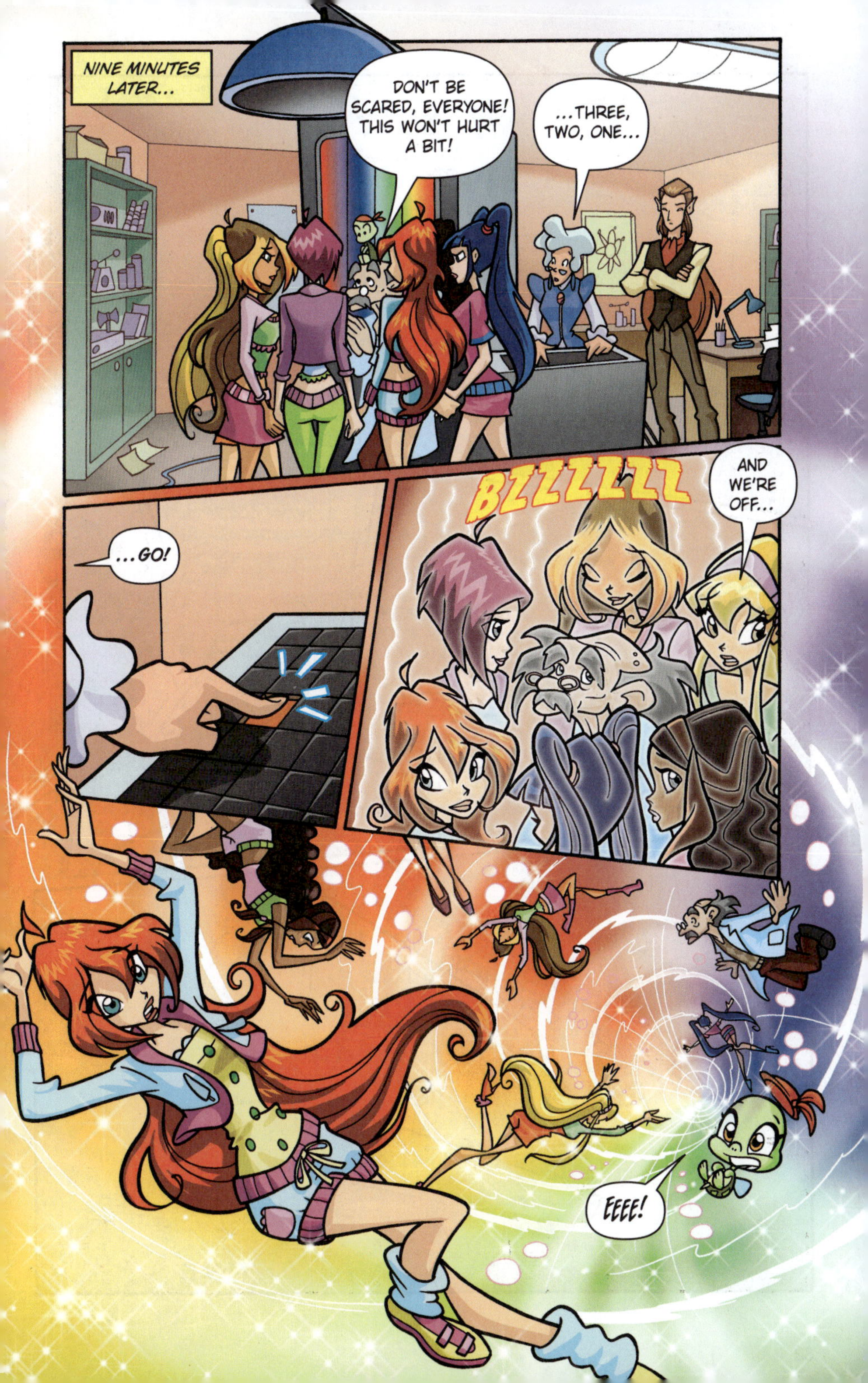
NINE MINUTES LATER...
DON'T BE SCARED, EVERYONE! THIS WON'T HURT A BIT!
...THREE, TWO, ONE...
...GO!
BZZZZZZ
AND WE'RE OFF...
EEEE!

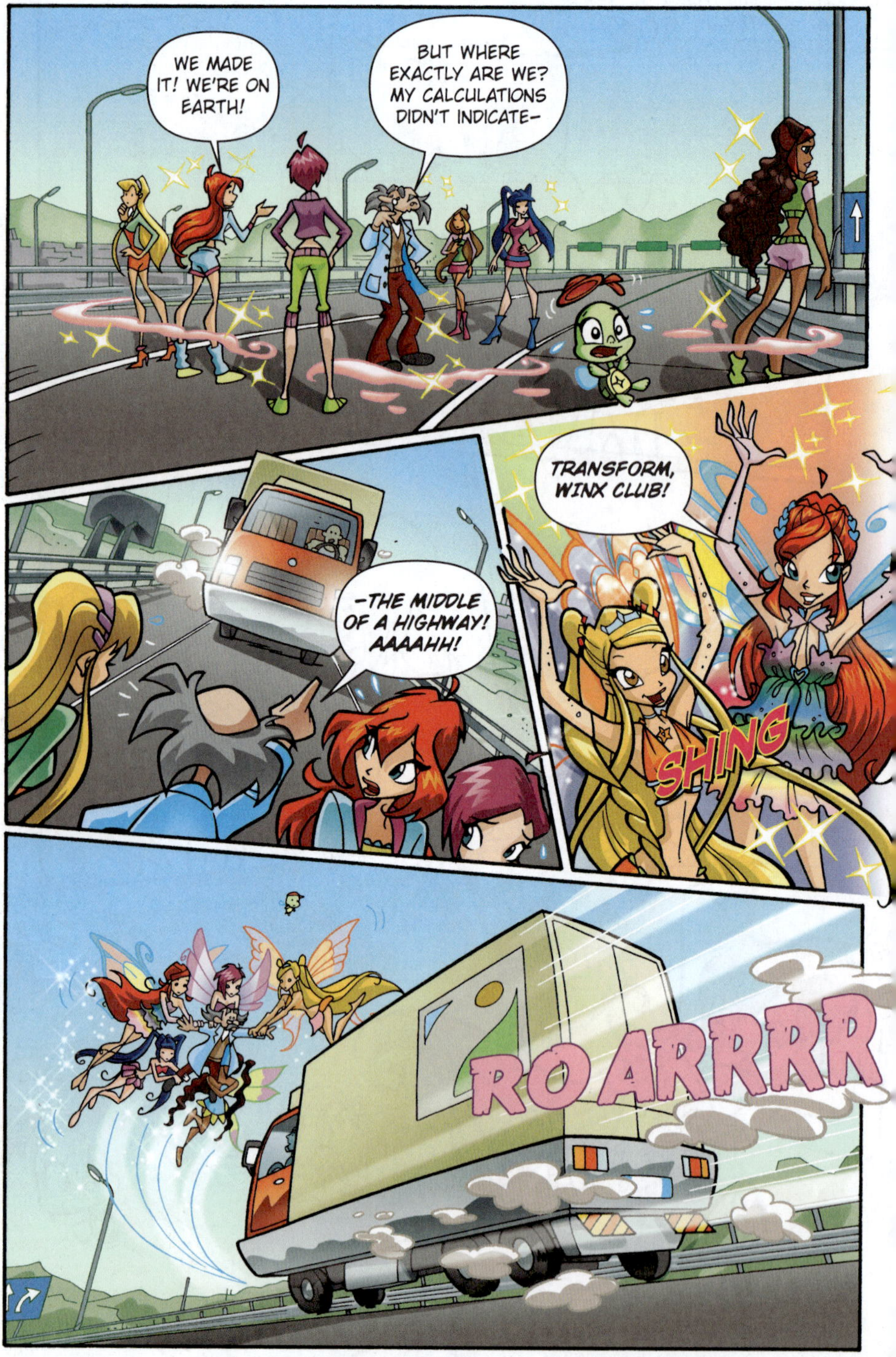
WE MADE IT! WE'RE ON EARTH!
BUT WHERE EXACTLY ARE WE? MY CALCULATIONS DIDN'T INDICATE—
—THE MIDDLE OF A HIGHWAY! AAAAHH!
TRANSFORM, WINX CLUB!
SHING
ROARRRR

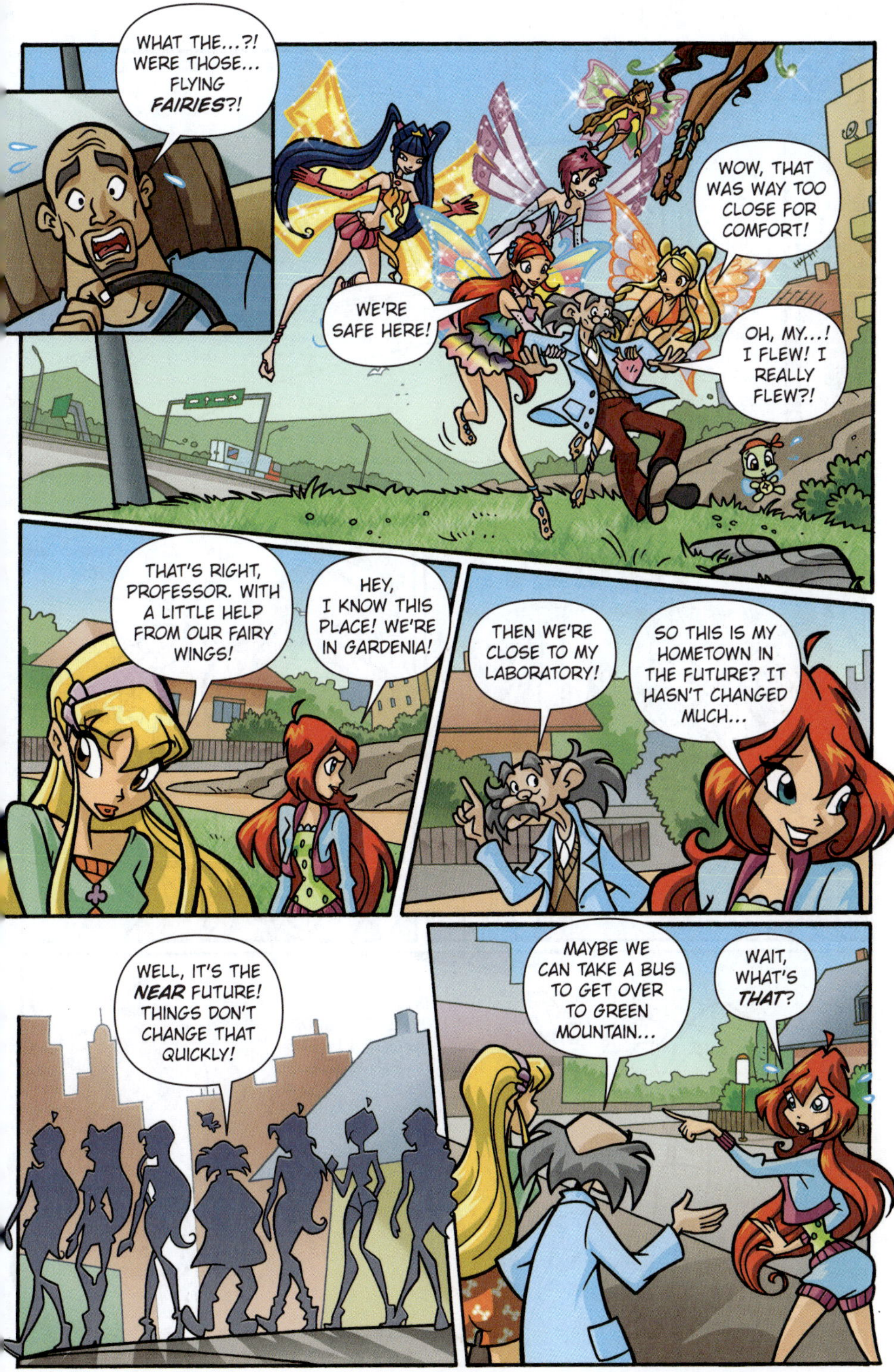
WHAT THE...?! WERE THOSE... FLYING FAIRIES?!
WOW, THAT WAS WAY TOO CLOSE FOR COMFORT!
WE'RE SAFE HERE!
OH, MY...! I FLEW! I REALLY FLEW?!
THAT'S RIGHT, PROFESSOR. WITH A LITTLE HELP FROM OUR FAIRY WINGS!
HEY, I KNOW THIS PLACE! WE'RE IN GARDENIA!
THEN WE'RE CLOSE TO MY LABORATORY!
SO THIS IS MY HOMETOWN IN THE FUTURE? IT HASN'T CHANGED MUCH...
WELL, IT'S THE NEAR FUTURE! THINGS DON'T CHANGE THAT QUICKLY!
MAYBE WE CAN TAKE A BUS TO GET OVER TO GREEN MOUNTAIN...
WAIT, WHAT'S THAT?

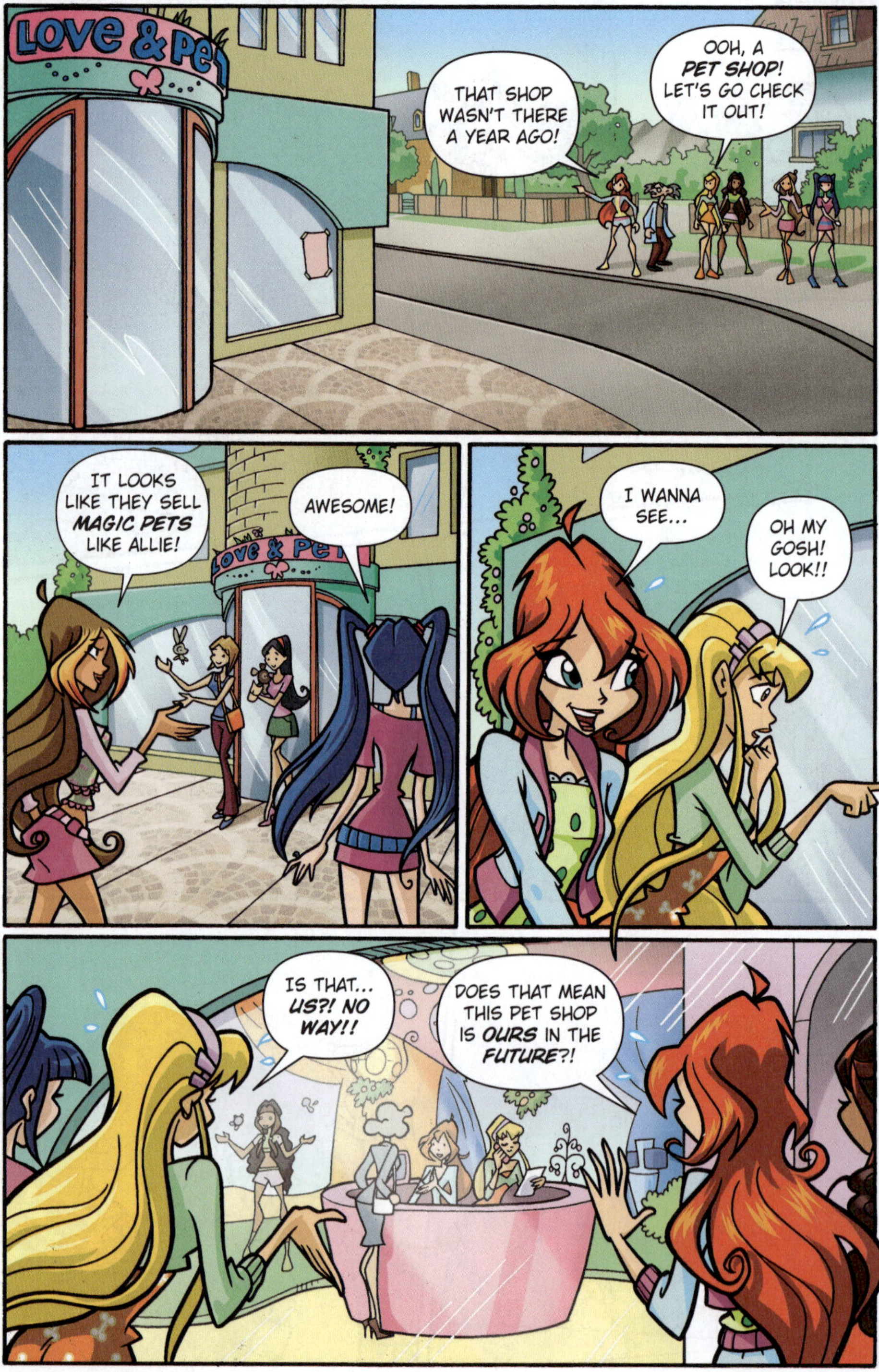
Love & Pet
THAT SHOP WASN'T THERE A YEAR AGO!
OOH, A *PET SHOP!* LET'S GO CHECK IT OUT!
IT LOOKS LIKE THEY SELL *MAGIC PETS* LIKE ALLIE!
Love & Pet
AWESOME!
I WANNA SEE...
OH MY GOSH! LOOK!!
IS THAT... *US?! NO WAY!!*
DOES THAT MEAN THIS PET SHOP IS *OURS* IN THE *FUTURE?!*

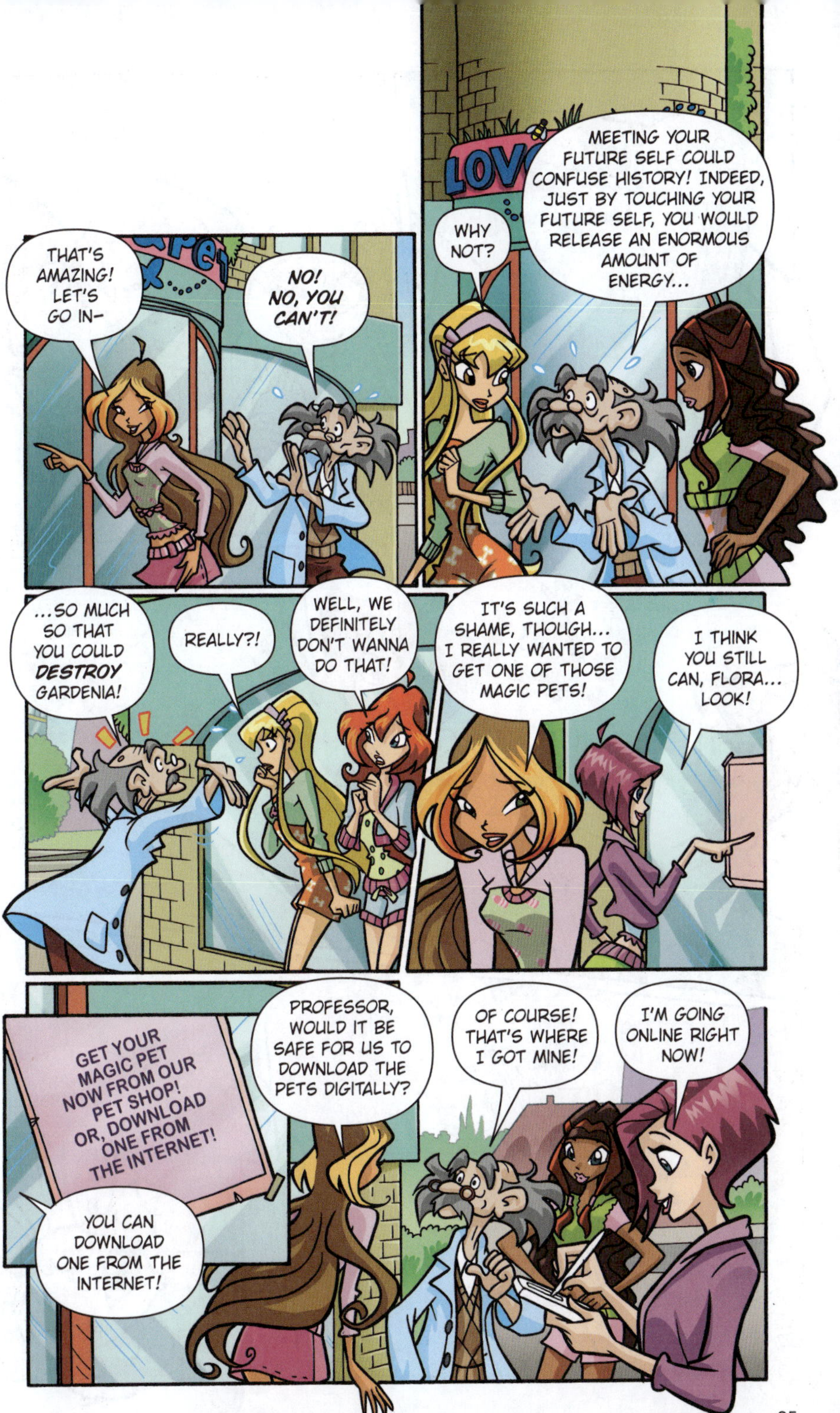
THAT'S AMAZING! LET'S GO IN-
NO! NO, YOU CAN'T!
WHY NOT?
MEETING YOUR FUTURE SELF COULD CONFUSE HISTORY! INDEED, JUST BY TOUCHING YOUR FUTURE SELF, YOU WOULD RELEASE AN ENORMOUS AMOUNT OF ENERGY...
...SO MUCH SO THAT YOU COULD DESTROY GARDENIA!
REALLY?!
WELL, WE DEFINITELY DON'T WANNA DO THAT!
IT'S SUCH A SHAME, THOUGH... I REALLY WANTED TO GET ONE OF THOSE MAGIC PETS!
I THINK YOU STILL CAN, FLORA... LOOK!
GET YOUR MAGIC PET NOW FROM OUR PET SHOP! OR, DOWNLOAD ONE FROM THE INTERNET!
YOU CAN DOWNLOAD ONE FROM THE INTERNET!
PROFESSOR, WOULD IT BE SAFE FOR US TO DOWNLOAD THE PETS DIGITALLY?
OF COURSE! THAT'S WHERE I GOT MINE!
I'M GOING ONLINE RIGHT NOW!

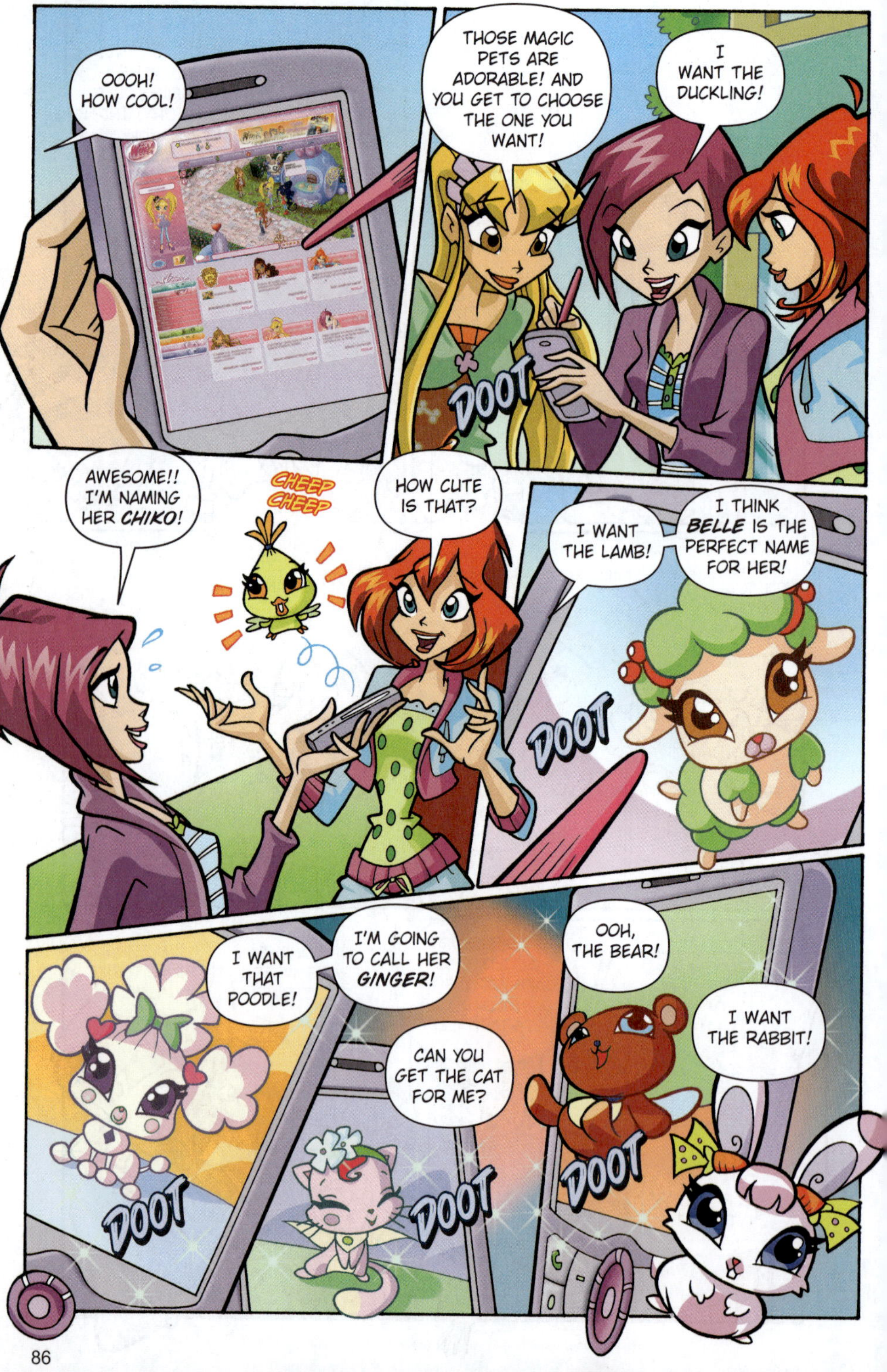

OOOH! HOW COOL!
THOSE MAGIC PETS ARE ADORABLE! AND YOU GET TO CHOOSE THE ONE YOU WANT!
I WANT THE DUCKLING!
DOOT
AWESOME!! I'M NAMING HER CHIKO!
CHEEP CHEEP
HOW CUTE IS THAT?
I WANT THE LAMB!
I THINK BELLE IS THE PERFECT NAME FOR HER!
DOOT
I WANT THAT POODLE!
I'M GOING TO CALL HER GINGER!
OOH, THE BEAR!
I WANT THE RABBIT!
CAN YOU GET THE CAT FOR ME?
DOOT
DOOT
DOOT

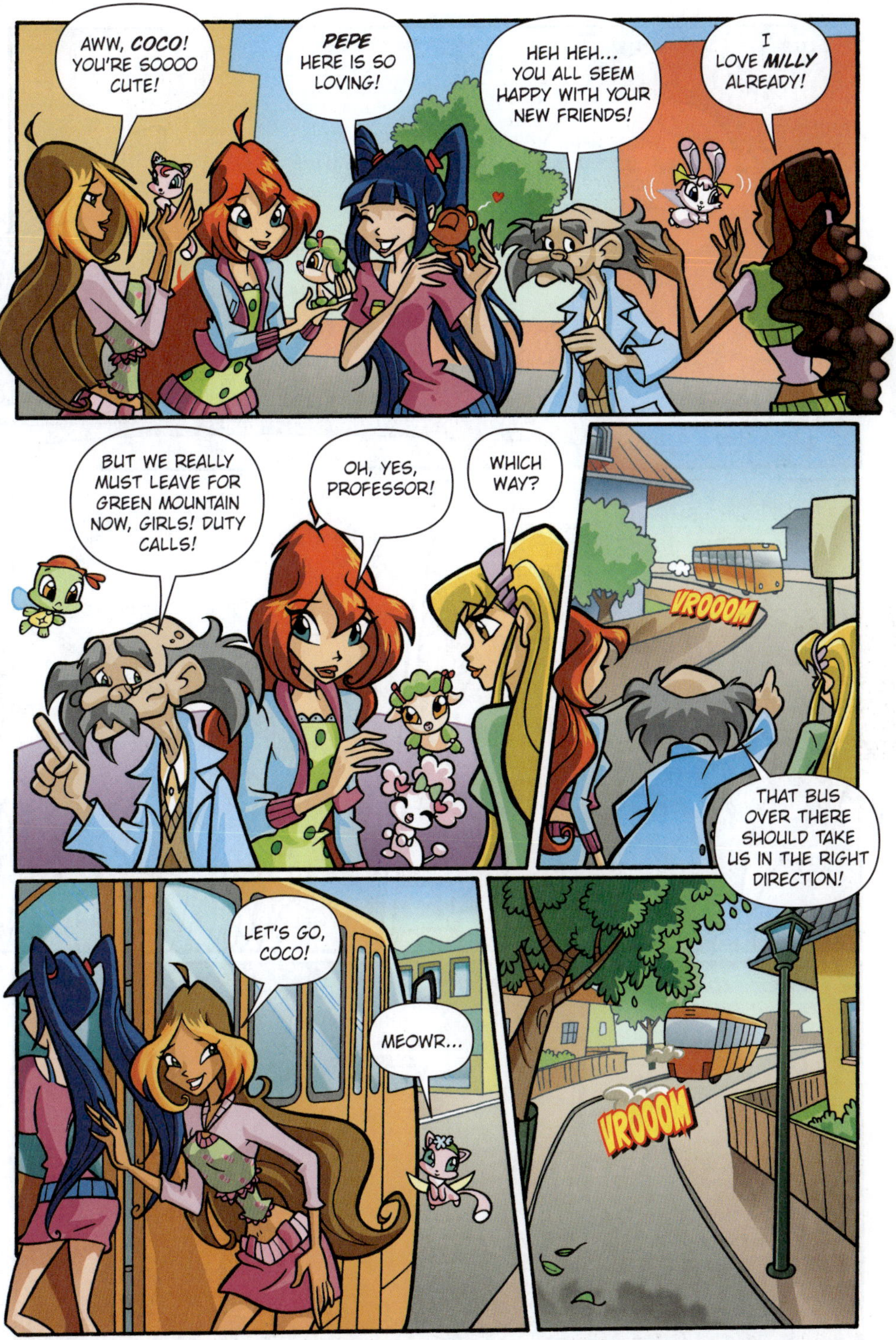
AWW, COCO! YOU'RE SOOOO CUTE!
PEPE HERE IS SO LOVING!
HEH HEH... YOU ALL SEEM HAPPY WITH YOUR NEW FRIENDS!
I LOVE MILLY ALREADY!
BUT WE REALLY MUST LEAVE FOR GREEN MOUNTAIN NOW, GIRLS! DUTY CALLS!
OH, YES, PROFESSOR!
WHICH WAY?
VROOOM
THAT BUS OVER THERE SHOULD TAKE US IN THE RIGHT DIRECTION!
LET'S GO, COCO!
MEOWR...
VROOOM

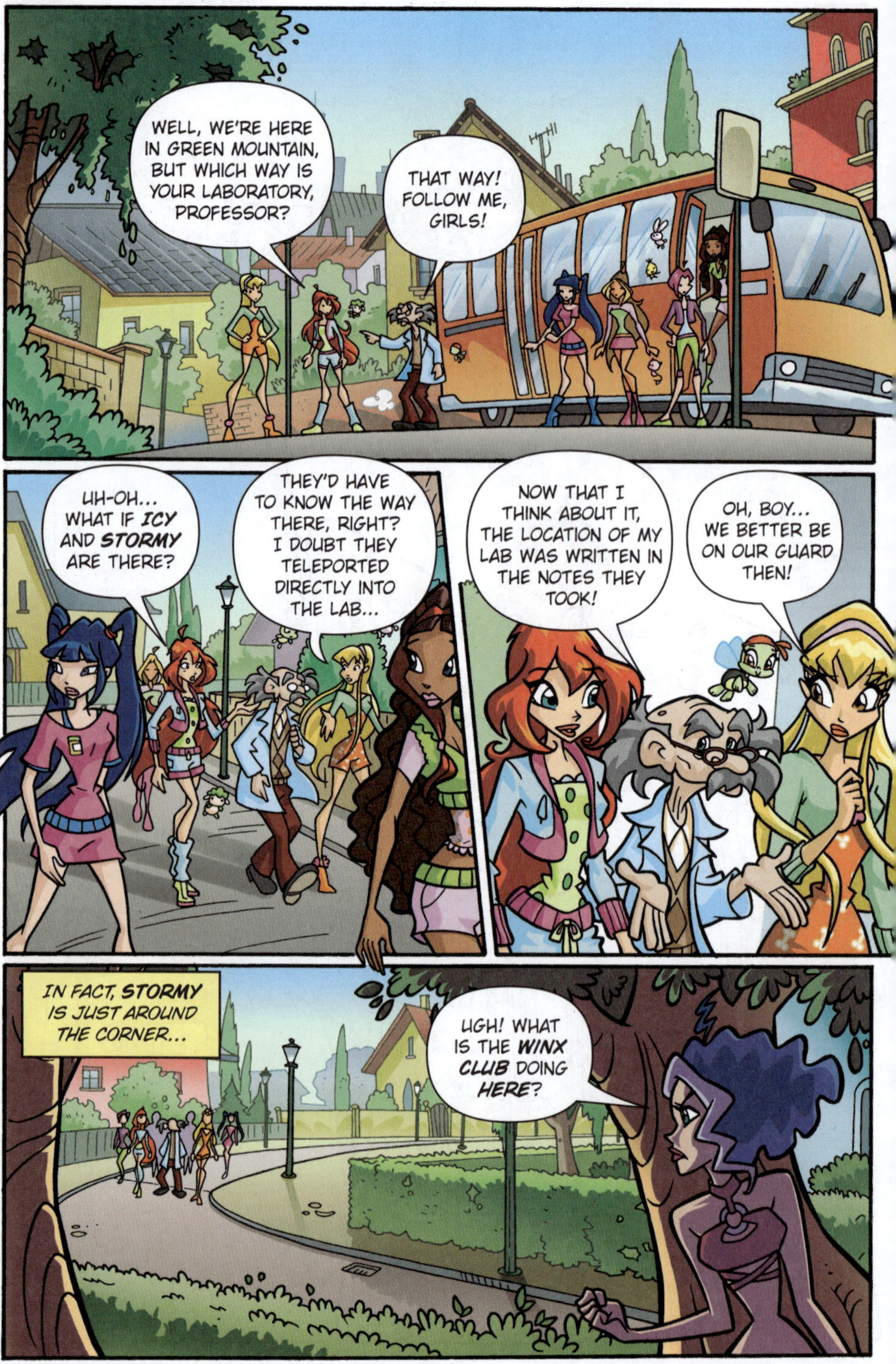
WELL, WE'RE HERE IN GREEN MOUNTAIN, BUT WHICH WAY IS YOUR LABORATORY, PROFESSOR?
THAT WAY! FOLLOW ME, GIRLS!
UH-OH... WHAT IF ICY AND STORMY ARE THERE?
THEY'D HAVE TO KNOW THE WAY THERE, RIGHT? I DOUBT THEY TELEPORTED DIRECTLY INTO THE LAB...
NOW THAT I THINK ABOUT IT, THE LOCATION OF MY LAB WAS WRITTEN IN THE NOTES THEY TOOK!
OH, BOY... WE BETTER BE ON OUR GUARD THEN!
IN FACT, STORMY IS JUST AROUND THE CORNER...
UGH! WHAT IS THE WINX CLUB DOING HERE?

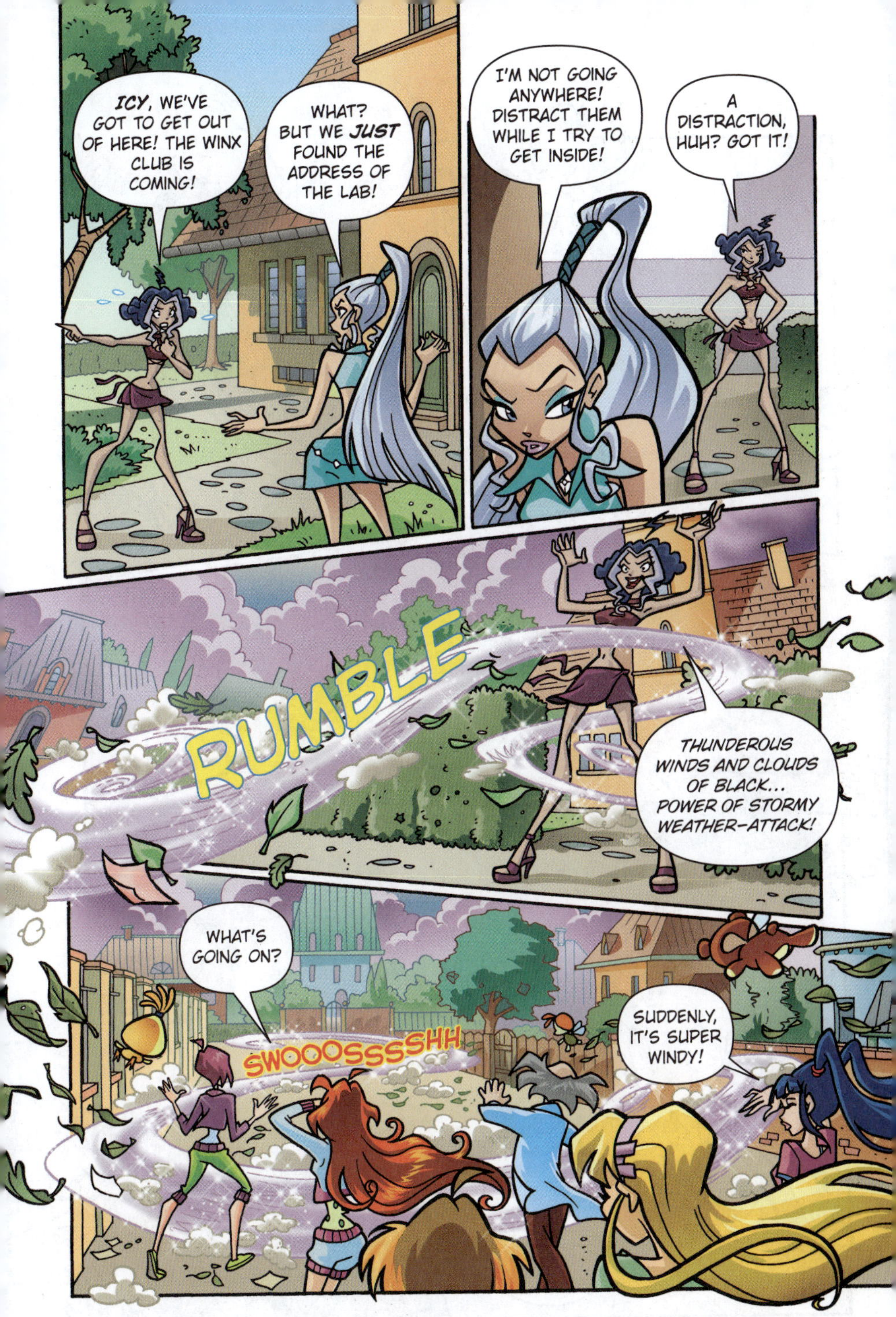
ICY, WE'VE GOT TO GET OUT OF HERE! THE WINX CLUB IS COMING!
WHAT? BUT WE JUST FOUND THE ADDRESS OF THE LAB!
I'M NOT GOING ANYWHERE! DISTRACT THEM WHILE I TRY TO GET INSIDE!
A DISTRACTION, HUH? GOT IT!
RUMBLE
THUNDEROUS WINDS AND CLOUDS OF BLACK... POWER OF STORMY WEATHER-ATTACK!
WHAT'S GOING ON?
SWOOOSSSSHH
SUDDENLY, IT'S SUPER WINDY!

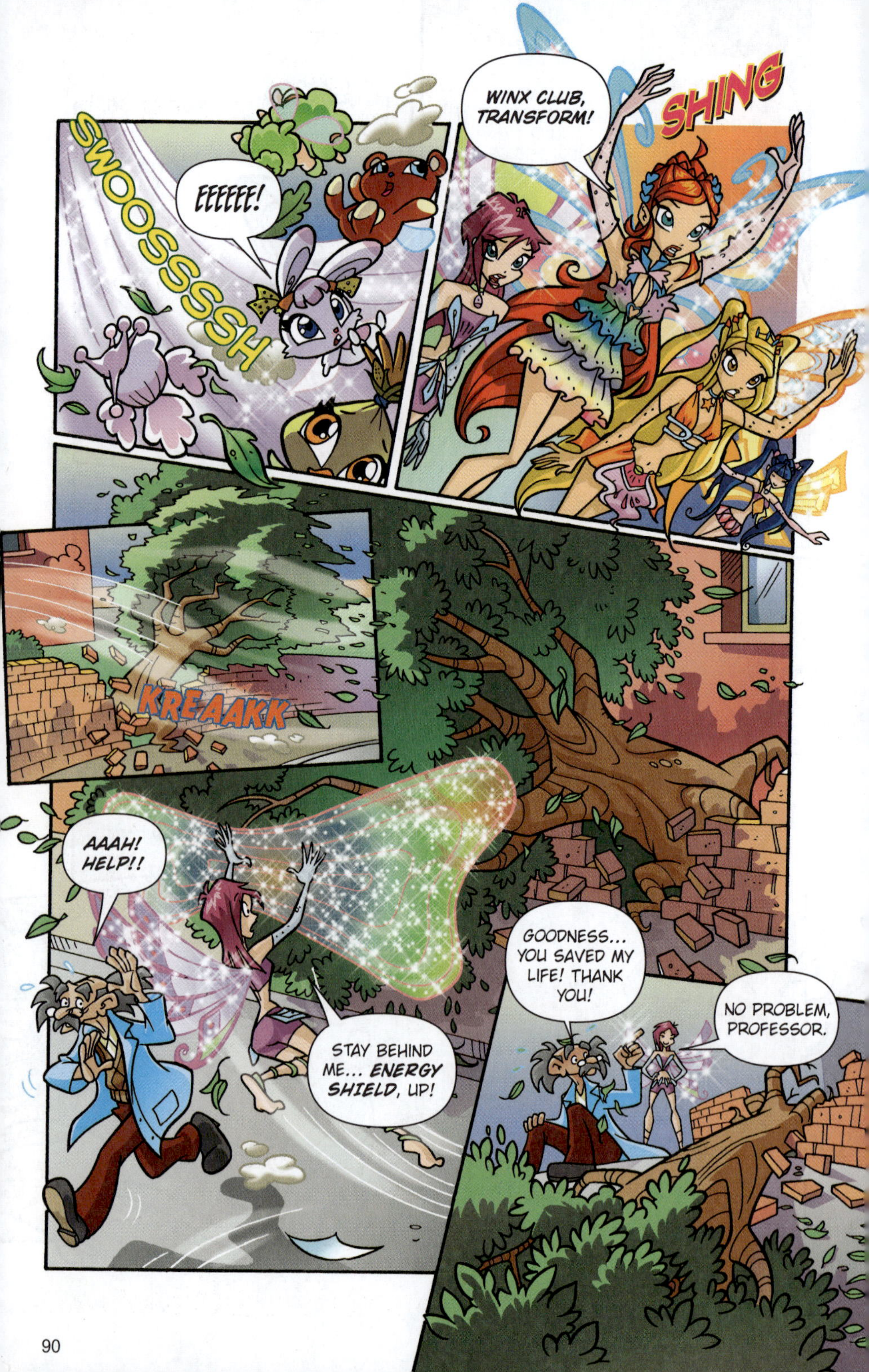
SWOOSSSSH
EEEEEE!
WINX CLUB, TRANSFORM!
SHING
KREAAKK
AAAH! HELP!!
STAY BEHIND ME... ENERGY SHIELD, UP!
GOODNESS... YOU SAVED MY LIFE! THANK YOU!
NO PROBLEM, PROFESSOR.

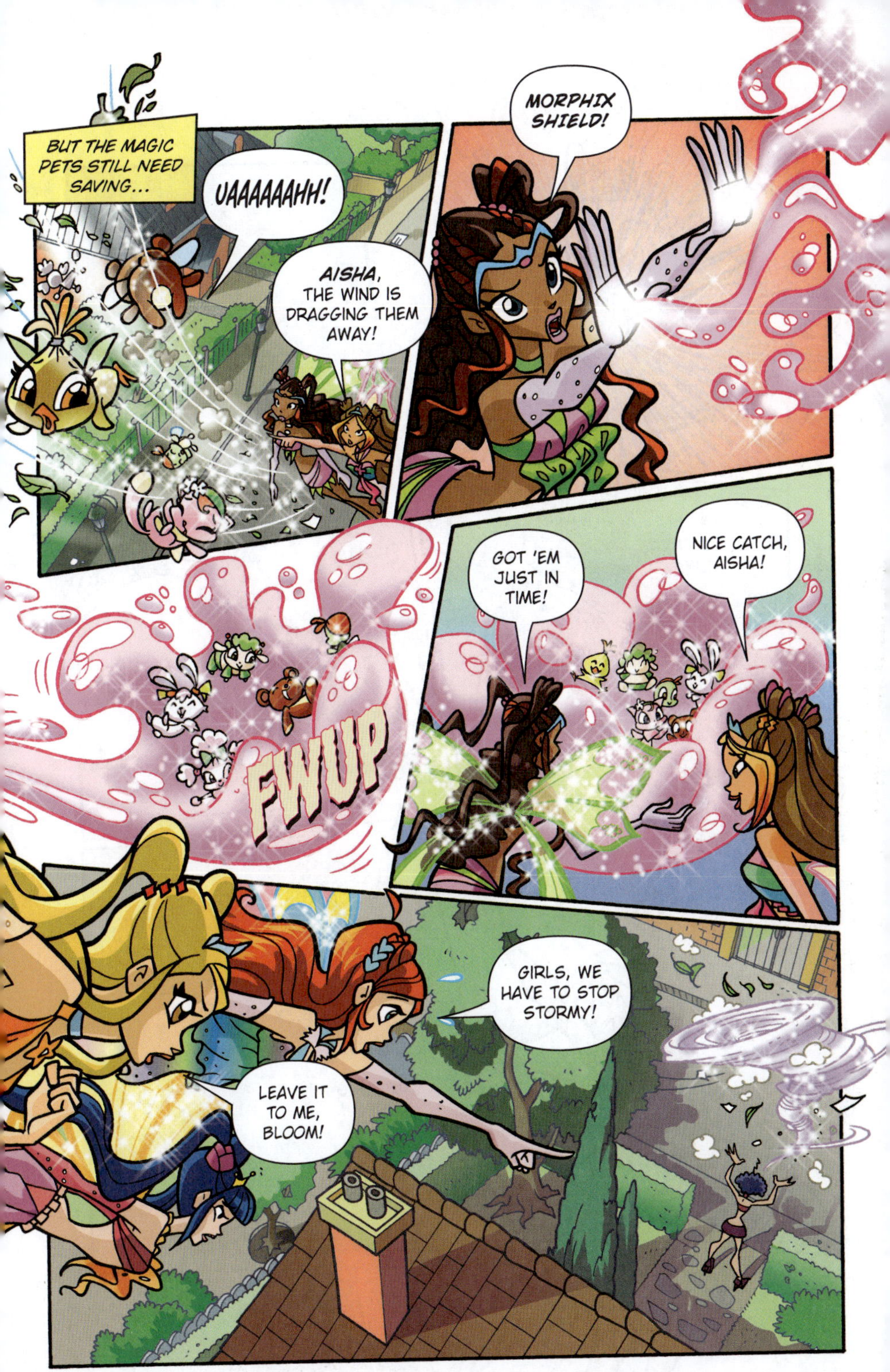

BUT THE MAGIC PETS STILL NEED SAVING...
UAAAAAAHH!
AISHA, THE WIND IS DRAGGING THEM AWAY!
MORPHIX SHIELD!
FWUP
GOT 'EM JUST IN TIME!
NICE CATCH, AISHA!
GIRLS, WE HAVE TO STOP STORMY!
LEAVE IT TO ME, BLOOM!

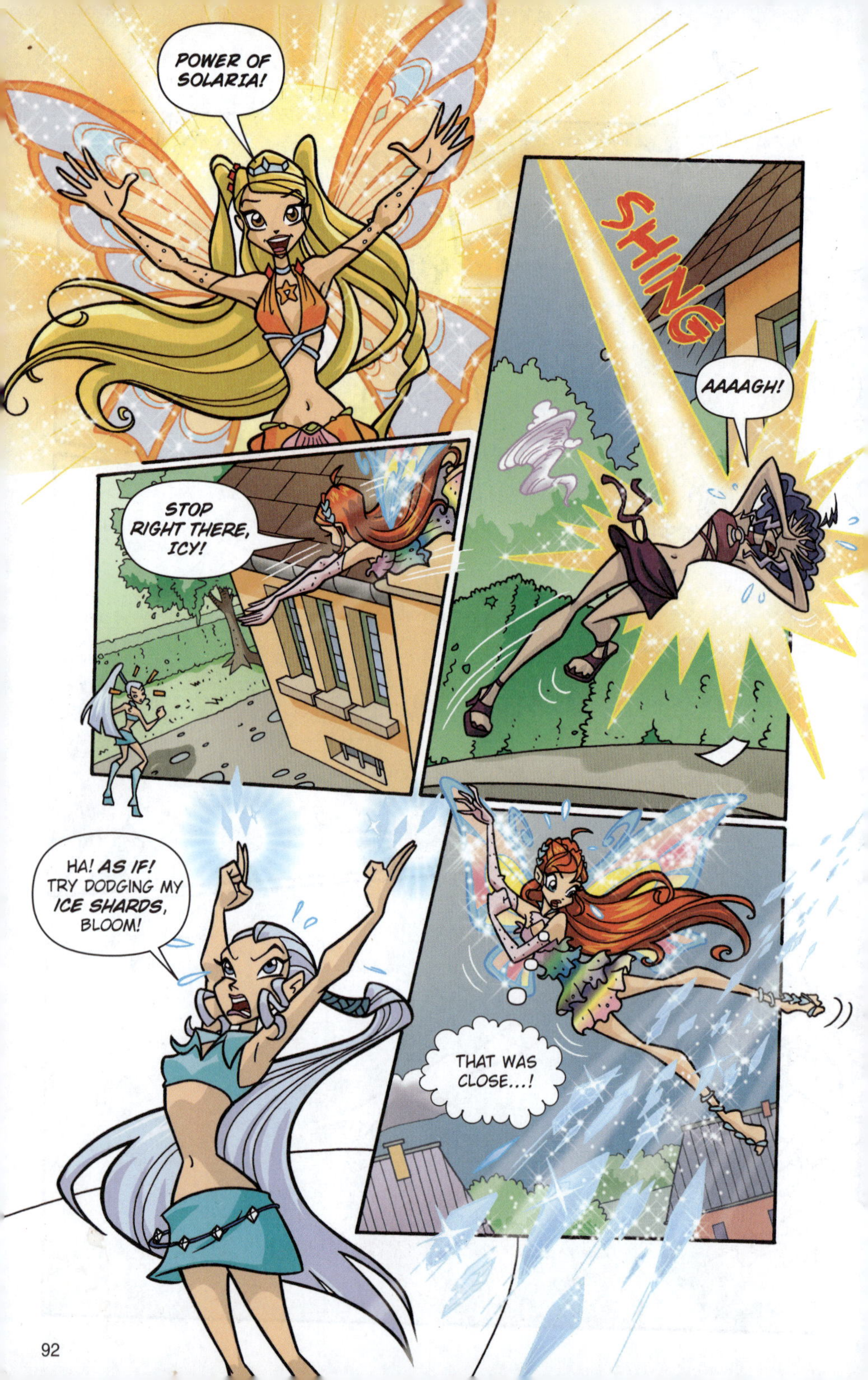
POWER OF SOLARIA!
STOP RIGHT THERE, ICY!
SHING
AAAAGH!
HA! AS IF! TRY DODGING MY ICE SHARDS, BLOOM!
THAT WAS CLOSE...!

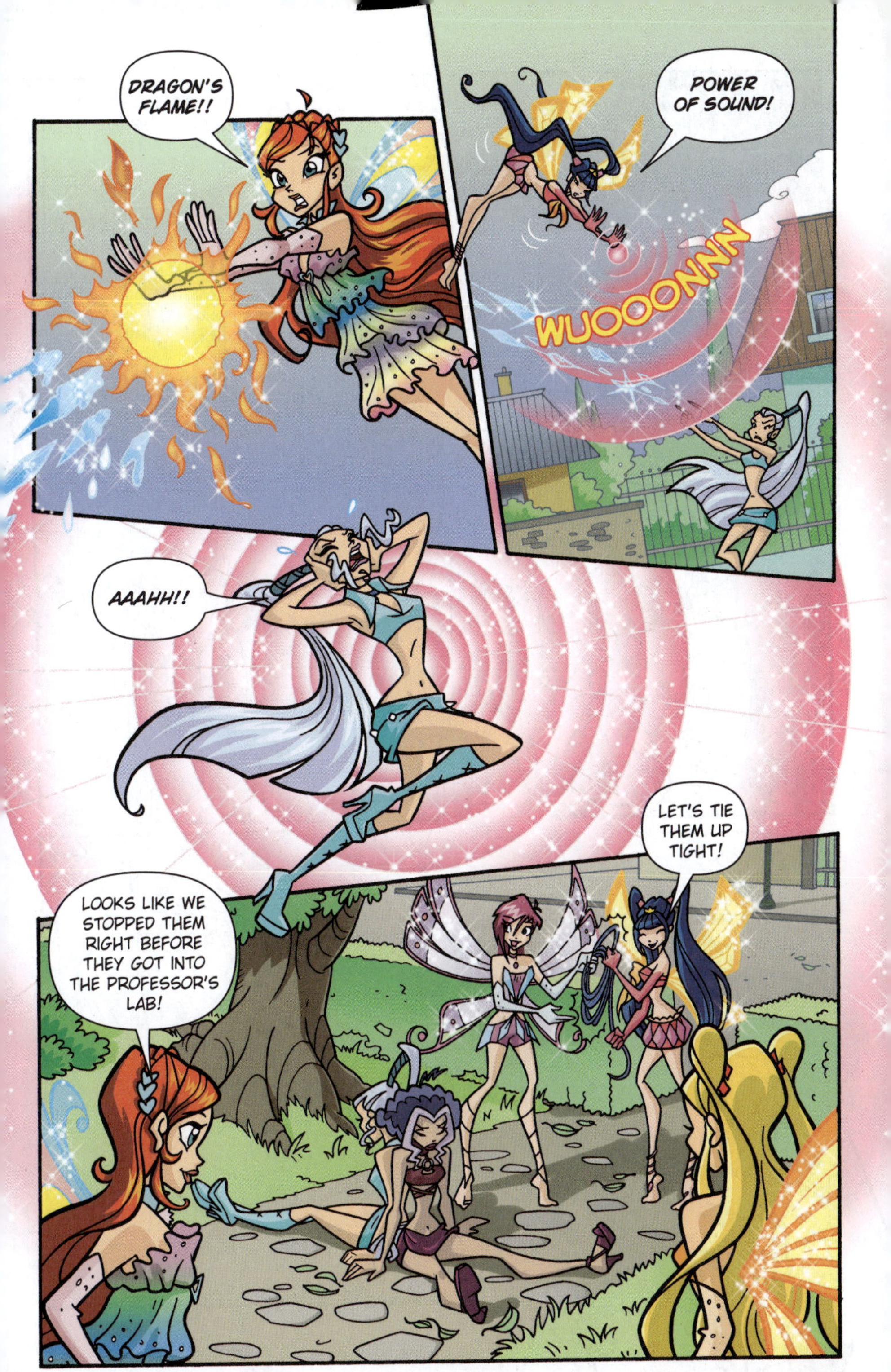

DRAGON'S FLAME!!
POWER OF SOUND!
WUOOONNN
AAAHH!!
LET'S TIE THEM UP TIGHT!
LOOKS LIKE WE STOPPED THEM RIGHT BEFORE THEY GOT INTO THE PROFESSOR'S LAB!

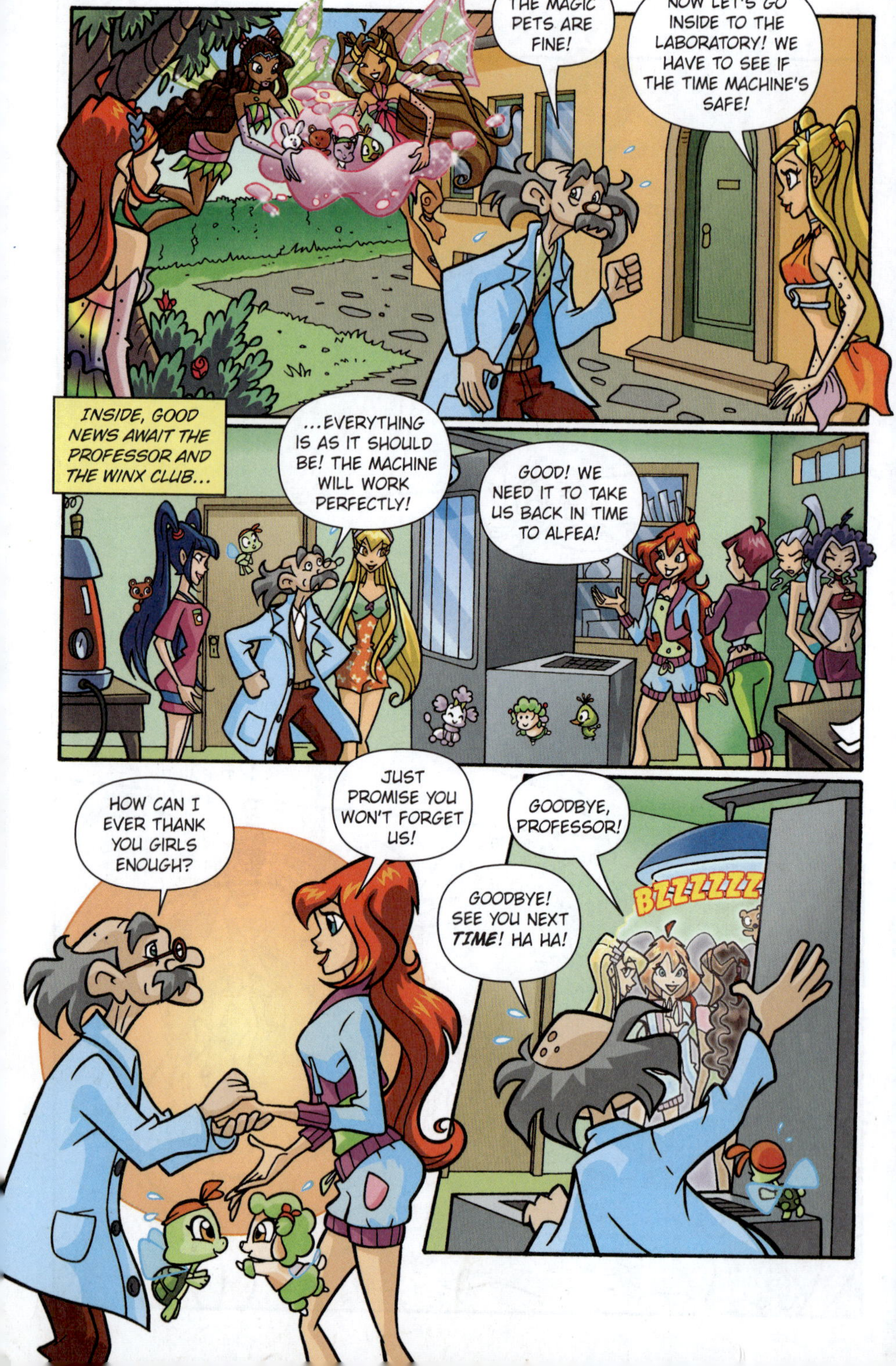
THE MAGIC PETS ARE FINE!
NOW LET'S GO INSIDE TO THE LABORATORY! WE HAVE TO SEE IF THE TIME MACHINE'S SAFE!
INSIDE, GOOD NEWS AWAIT THE PROFESSOR AND THE WINX CLUB...
...EVERYTHING IS AS IT SHOULD BE! THE MACHINE WILL WORK PERFECTLY!
GOOD! WE NEED IT TO TAKE US BACK IN TIME TO ALFEA!
HOW CAN I EVER THANK YOU GIRLS ENOUGH?
JUST PROMISE YOU WON'T FORGET US!
GOODBYE, PROFESSOR!
GOODBYE! SEE YOU NEXT TIME! HA HA!
BZZZZZZ

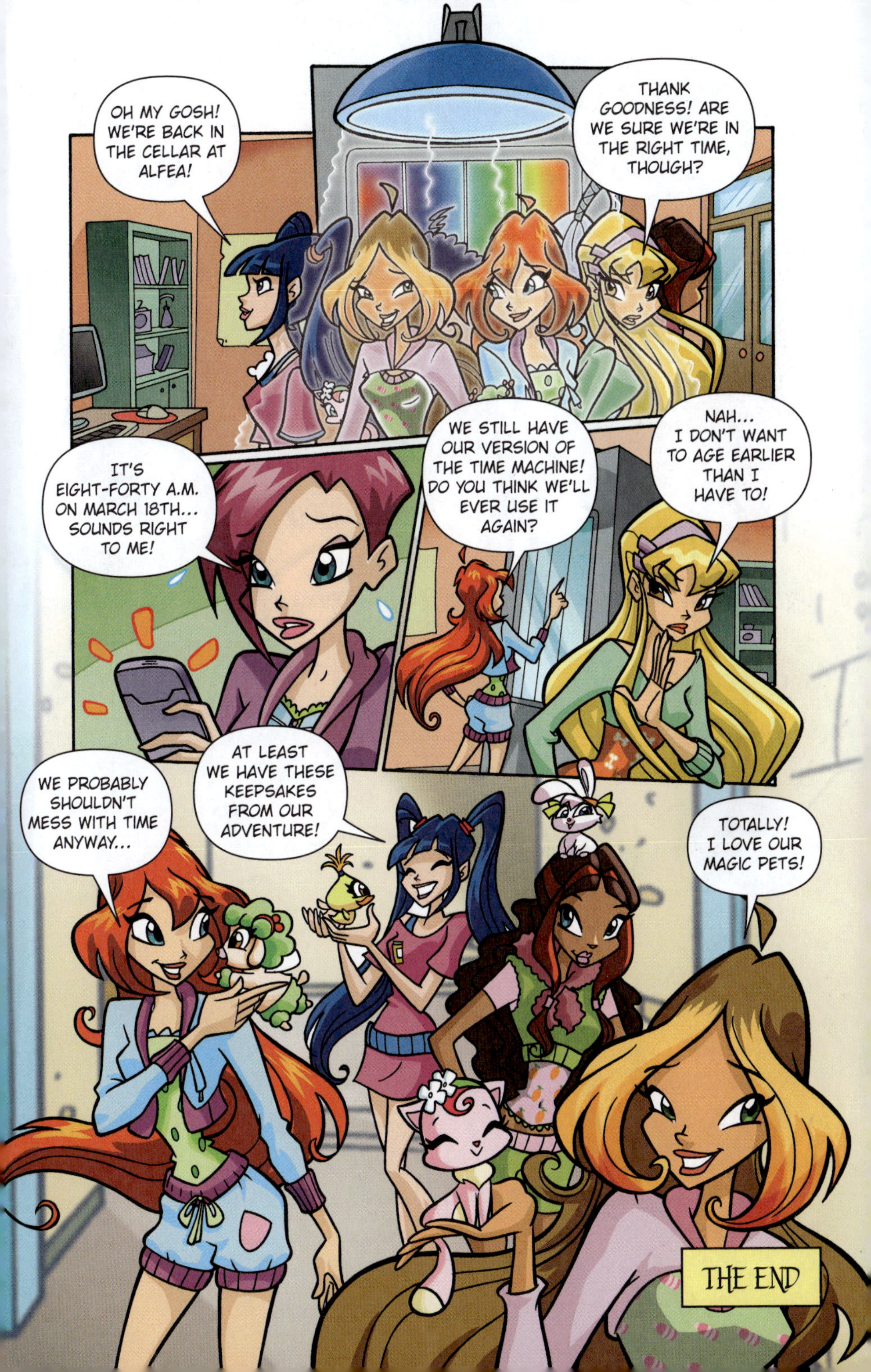
OH MY GOSH! WE'RE BACK IN THE CELLAR AT ALFEA!
THANK GOODNESS! ARE WE SURE WE'RE IN THE RIGHT TIME, THOUGH?
IT'S EIGHT-FORTY A.M. ON MARCH 18TH... SOUNDS RIGHT TO ME!
WE STILL HAVE OUR VERSION OF THE TIME MACHINE! DO YOU THINK WE'LL EVER USE IT AGAIN?
NAH... I DON'T WANT TO AGE EARLIER THAN I HAVE TO!
WE PROBABLY SHOULDN'T MESS WITH TIME ANYWAY...
AT LEAST WE HAVE THESE KEEPSAKES FROM OUR ADVENTURE!
TOTALLY! I LOVE OUR MAGIC PETS!
THE END